NAN DALTON was born in Essex but has lived in Devon for the past forty years enjoying time spent exploring Dartmoor, South Devon and the South Hams. A former secretary and landlady, winning prizes for poetry and the Peninsula Prize for Fiction 2002 with *Tansy*. This book continues the latter's story moving between the town of Chagford and Teign Head Farm.

By the same author

Poetry
Beachcombing
Gleaning the seasons
A Trick of the Light

Fiction
Tansy

Tansy's Moor

Nan Dalton

Best wishes
Nan Dalton

PERRY MEADOW PRESS

First published in Great Britain by
Perry Meadow Press 2005

© Nan Dalton 2005

The rights of Nan Dalton to be identified as the author
of this work has been asserted in accordance with the Copyright,
Designs and Patents Act 1988.

British Library Cataloguing-in-Publication Data
A CIP record for this title is available from the British Library

ISBN 0-9543196-1-3

Cover design by Nan Dalton
Cover photograph by Ruth L. Price

Perry Meadow Press
12 Fairfield Terrace
Newton Abbot
Devon TQ12 2LH

Text design and typesetting by
Short Run Press Ltd, Exeter

Printed and bound in Great Britain by
Short Run Press Ltd, Exeter

For Bruno, John, Theo, Rachel and William

ACKNOWLEDGEMENTS

I acknowledge help and encouragement in writing this sequel to 'Tansy' from Christina Green, Ruth Price who visited the ruins of Teignhead Farm both in Spring and Autumn, Anne Rolls for advice on matters equine and Jean Ward for her invaluable help reading the draft twice. Also thanks are due to family and friends for their patience during the two years it has taken me to research and write *Tansy's Moor*.

I also acknowledge permission to copy Robert Burnard's 1899 photograph of Teignhead Farm from Crossing's *Dartmoor Worker* (Peninsula Press) and to reproduce the words of 'Strawberry Fair' from *Songs of the West* collected by Sabine Baring Gould (Wren Trust).

1

DECISIONS

Tansy slept for forty eight hours; slept the sleep of shock and exhaustion caused by her flight from the Methodist Court at Newton Abbot. Slept without waking even when Tom Osborne came twice each day to milk the cow and rattle the door of Teignhead Farm then, getting no response, had gone home to Fernworthy. When Tansy finally awoke she remembered what had passed between her and Martin; remembered how he had asked the question.

'Why have you come?' and her reply
'I needed to see you' followed by another question
'Do you mean you have come to stay?' and her reply
'If you'll have me?'

Remembered too how he had wanted to wait a little longer before deciding her future and, dependent on her answer, his. Now Tansy laughed out loud as she rose from the truckle bed; recalling the relief she had experienced with the arrival of her monthly flow, releasing her from any obligation to Martin, the bleeding which told her she was not carrying his child, knew she could leave Teignhead Farm and Martin and never return, knew also that she did not want to return to a life of domestic service, had no money to pay for the travel she longed for without taking a position perhaps as companion to a rich woman. Yet, if she stayed here at Teignhead with Martin wasn't she accepting another

1

form of bondage – living Martin's life – not her own. But then wasn't it Martin who had himself sought freedom from his family's expectations trapped in the Wrey Valley? Given up his inheritance for the hard life raising sheep on Dartmoor? Wasn't it Martin who had introduced her to the high hills and magnificent moorland; he who had taught her to ride? Why not accept what he offered and let the future take care of itself?

Tansy dressed quickly and left the farmhouse with Moss at her heels to cross the yard and climb wet turf to Sittaford Tor. Still deep in thought a feeling of guilt surfaced, caused by the fact that she hadn't come to Teignhead until now when her own needs had driven her; not because she wanted Martin but because she needed to escape the truth, Geoffrey Llewellyn didn't love her, had never loved her. Bitter knowledge indeed. Bad enough that he had never loved her, worse still that it was Norah, her own sister, who held his heart. The thought of the tall man with hair the same red as her own, the man who had become an all embracing part of her life brought again the knot of misery to her stomach, the knot of misery that would not go away. Life without Geoffrey was hard to contemplate; not to see him ever without the knowledge that he belonged to another, and not just anyone but her own sister was hard to bear. Feeling like she did would it be fair to stay with Martin, Martin who had rescued her once again, brought her here to Teignhead without seeking an explanation, had looked after her and once more asked her to be his wife?

She looked down at the granite on which she sat, traced the pink star like stonecrop with a finger, shifted her gaze to the flock of sheep which didn't seem to move from their circles beneath White Ridge. She wondered why they kept so still. She knew they couldn't be Martin's; knew he owned but a dozen, looked down at the bog ridden valley below, looked at the bog which had threatened to engulf both herself and Norsworthy's pony when she had galloped from Lustleigh on the night of the storm, the night after the Methodist Conclave had absolved Geoffrey of all the charges except that of 'conduct unbecoming to a minister of the church.'

Tansy smiled as she remembered the day of the chapel outing; a day that had begun with such promise, the boat ride down the River Teign, the picnic on the beach then Martin and Geoffrey racing against each other in the swimming race, swimming through the waves in their long johns. Yes, she thought, Geoffrey had indeed behaved in a manner unbecoming to a priest but then he had won!! Her smile faded as she remembered her shame as Geoffrey had chosen Norah to share his prize; a ride in the handsome car to the Passage House Inn, her face burned at the memory of the moment she Tansy had stepped forward expecting him to choose her to ride beside him only to be passed over for her sister. Remembered how Martin had appealed to her pride, made her dance with him and join in the Chapel party. She remembered how she had left him at Newton Abbot Station without a backward look to hurry home to sob out her heart. Now she felt guilty at her treatment of him that day having experienced the journey for herself.

Her thoughts went back again to the moment her misery began; the reading in Court of Geoffrey's letter committing himself to Norah; read out in front of the Ministers Council, her Father and her friends. Yes, that had been the moment that had sent her running from the Court to take the train to Lustleigh to seek Martin and, finding him gone, had taken Norsworthy's pony and ridden through the storm to end up in the bog below Teignhead Farm and Moss it was who had sensed their presence and brought his master to rescue them. She turned to stroke Moss's soft head causing him to turn toward her, whine quietly, look across the valley for his master, missing him. Heather coloured the slopes of White Ridge, bracken beginning to turn russet in the late summer sun which now disappeared behind

3

lowering clouds. Cold began to chill Tansy's back and she turned to see mist approaching from the West, mist which soon thickened into rain and she rose to run downhill back to Teignhead Farm.

Late afternoon brought Moss to his feet his throat issuing welcoming whimpers that heralded Martin's return. The man raised a hand in acknowledgment as Tansy and Moss rushed out through the stone porch into the rain and wind.

'Get back inside you little fool' he shouted 'I've to see to the Cob.'

Crestfallen Tansy retreated inside to stir up the peat into a blaze, fill a pot with water and set it on the trivet. Of course Martin was first and foremost a farmer, of course it must be animals that received his attention, a hard lesson to learn. She listened as the noise of hoofs on cobbles faded – this, she thought, must be the horse Martin had gone to Okehampton to buy. Time passed slowly as Tansy mixed oats with water, thickened them over the fire until the heavy door opened and Martin came in, clothes soaked, face reddened by rain and wind. He stood, uncertain, looking at Tansy across the dark kitchen till she left her stirring to kneel at his feet, pull off worn boots, wet coat, leggings and shirt. For the first time she noticed lines around the firm mouth, a reserve about the blue eyes. She handed him a towel, took wet clothes, spread them before the hearth to dry while he rubbed his body with the towel then took the rough blanket she offered and wrapped it around his body.

'Can you eat?' Tansy asked and his face split into a huge grin.

'Can I eat – just show us the vittles!' He sat down at the scrubbed table.

'Now it's my turn to look after you' she said, setting a skillet on the fire where soon sounds of crackling and a smell of frying filled the room. She ladled porridge into a wooden bowl and set it down in front of him. He seized a spoon and began to eat but, after a few mouthfuls, made a face.

'What's wrong?' Tansy demanded.

'Forget the salt did ee my maid?' was his response and a spurt of anger filled her. In silence she removed the porridge, threw the cooked bacon and eggs onto a plate, slapped it down in front of him.

'Eat this if you can' she shouted 'or go without. I didn't work as cook at 'Courtenay House' but if it's a cook you want then I'd best be gone.'

Martin gave her a long level look then picking up knife and fork began to eat while Tansy peered through the square of glass to check the weather. Moss whined and rubbed his body around her legs. She put her hand down to stroke his smooth black head and looked across at Martin, already cleaning an empty plate with the bread she'd added to the meal.

'At least Moss is glad I'm here!' she stormed, not really wanting to leave. Suddenly Martin was on his feet, the blanket falling to the floor, his body strong and alive with the warmth from the fire, the fill of food. Anger erupted from his face and Tansy felt afraid she had gone too far.

'I thought it wouldn't last – the biddable Tansy. At least now I know I've got the real Tansy here with me. But if she's going to take offence each time there's a fall out then tis best she goes now.'

He grabbed dry drawers, shirt and trousers from a chest by the side of the fire, opened the door and strode out into the drumming rain. Tansy sat down at the table, regretted her angry words, felt a new misery fill her body. When would she ever learn not to speak out of turn. When would she ever consider her words before voicing her opinions. Now she had placed herself out on a limb. Where was she to go? Home to face Eva and Edward; she knew her parents would forgive her for leaving Newton without so much as a word of explanation but to face Norah and Geoffrey now making wedding plans? Unthinkable. Nor could she return to 'Courtenay House' even if the Vallance's would have her back after she had left without notice. No, there was no going back. She had burnt her bridges; must make the best of things here at Teign-head with Martin. At least here she had the chance of a new life with a man who wanted her, a man who had told her he loved her on more than one occasion, whose body excited her even though she didn't love him. Perhaps that would come later? Suddenly she smiled; best make amends, she seized a pot, filled it with water from the pot well outside the door, placed it on the fire, paced up and down, impatient for the water to boil, put tea in a strainer, passed the boiling water through, added milk and sugar and, taking a deep breath, passed through the heavy door into the darkening night and made her way to the stable where she found Martin drying and grooming a large black animal. Martin paused in his work looked quizzically at her, while Tansy reached up and rubbed the horse's soft nose.

'So have ee come to steal another animal and gallop off into the night?' Martin asked and Tansy swallowed back the rude retort that immediately rose in her throat.

'No,' she paused then continued determinedly 'I've come to ask if I can stay and try to earn my keep' she gulped then added 'that is if you'll let me' and Martin knowing what an effort must have gone into this short speech smiled at last, placed the curry comb on the shelf, and said.

'Very well, first task then is to give a name to this animal' he paused to stroke the cob 'which, when I bought him, was Jack, but, from the way he tackled the ride across the Moor and a feeling I have in my bones, I've decided Lucifer would be a better one. What do ee say to that?'

Tansy laughed with relief and amusement. She eyed the cob's broad back, the wild look in the animal's brown eyes showing white the body long but broad, the short legs making two of Norsworthy's pony Fairy. She wondered how long it would take her to bestride this animal, to ride the black beast across the Moor. Did Martin suspect a streak of evil inside the large work horse? She looked round the stable, wondered if Martin ever thought of the time she had accompanied his mother from 'Staddens' earlier in the year and they had lain together in the linhay. As if he had read her mind Martin was suddenly behind her, his arms coming around her waist, turning her to face him.

'Tis a hard life here Tansy; long days with just sheep and dog for company, far from town, family and friends, far from all you've grown up with, but' he added 'Chagford's but an hour's ride when there's time to spare' he paused to hold her away from him. A sudden impulse brought Tansy's arms up around his neck and he drew her close, searched her face, closed her lips with his and at once she felt a warmth spread through her body, her breasts begin to respond to his touch, felt his body hardening against hers, her mouth opening to his tongue. Suddenly Martin pulled away from her.

'Tidn't right that an unmarried maid should live here with no other woman. If you really want to stay with me then we must marry as soon as banns can be called.'

Tansy, only half listening, didn't want the kissing to stop, didn't want the delicious feel of her body to stop. She nodded and moved closer to Martin who now took her arms from around his neck and put her away from him.

'Not so fast my maid' he said 'First I must visit your Feyther, get his permission, ask your family for their blessing.' This plan, so sudden in its presentation, shocked Tansy; the thought of going home, going back to Newton, back to face Eva and Edward, back to face Geoffrey and Norah, was she ready for it?

'I can't face them Martin – can't go back to Newton, not yet – I want to stay here with you.'

7

She wanted the here and now to continue, wanted to lose herself in Martin's arms, to lie with him, to let go all the pent up emotion of the past year.

Martin spoke to her through lips thickened by emotion.

'Until we'm married Tansy Drewe I will sleep out here in the stable and you will sleep in the house on your own.' He pushed her toward the door and she could do nothing but stumble out into the night. She felt unsettled, not wanting to go back into the house, climbed the hill in an effort to still her seething thoughts, calm her awakened body. At last the rain and wind stopped and a ringed moon emerged from the hasting clouds. For the second time that day she climbed Sittaford where she would go whenever the need arose. She stumbled over the uneven ground, dark now, and thought of the future and all that lay ahead.

The first sound Tansy heard next morning was the jingle of harness, the clop of hoofs on stone and, although it was still quite dark, she rose to peer through the small window to see Martin astride Lucifer's back, watched as Moss followed man and horse from the courtyard.

She stirred the peat fire, took a spill from the crock on the overmantel to light a candle, sought the oil lamp, the lamp which had spread light and warmth through the large bare room each night of Martin's absence. She removed the glass funnel to raise the wick and apply the candle flame without success. Shaking the lamp she found no answering movement of liquid. She sighed realising the oil was used up, took the candlestick and sought a fresh supply of oil, found only a pile of dried peat bricks, a sheepskin and in the opposite corner a basket of brown eggs, covered with dung and feathers clinging to shells. Disheartened she put the sheepskin on top of the bed, threw herself down once more and fell into a deep sleep. The sun was high by the time

Martin returned; he frowned when he found Tansy still asleep but then he remembered how his life had changed, changed dramatically in the last few days, how he had achieved his heart's desire – a result he had stopped hoping for – Tansy was here with him, had at last agreed to be his wife. He knelt beside the truckle bed, smiled down at the slight figure swamped in his night shirt, auburn curls fanning out across the herb scented pillow his mother had brought on one of her monthly visits. Long eyelashes lay above freckled cheeks and a rhythmic sound of breathing lifted the soft breasts. A wave of tenderness filled Martin's heart tempting him to touch the sleeping girl but then he reminded himself of his resolution – no love making until he and Tansy were wed. He rose from his knees to reach down the ever depleting ham and set about making a meal for the two of them; the smell of this meal finally roused Tansy, caused her to wake, stretch luxuriously and open her eyes. So deep had been her sleep that for a moment she didn't know where she was until Martin's voice reached her across the cool dark of the room.

'Hallo, lazybones. Time to get up, the day is well on.'

'Where have you been?' Tansy demanded, amazed to see Martin standing over the skillet, thinking how her Father never so much as made a cup of tea or toasted a slice of bread.

'What are you doing?'

Martin laughed, broke eggs into the pan and set knives and forks on the rough wooden table.

'Since April I've been shepherd, woman of all work and cook; who would have looked after me if I hadn't?' He smiled at Tansy adding an invitation.

'Here, come and set down and eat.'

Barefoot Tansy crossed the room to join him.

'Tis good' she licked her lips after the first mouthful of crisp ham and looked at Martin as she began on the eggs.

'Why these are just the way I like them.'

9

She mopped her plate with the hunk of bread Martin had added at the last minute.

'All we need now is some tea and a Chudley.'

Martin who had watched the enjoyment she had shown while eating laughed shortly.

'That's your job.'

Tansy had however already noticed the lack of an oven, could find no means to cook except over the peat fire.

'Can't make bread and Chudleys without an oven.'

A vision of the black iron range at 'Courtenay House' came to her with it's hot plates, two ovens, one close the fire, the other cooler for slow cooking stews and large fruit cakes. Remembered the battery of hooks hanging above the hot plates, the roasting spits for huge joints. Thought of Cook standing stirring the huge iron pots, stopping to wipe sweat from her brow and ease the pressure from her corset. Not for the first time Tansy realised the barrenness of this room; silently listed the items lacking here at Teignhead, flat irons, curtains for the square of glass, ornaments for the over mantel, sewing box to mend the rough clothes Martin wore, no dressing table, no hair or clothes brushes, worst of all no settle to keep draughts at bay between porch door and fire. How, if indeed she was to be mistress of Teignhead, was she to manage to keep Martin and herself spick and span? More pressing still, how was she to make herself presentable for her return to Newton and her family? Amos Webber's words came back to her, words Martin's father had spoken when first he took her to his parents' farm that Sunday last Spring .

'Set on living on Moor, our Martin is. 'Staddens' not good enough for ee. Good enough for my Feyther and his Feyther afore him, but not good enough for my son.' How he had turned to look at Tansy across the family meal table.

'So, young woman, if you'm set on being a moorman's wife I hope you'm used to a hard life.'

She remembered how Martin had tried to interrupt his Father, only to be silenced.

'When snows come you'll be shut in for days, even weeks with only new born lambs for company, praying for Spring to come and, mark my words, Spring comes late on Moor.'

'Penny for them?' Martin asked pausing to wipe his mouth with the back of his hand. Tansy still busy in her mind with the ever growing list looked up and shrugged, perhaps a change of thought a wise move.

'What time did ee leave this morning? Why, it was hardly light?'

'Thought you'd a been used to starting work in the dark?' He teased, while Tansy nodded remembering all too well the carrying of heavy hot water jugs, sweeping of hearths, laying and lighting of fires all carried out by oil light. Now she listened as Martin spelt out his own list of early morning activities.

'Checked sheep, made sure they was safe, can't afford to lose em to fox or bog, need their coats next summer to pay off loan for the Cob and perhaps buy netting to make a rabbit warren.'

'Rabbit warren!' Tansy exclaimed, remembering the crates of rabbits being put on the London train the night she'd been dismissed from 'Courtenay House' and had taken the train to Norah how her ticket had been bought with the proceeds of her shorn hair. Martin stopped his talk of warrens, remembered Tansy's soft heart where all wild creatures were concerned and shrugged.

'We'll see how much money we can get for the wool before we thinks of other ways of making income.' He added as an afterthought.

'Perhaps we can build ee an oven beside the fireplace for your baking, Tansy Drewe.'

Distracted from the thought of rabbit warrens and comforted by Martin's promise to build an oven for her, Tansy began on another train of thought. This one ran on wedding plans and a dress to be married in; first she

11

must retrieve her few belongings from her old room high above the front door of 'Courtenay House'. Small but cosy with a fire burning in the tiny hearth; the regular wage and good food, close to her family and friends. What was she giving this up for? The hard life Amos Webber had promised up here in a wilderness she knew nothing about. On the other hand, she mused, here at Teignhead Farm she would be her own mistress, could choose how to spend each day, could ride out across the Moor and make a home in this long bare room. Aware suddenly that Martin was speaking to her with an invitation.

'Would ee like to come and see sheep? We can walk, tidd'n far' he paused smiling at her 'I'll wait outside while ee gets dressed'.

2

RETURN TO NEWTON

Tansy felt nervous as Sunday drew near; her shirt and skirt had blown clean and dry in the sweet moor land air but there was no iron to banish the creases and her straw hat had suffered from its immersion in the bog. Battered now she tied it to her head with the stained scarf and prayed that Sunday would prove another fine August day. Martin announced his plans for the journey beginning with a ride on Lucifer to 'Staddens' where the Cob would be stabled. From there, after breaking their news to Sarah and Amos, they were to take the train from Lustleigh to Newton Abbot, then climb the hill to the Post Office. Sunday arrived with speeding clouds which parted to let through shafts of sun followed by a clear blue sky. Lucifer excited by the wind pawed the ground eager to be off and, almost before Martin had seated Tansy in front of him where he sat astride the Cob's broad back, was trotting down the stroll to cross the Teign then turn right along the valley bottom before climbing Sittaford Tor and on to Grey Wethers where Martin stopped briefly so Tansy could see the two stone circles for herself.

'Oh, so they'm not sheep at all! You might have told me!' Now Martin hauled the Cob round both circles so Tansy could inspect each one – she laughed to think that she had believed them sheep. Laughter which Martin was pleased to share as he explained.

'Bronze Age people put them there – History Men keep coming to see them and have stood them upright but the locals at Warren House Inn try and sell them to strangers. Yes, they look like sheep too from the Postbridge road as well as from where you sat on Sittaford Tor.' Tansy realised just how much she had to learn about her new neighbourhood. Martin set Lucifer's head toward the East and soon the Cob had broken into a brisk trot along the Postbridge Road past the Warren House Inn to Bennett's Cross. Now Martin turned the Cob's head to pick out a path through old heaps of spoil with Birch Tor on their left. Tansy looked at the huge wheel, tall chimney and buildings huddled together beneath the Tor.

'What's all that, Martin?'

'Tis Vitifer and Birch Tor Mines.'

'What do they mine?' Tansy wanted to know remembering after she had spoken that it was at Vitifer that Avril Moore's Tom had come to work at the instigation of her Father.

'Black tin, that's what they goes underground for! Been drilling rock there for hundreds of years! This is the spoil that's been left. Hold tight – it gets rough now.' Tansy clung to the front of the saddle as they rode down through the valley past Headland Warren Farm where the farmer and his family came out to stare at the flying horse and pair of riders on its back.

'Going 'ome, Martin Webber?' came the question but Martin waved his whip and kept going edging past Grimspound to Natsworthy Gate and across the Moor then track past Kitty Jay's Grave where Tansy wanted to stop but Martin urged Lucifer on. 'Us'll come and take our time looking another day or us'll not get to Newton!'. On and on to Manaton then along the main road to Lustleigh and as they passed under the railway arch to 'Staddens' Tansy remembered how the horses had bolted on the day she and Beatrice Vallance were jolted from their seats in the hired coach. Was it only just over a year ago? Aware of all that had happened since Tansy was overwhelmed with doubts and wondered what she was doing here with Martin about to announce to his parents that they were to be wed. If the bolting horses hadn't hit the roadside hedge and cast a wheel would she ever have got to know Martin? If Beatrice hadn't sent her here to 'Staddens' would she be here now listening to sounds of churning coming from the dairy. Tansy looked beseechingly at Martin, not wanting to face Fanny Luscombe whose sister Janet had caused Tansy so much trouble; caused her to be dismissed from 'Courtenay House' falsely accused of stealing Emma Vallance's watch. Tansy hurried past the open door into the passage between dairy and house and Martin caught her hand and drew her into his mother's warm kitchen where Sarah Webber stood over a mixing bowl.

Surprised to see them she paused in her kneading, flour up to her elbows. She pushed a strand of hair from her eyes and smiled a welcome.

'What a surprise our Martin' her gaze shifted to Tansy. 'Tis good to see you too my maid' she said moving to wash and dry her hands. 'So have you decided to wed our Martin then?' she asked and when Tansy nodded Sarah came over and took her into her arms. 'Martin wouldn't have been happy without you Tansy and now you must make him happy with you.'

At these words Tansy realised Sarah must have known what had been happening at Teignhead. Martin must have called here during the three days he was away at the Horse Fair. Tansy felt a sudden spurt of anger that Sarah had known what Martin had decided before she had. She reached to tug at her hat and the sudden movement caused the ribbon to slip from around the bonnet and allow her pinned up hair to fall in a cascade of auburn. Sensing her change of mood Martin announced.

'Going to the Post Office now to tell Mr & Mrs Drewe.' Sarah looked Tansy over, taking in the creased clothes, the stained scarf and battered straw.

'P'raps we'd best heat up the iron and take the creases out of your clothes avore you go home, my maid. There's nothing I can do about the hat but tis you your parents will want to see after all. Sit you down and she produced cider from a small barrel in the corner, set it in front of the couple, put an iron on the new stove and after drinking Martin turned to Tansy.

'I'll find Feyther while Mother sees to your clothes – I'll not be long.' Sarah sent her up to change into a wrap and an hour later Tansy and Martin boarded the train at Lustleigh Station. Tansy felt this should be the happiest day of her life, engaged to be married at 19 but in fact the closer they drew to Newton the more miserable she became.

'Do Mother and Father know we're coming?' she pressed Martin and he shook his head. 'They know you've been staying at Teignhead' he said 'but that is all' and Tansy had to be content with that.

Leaving the Station they crossed Courtenay Park to climb uphill to Southernhay Tansy felt her heart begin a slow pounding. How would she be received? Would Eva and Edward be angry with her for running away from the Assembly Rooms after Geoffrey Llewellyn's trial? Would Norah be at home? Still angry with her sister for stealing Geoffrey's affections Tansy had made no plans as to how she would greet her sister when next they met.

Suddenly the door of the Post Office was in front of them and Martin, looking equally nervous, was hauling on the bell chain. It was Tansy's little brothers, Robert and James, who opened the door and seeing Tansy seized a hand each, swung her round until she laughed with pleasure at the closeness of them, the excitement of their welcome, ruffled their red hair and kissed their soft cheeks.

'Look who's come' Robert shouted as he ran ahead through the Post Room and into the Sitting Room where the Drewe family sat at their Sunday meal. Eva was the first to rise and move toward Tansy, her face a mixture of pleasure and pain.

'You bad girl!' she said 'whatever did you run away for – causing us such worry?' Now Edward rose and took Tansy, his favourite always, in his arms and kissed and hugged her.

'You'm safe, you'm here my little girl – that's all that matters' and Tansy felt such happiness to be with her family once more. Edward shook Martin by the hand and invited him to join them. Room was quickly made at the table, chairs were forthcoming from the kitchen and the young couple settled. It was then that Tansy became aware of Norah and Geoffrey watching from the farthest end of the table. Norah's face wore a look of apprehension and Geoffrey's a wariness under-lined by a rising of colour in the now clean shaven face. Shocked by the change in his appearance Tansy exclaimed.

'Why Geoffrey you've shaved off your beard!' then she recovered her poise and a coolness filled her heart as she added.

'I didn't expect to find the secret lovers here!'

Turning to Martin, now seated with the family, she nudged him and announced. 'Martin and I have some-thing to tell you.'

Placed on the spot by Tansy Martin rose, cleared his throat and, turning towards Edward Drewe addressed him.

'This isn't the way it was planned' he said, easing the high collar of his best white shirt and undoing the top button of his chapel suit. Reproachfully he looked down at Tansy, whose face held a look of fierce deter-mination.

'Forgive me, Sir, if this seems too hasty but from the first day when I met Tansy at Lustleigh Fair it has been my hope that she would become my wife. So today I am here to ask your permission to wed Tansy' – now he stuttered 'I've asked her to be my wife and share my life at Teignhead Farm and' here he looked round the

17

table, where eating had long since ceased 'I am proud to say that she has said yes.'

Having delivered his message Martin relieved, sat down looking at Tansy who nodded her head in approval while everyone clapped their hands till Edward serious now rose to look from Martin to Tansy.

'If Tansy truly wishes to wed you Martin then we' (here he looked across at Eva who smiled and nodded) 'must give you our blessing and welcome you into our family.' Now he looked once more at Tansy and, after a long pause, asked.

'Are you quite sure this is what you want, our Tansy?' and she turning to Martin, took both his hands in hers then back to face her mother and father said with a fierceness that startled everyone in the room.

'I'm as sure of it as Norah is sure of wedding Geoffrey.' At these words silence fell until Geoffrey broke it by rising and reaching out his hand to Martin in answering gesture.

'Congratulations to you both – I trust you will be as happy as Norah and I intend to be.' Now Norah smiling rose and came round the table to add her congratulations to Geoffrey's but her sister drew back turning away from the kiss Norah intended to place on Tansy's cheek. Tansy turned to leave the room.

'I'm going to see Rosemary' she gasped and was gone leaving Martin alone with her family hardly believing the way his life had turned about, feeling he should be grateful to Geoffrey and Norah for causing this, for him, happy ending. He smiled down the table at the couple who responded in a fashion that caused him to think about the future which lay ahead of him.

'Don't let her have her own way, Martin' Norah said 'or she'll lead you a merry dance' and Geoffrey added.

'Strong young woman, your Tansy, but a woman with almost too much heart for her own good.' Shaking Martin's hand once more they left the room, Norah to help Eva in the kitchen, Geoffrey to talk chapel affairs

18

with Edward leaving Martin alarmed and wondering what he'd let himself in for.

Tansy leapt up steps to push open the gate into the Brimmacombes' garden, sending chickens scattering squawking across bare soil. She knocked at the worn oak door but then couldn't wait for it to be opened and barged in to find Bessie and Johnnie sat at dinner. Both paused in their eating to see who it was who hadn't waited to be invited in, then, seeing it was Tansy, Bessie rose and waddled over to take Tansy in her arms.

'Why, tis Tansy – sit you down' she pulled up a chair 'you can christen our Johnnie's latest piece of work' and Tansy remembering her manners at last, stood blushing, then ran her hands over the light curved frame.

'You made this Johnnie?'

When the lad nodded and smiled she sat down to look longingly at the remains of their meal. Bessie recognized the look and asked.

'Would ee like a piece of homity pie, my dear?'

Tansy, her stomach empty, her mouth watering, nodded and said.

'Always made a good homity, Mrs Brimmacombe' confessing with rising colour 'Martin and I were too late to eat at home' which was hardly the truth but, in the emotion of her return to the Post Office, had caused her Mother's food to stick in her throat and all she had wanted was to escape the attention of both her family and Geoffrey Llewellyn. All she had wanted was to see Rosemary Brimmacombe, needed her best friend's company, needed to tell her all that had happened since they had last met. Was it so long ago? Now she relaxed warmed by the familiar room, cheered by Bessie's welcome, the food and comfort.

'Rosemary – where is she?' Tansy asked and Bessie smiled and looked proud as she explained.

'Rose, why she's in London at Guildhall school. Just begun first term.'

At this, Tansy felt an instant lowering of spirits;

19

longing to pour out her story to the only one who would listen without comment or, if she did comment, would not criticize but would say something supportive. Tansy felt Bessie's eyes on her and struggled to respond.

'Of course, I forgot she was going to be away this winter and I wasn't even here to wish her luck and give her my present. Tansy thought of the manuscript sheets wrapped in tissue and tied round with blue ribbon lying in the chest of drawers in her room at the top of 'Courtenay House'. As if Bessie could read her thoughts she reached out to touch Tansy's arm.

'She'll be home at half term – October tis, I do believe, you can give it her then, my dear.'

Somewhat comforted Tansy went back to the food on the blue and white plate.

'This is so good.' she turned to Johnnie to ask 'Are you making furniture to sell now? Have you left the Mill?' Johnnie shook his head.

'No, still at Mill but, if I hear of a tree coming down then I rush off to try and get some of the wood. Perhaps one day I'll have my own workshop. Your Father lends me tools so's I can prepare the wood; this chair is made of beech from a faller at Steppes Meadow!'

Tansy stood to run her fingers once more over the smooth rungs of the chair back, admired the way they connected seat to back.

'Perhaps you could make a settle for Teignhead Farm, Johnnie?'

She blushed as Bessie, realising the implication of Tansy's request, rose to her feet and held out her arms, took Tansy into a huge embrace.

'There, I knew it the moment I saw that Martin Webber at Lustleigh May Fair – knew he was going to be the one for ee our Tansy!'

Tansy laughed and pulled herself away, wishing it was Geoffrey Llewellyn Bessie was matching her with; realised she would have to go through much of this comment before her wedding day. Now Bessie produced a bottle of port from the larder, added three glasses and, after pouring generous measures into each, held hers toward Tansy who sat there embarrassed and uncertain. Johnnie, as if aware of her feelings spoke up.

'There's talk of felling oak tree in St Paul's Road, tis thought the next gale could bring un down, perhaps t'would block the road from town to Station. That tree would provide enough planks to make a settle' he paused to rub his head 'though I've not made one yet'. Now Tansy's emotions took a sudden somersault. After all their meetings at the oak in St Paul's Road was she and Martins trysting tree to be cut down? It would be fitting if Johnnie could make them a settle from the tree which had played such an important part in their early courtship when she ran downhill from 'Courtenay House' on a Sunday to meet Martin after Chapel. She laid a hand on Johnnie's arm.

'That would be wonderful Johnnie' she hesitated 'how much would it cost you to make?' and, after writing some figures on a piece of paper he frowned and announced.

'T'would be more than you could afford, Tansy Drewe. At least five pounds I would think although I could say for certain when I knowed the width and height you'm thinking on.' Now Bessie changed the subject.

'Is it true that your Norah is to wed the Preacher?' She wanted confirmation of Eva's hint when she had confided to her the result of the Chapel Elders' hearing.

'Your Ma said you was visiting with the Webbers for a few days?'

Tansy's temper rose, her head went up and she spoke coldly and slowly.

'Yes, Norah and Geoffrey Llewellyn have been courting all summer behind our backs it seems – all came out at the Chapel Hearing!'.

Tansy restrained her temper with difficulty, stopped

herself from stamping a foot. Bessie looked wise.

'If you'm going to marry Martin – why you and Norah might as well have a double wedding' then added as Tansy's eyes widened in horror 'Save your Ma and Pa a deal of money – after all guests would be the same for both weddings?' Now Tansy felt she could bear no more and, thanking Bessie for the food and wine, hurried out of the house and continued on up 148 steps till she reached the top of Wolborough Hill where a strong north wind blew straight off the Moor. She hesitated, undecided as to which way to go; the drive leading to 'Courtenay House' lay to the left, the path down to St. Mary's Church and Steppes Meadow to the right. For the first time she wondered who now filled her place as Lady's Maid to Caroline and Emma Vallance? Who slept in her room at the top of the house? Other thoughts came thick and fast. In her flight from Geoffrey's trial she had not given a thought to her workplace; had dwelt only on the fact that Geoffrey was in love with Norah, the possibility of returning to work at 'Courtenay House' had not occurred to her, not once, till now. She stood looking at the pineapple topped gate posts at the end of the drive; a sudden longing for the warm kitchen where even now Cook would be enjoying a post lunch rest, dozing in front of the range. Again she thought of her room with its view over the front door, the sewing machine and firegrate ablaze with glowing coals, both of these luxuries going with the job.

Memories rushed upon her, the sound of the Vallances' pony and trap catching up with her after her dismissal from 'Courtenay House', Harry Vallance's voice calling to her.

'Drewe, Drewe. When are you coming back? They won't tell me why you've gone. I want you to come and play Mafeking with me again.' She felt again the warmth of Geoffrey's hand supporting her as the pony and trap passed by them on their first walk about the parish when Geoffrey as new Minister had arrived.

Tansy shook herself, she must forget the past and, taking a deep breath, she turned right and strode along the road towards St Mary's Church only pausing to look down at her favourite views of the town below. There was Vallance's Mill which had made serge for the British Army fighting in the Boer War, the Market buildings where every Wednesday animals were bought and sold, the Cricket Field where white figures could be seen on Saturdays playing against local teams, the familiar streets. Suddenly a figure came into view, growing larger by the moment; a familiar figure and a man that was for sure. As the person in its dark clothes grew nearer her heart began a slow pounding. Was it? No, she shook herself. It couldn't be Geoffrey. He would never come looking for her again. This figure was shorter than Geoffrey and more solid. This one also dressed in black but with a bowler hat perched on the back of it's head. What a ridiculous piece of head gear thought Tansy then recognized it's owner.

'Thought I'd find ee up here!' Martin exclaimed as he stopped in front of Tansy, his eyes holding a question. He turned to look down at the race course with its white rails, at the river retreating on a low tide towards the sea at Teignmouth. Tansy bit her tongue, she wasn't ready for this, wanted more time to think. What was she doing marrying Martin when all her instincts told her it was Geoffrey who held her heart.

'Your Mother gave me a plate of roast in the Kitchen'. Martin said turning back to Tansy. 'Rushing off like that you must be hungry too?'

Tansy swallowed hard, struggled to collect her thoughts.

'I had some dinner at Rosemary's house – she's not there – gone away to London to Music College – just like Norah . . .' she bit her tongue and Martin immediately picked up her words as she had feared he would even as she had uttered them.

'I suppose you wish you were going to London too?' but Tansy didn't respond to Martin's question. She wanted to get away from Newton which held Norah and Geoffrey; she turned to face him and ask.

'Have they gone?' and Martin knew at once whom she meant.

'Gone to Chapel to arrange tonight's service'. Silence fell as both looked out toward the Moor and it was Martin who broke the silence.

'Tis indeed a fine view. Haytor looks so clear today.' Tansy's attention captured, her green eyes followed Martin's gaze.

'See beyond Highweek Church, a rounded hill with a gap beyond? That's the way to Bovey and the Wrey Valley – take us to Lustleigh and 'Staddens' that does.'

'And Teignhead?' Tansy asked now thoroughly involved 'Where's Teignhead Martin?' He smiled.

'Tis further out by miles, beyond Haytor and Manaton beyond Chagford . . .' He turned to Tansy 'but now you know the way from there my maid . . .' Both fell silent, busy with their own thoughts.

'Having doubts already?' Martin asked 'Want to go back to being a lady's maid at 'Courtenay House'? Not enough of a challenge for you – just me, the sheep and Dartmoor?' Now Tansy, rising as always to the thrown gauntlet, turned to Martin. She pulled the bowler hat from his head hurled it out over the sloping field towards Cull's cows grazing at the bottom.

'I'll come to Teignhead if you can catch your hat!' She shouted and Martin was gone, leaping and jumping down the slope to catch the black hat as it sailed on the wind falling almost into his hands. Tansy ran to meet him as he scrambled to the top of the field and, laughing, they ran hand in hand down past the Williams' home in Bowden Hill and so to the Post Office and Eva, seeing the glow on Tansy's face, the sparkle in her eyes, felt relieved and reassured that the marriage plans mooted earlier in the day were after all for the best.

'Thank you for dinner' Martin twisted the now muddy hat between his hands 'we must be away or twill

24

be dark avore us gets home.' He blushed on the word 'home'. Eva followed them to the door then demanded.

'You'll stay here till you'm wed our Tansy?' There was a moment or two's silence then Tansy's voice came firm and sure.

'No, Mother. I'm to learn to be a sheep farmer's wife now and must get settled avore winter comes.'

'Then when should Father arrange for the banns to be called?' Eva wanted to know.

'Harvest Festival would suit us' Tansy said turning to Martin for his nod of approval then adding 'Mrs Brimmacombe says Norah and I should wed same day so, if that's alright with you and Father shall we say September 29th?' Now Eva caught both by the hand looking from one to the other and asking.

'Are you sure this is what you both want?' and when Tansy and Martin smiled their agreement, she kissed Tansy and let them out through the Post Office door.

'Then come next Sunday Tansy and we'll arrange everything.'

3

CHAGFORD

Tansy had had to assure Martin on the way home from the Post Office that she really did want to spend the three weeks before their wedding at Teignhead. Not at the Post Office.

'To stay at home, share our old bedroom with Norah – no, Martin, I couldn't bear it.'

Her colour high she thought of all she had wanted to say to Norah when first she heard that she it was who had stolen Geoffrey Llewellyn from her – instead she had run here to Martin who now told her she could buy tea, sugar, flour, candles and paraffin at Chagford where there were dressmakers, milliners and a dairy where when she had learned how to make cream she could sell it together with eggs from the hens they would have soon. On receipt of this information Tansy was all agog to see her local town. She realised Martin was watching her and, turning her back, she gathered up a large basket, took her jacket and hat from a peg behind the door.

'I'm going to Chagford now, Martin. Do you want me to get anything for you?'

''Tis four miles there and four miles back, Tansy. Do you want me to take ee?' Tansy shook her head.

'Just tell me the way. I'll enjoy the walk.' Martin looked unsure, thinking of the moorland he wanted to clear to make new pasture.

'Take the track from the clapper to the stone circle, keep to the track through Fernworthy Farm, this is where Tom Osborne lives -he's been milking the cow when I'm not here. Cross the Teign at the bridge then follow the river to Thornworthy and take the right fork at Waye Barton that'll see ee right for Chagford!' Martin laughed.

'Tis a fair step Tansy – are you sure you'm up to it?' Tansy always ripe for a challenge tossed her head and opened the door and was gone.

She enjoyed the walk across the Moor pausing at the stone circles to wonder who had placed them there and why. Reaching the first group of buildings she was greeted by three dogs who ran round her, barking and jumping up till they were brought to order by a woman and three children. Tansy stopped to greet them.

'Is this Fernworthy Farm?' she enquired and when the woman nodded in the affirmative Tansy offered to purchase anything the family required in Chagford?

This offer was greeted with a grim shake of the head, a frown growing on her plain countenance. One of the girls seemed about to speak but was immediately shushed by the mother who, sensing disappointment on the faces of the children now offered.

'Come you in on the way back and I'll make tea.' Tansy nodded her thanks and hurried on but not before noticing how run down were the farm buildings, roofs sagging, thatches needing attention. The house itself showed peeling paint on casement windows, indeed some windows were broken and patched over with brown paper. The dogs, no longer interested in her, lay in a heap outside a barn. There was no sign of activity and Tansy wondered where the men were?

Thornworthy was a different story altogether – more like the state of Martin's family's farm at 'Staddens' with its air of bustle and activity. No dogs to greet her but a pretty woman with her hair tied back above rosy cheeks and a fat baby balanced on one hip. She invited Tansy in but she anxious to be on her way refused the invitation but accepted an errand to buy lamp wicks and accepted too the coin pressed into her hand.

As moorland and farm field gave way to lane edged with the last flowers of autumn Tansy stopped to savour the sweet smell of meadowsweet, late honeysuckle and pick ripe blackberries until houses began to appear at the road side. She noted the size of the Church and substantial square and The Three Crowns Hotel with its handsome porch, she walked along the main street, crossed over and returned up the other side counting no less than 9 blacksmiths. Very impressive thought Tansy but so different from her home town Newton Abbot. Reaching the market square once more, Tansy decided to look in at Jacob Blackstone's Emporium which had sounded imposing and so it proved. Everything from saucepans, crocks, boots and tools covered the shelves, seed, firewood, paraffin, candles, lamps covered the floor and in a far corner bolts of cloth. Tansy was immediately drawn to a coloured bolt of turquoise taffeta which she couldn't resist touching. What a wonderful dress it would make. She thought of her wedding day. What was she to wear? Not her mother's old green suit which had seen such hard service when she had ridden over the moor with Martin. It would in any case be too thick for September. She wondered what Norah planned to wear, something sober as was her style – grey probably – Tansy's mouth twisted in a smile. She would be different. Looking round for an assistant she pondered on the price and the length she would need.

'How much a yard?' she called and an assistant, a thin young man came toward her.

'That's new in Miss. Just arrived yesterday. I'll enquire the price for you.'

He set off for a door at the back of the shop and disappeared from view. Tansy continued to muse on her wedding dress – she had the muslin but that hadn't been the same since she'd been caught in the thunderstorm at Kingsteignton's Ram Roast. Wistfully she turned from the cloth. Aware of movement from the door at the back of the shop Tansy looked up to see the assistant approaching again wringing his hands, looking back towards a large man who stood button booted feet planted apart, dressed in pin striped trousers and black tail coat, his waxed moustache matching thick black hair parted in the centre, watching his assistant who now enquired.

'Was it for some special occasion Miss?' Tansy nodded.

'I'm to be wed in three weeks' time.' At this the assistant, sensing a sale, took down the bolt of turquoise and threw it across the counter where it glistened and shone.

'Show Madame the new hats, Thomas.' Tansy hadn't noticed the approach of the store owner, for surely such an imposing figure must be he. This figure now gave a small bow.

'Jacob Blackstone at your service, Madame.'

Tansy flushed, embarrassed at being addressed as 'Madame' for the first time in her life. Thomas fetched steps and brought down a toque which perfectly matched the bolt of taffeta and, before she could resist, set it on her head. It sat on her auburn curls matching her eyes and she was aware that both master and assistant were regarding her in admiration. She shook herself and thought of the motoring hat she had brought at Widecombe's in Newton Abbot. Surely that would do if she trimmed it with a piece of the taffeta.

'How many yards would it take to make an ankle length dress with leg of mutton sleeves and a bustle?' While Jacob Blackstone and Thomas measured and figured she thought to herself 'I must be mad, where on earth can I get enough money to buy this?' Thomas produced a yard stick and measured 'Four and a half yards should be plenty' He looked to Jacob Blackstone for confirmation. He pressed his fingers together and smiled.

'Yes, yes. Plenty for such a petite figure as Madame's'.

Again Tansy blushed, aware of Jacob Blackstone's gaze eyeing her figure from top to toe.

'How much?' she asked. Might as well get it out of the way once and for all. Then she could banish the turquoise cloth and get the lamp wicks for the woman at Thornworthy, the groceries and return to Teignhead.

Jacob Blackstone waved away the assistant who hovered anxiously in the background awaiting developments.

'Bring the grey boots, Thomas' he clicked his fingers and Thomas brought down boxes of boots, a chair appeared as if by magic and Tansy began to enjoy herself as she sat down with a bump and unlaced her black workaday boots, boots covered in the dust of moor and lane. Jacob himself knelt at her feet, trying soft grey boots on her slim feet, touching her arches and producing a button hook to fasten the mother of pearl buttons which ran up the side of the suede boots. She stood to try them out and Thomas encouraged by his master held the bolt of material against her figure; Jacob placed the toque on her head tucking the wriggling locks of hair beneath the hat. Together the men led her towards a cheval mirror in the corner of the shop. Tansy gasped with delight at the effect. Why she looked every bit as elegant as Emma Vallance had in her new chapel outfit of the autumn before. Dreading the answer again she enquired 'How much?' Jacob shook his head at Thomas busy with notepad and pencil.

'Together – taffeta, hat and shoes' here he paused to smile at Tansy 'and I would include grey gloves to match for nothing – eight pounds'.

Tansy's face fell with the realisation that this figure was more than two months wages at Courtenay House. Jacob bent toward her.

'Don't concern yourself, Madame, a pound down would be sufficient to secure everything and a pound each month after could be arranged.'

Quickly Tansy unbuttoned the elegant grey boots

removed the turquoise toque which had so perfectly matched her eyes and turned her back on the length of taffeta covering the counter.

'Thank you, sir' she said 'but I haven't brought money with me to buy today.' Quickly she slid feet into black boots and stood up preparing to leave. Jacob's smile never wavered.

'Tell you what I'll do, Madame' he said pressing his finger tips together 'We will keep 4½ yards of material for you, Madame, should you find this meets your needs. Keep it for a week. Still leave enough time to make it up' Here he raised an eyebrow in query 'has Madame a dress maker?'

Tansy found herself nodding – confident her Mother could make up the material in time for the wedding.

'Well then, we will keep the hat and shoes too until a week today. Madame wouldn't find a better colour or material for such an important day.' Here he bowed from the waist and Tansy fled from the shop forgetting all about the lamp wicks she had promised to buy for the farmer's wife at Thornworthy. She was unaware of curious eyes following her as she paced the streets. If she took the taffeta home at the weekend there would just be time for her mother to make it up. Would a bustle pose a problem? She shook her head – unthinkable to spend such a large sum of money then remembering the wages owing her at Courtenay House she stopped – would they be enough?

How could she go and ask for her money when she had left without notice. Then too her spare drawers and chemise still lay in her room and, she drew in her breath remembering, her precious books. Now she wondered if there was a new lady's maid looking after Emma and Caroline Vallance. Would she have the nerve to go to 'Courtenay House' and ask for those wages. Her chin went up and smiled – decision taken – and finding a small general store, not so grand as Blackstone's she went in and bought candles, twine and matches for Martin, lamp wicks for the Farmer's wife and, making up her mind at last, returned to Blackstone's, leaving ten minutes later with a brown paper parcel in her basket and began the long walk back to Teignhead. At Thornworthy she disturbed farm dogs returned from the fields, heard hoofs moving in the linhay, sounds of grooming going on and a general air of activity and when Tansy approached the farmhouse door it stood open and beyond the sound of meal preparation taking place.

'Hallo' Tansy called and one of the children came running 'tis the lamp wicks for your Mother' she placed them into young hands. The woman looked up from carving a large ham, just nodded but made no move to invite Tansy in. She, rather disappointed at this lack of welcome, continued along the track to cross the bridge to Fernworthy. There the dogs greeted her again with much barking and jumping but this time tails wagged in welcome and when the smallest and youngest sheep dog rubbed against her legs she put down a hand to stroke its head and was rewarded with a friendly whine and lick from the rough tongue. Now the farmhouse door opened and the young woman appeared, smiling a welcome and inviting Tansy, who by now was growing tired, into the house.

'Would ee like a sup of tea?' the woman asked and Tansy nodded in gratitude. The woman, tall and painfully thin, moved quietly about the long kitchen, worn boots tapping on the blue slate floor, the only light some rushes in holders by a huge open fireplace where a meagre peat fire smouldered just breaking the evening chill. Three children sat at table eating bread and jam.

The small dog had crept in with Tansy and now lay by her feet where she sat on a settle placed between fire and door to combat draught. The woman placed a small oak table beside her and set down a fine bone china cup and saucer holding steaming liquid and enquired.

'Some bread and jam too perhaps?' adding a

32

matching plate to the table and bringing slices of bread and a small jar of jam.

'Is this home baked? The jam home made too?' and when the woman nodded she fell to wondering if this was the evening meal or just something to fill the gap between dinner mid day and supper at night.

'Yes, I bake all our bread and the jam is from bilberries; we make a day of the gathering in August – all the women from the moorland farms and some from Chagford. Tis a day out for the children too – we takes a picnic with us.'

'That sounds good – perhaps next August I can come too? Perhaps tis time I introduced myself? I'm Tansy Drewe and I am come to live at Teignhead Farm'. She announced as she lifted the cup and saucer to her lips. The woman responded.

'Wilmot Osborne I be. Tom is my husband.'

'And the children?'

She smiled proudly and as she introduced each child they stood and gave a short bow to Tansy.

'Rebecca is the oldest, then Anne and Judd the youngest.' Dressed very simply in much patched dresses and trousers their figures reflected in the rushlight which cast shadows about the room. Tansy drank and ate, stealing looks about the room.

'Such lovely names' Tansy commented 'The old names are best I do believe. Do you go to school at Chagford?'

Here the children exchanged looks with their mother who shook her head in denial, colour rising in her pale face.

'Need good shoes or boots to walk to Chagford each day. No, I teach them at home just now.' Wilmot refilled Tansy's cup and enquired.

'What be doing at Teignhead then?'

Now it was Tansy's turn to blush as she tried out her news for the second time that day.

'Me and Martin Webber are to be wed three weeks

last Sunday.' Wilmot Osborne smiled and all three children looked up from their meal.

'And where be wedding taking place?'

'Methodist Church in Newton Abbot. Tis where I comes from. My father keeps the Post Office up Bowden Hill.' Now Wilmot smiled and pointed to a gilt photo frame set on the mantelpiece. Tansy rose to walk the few steps across the kitchen and gaze at the young couple posed against a background of studio ferns and velvet drapes. Wilmot, younger and plumper, dressed in white and Tom wearing a dark suit, hair brushed from a high forehead hands holding a bowler hat. Both looking at the Photographer with an anxious look as if they mistrusted his ability to take their likeness.

'Yes, tis me and my Tom on our special day . . .' she made as if to continue then stopped and turned back to the table, began clearinq plates while the children rose to fetch books from a small shelf against the wall. Wilmot lit a lamp with a spill from the rushlight and soon they were immersed in their reading.

Their mother began to wash the crocks and Tansy took the hint that it was time to leave. Thanking Wilmot for her hospitality she set off on the last lap homeward wondering at the absence of Tom Osborne and the paucity of the Osborne life style. She thought of the contrast in hospitality she had received between the two farms.

She was tired and when she saw a horseman coming toward her was pleased indeed to recognize Lucifer with Martin astride his back.

'You'm late my maid' Martin greeted her before reaching down to sweep Tansy up in front of him, knocking the brown parcel from her grasp. Tansy shouted until he stopped.

'Go back, go back. My parcel, my parcel.'

Wheeling the cob Martin went back, jumped down to retrieve the parcel.

'What have ee here?' Tansy sat clutching her basket, reached out for the parcel, shook her head.

'Tis a secret, you'm not to see it till the 29th September.' Martin looked puzzled but put no more questions while he tried to manage the cob, Tansy and parcel all at the same time. Half an hour saw them at Teignhead, dismounted, Martin to see to Lucifer, Tansy to begin on the evening chores of lamp lighting, fire stoking, stew heating and by the time Martin came into the kitchen the brown paper parcel had been hidden away.

4

PREPARATIONS

Sunday saw Tansy clutching her precious parcel delivered by Martin to the Station at Lustleigh bound for Newton Abbot and the Post Office. He was taking the opportunity of her absence to visit with his family.

'When shall I come to meet ee, my maid?' he wanted to know as she boarded the train. Tansy shook her head.

'I don't know Martin. I have something to settle so it may p'raps be that I have to stay home a night or two. I'll come back on the post van so don't meet the train. Now I know the way I can walk from Chagford. Give my love to your Mother.' So with a clanking of wheels and an issuing of steam the train bearing Tansy away was gone leaving Martin puzzling as to what Tansy had to settle at Newton Abbot. Impatient now for the time to pass and for he and Tansy to begin their life as man and wife he unhitched Lucifer from the hitching ring outside the Station and walked the cob slowly to 'Staddens' where he was greeted with shouts and laughter emanating from the granary. Suddenly the door burst open and Fanny Luscombe flew down the steps, face rosy, still laughing and pursued by his brother Adam.

Eva Drewe greeted Tansy with a hug, standing her away to look searchingly at her daughter, noted the tanned cheeks, glowing eyes. Took the parcel from her daughter's arms and drew her to the table where the midday meal was laid ready.

'Tis a pity you couldn't have got here in time to hear the banns today, Tansy. Twas the first time of asking'. Tansy wondered if it was Geoffrey who had read the announcement of her and Martin's marriage plans. She wondered too if anyone ever raised any objection.

'It takes a while to get to Newton Abbot from Teign-head, Mother' then added in a rush.

'Twill be good when you and Father can come and see the Farm. Robert and James will love it – they can run and run till they'm all puffed out. The moors are full o' birds, rabbits and foxes too,if you'm quiet and still enough. Where are they, the boys?' Eva laughed and explained.

'Given the job of collecting up hymn books at Chapel and now both are singing in the choir. They'll be home drekly.' Tansy knew what 'drekly' meant – any time from five minutes to five hours – she looked wistful.

'Only been away a few weeks and already everything has changed.' She remembered why she had come. 'I've something to show you.' Eva took up the parcel.

'I guess this is the something?' she smiled and Tansy suddenly shy with the importance of what she wanted from her Mother hesitated.

'After dinner Mother. After dinner – can we go somewhere where we won't be disturbed?'

Eva smiled, guessing the contents of the parcel, equally excited at the coming double wedding of her two daughters but slightly worried at the shortness of time till all should be ready. If Tansy had brought material to be made up it would indeed be a rush to get it done. Thank goodness she thought Norah had already decided to wear the new suit Eva had made for her to take to College. Practical Norah, preferring to economise on her own dress and think of books she would need when she became a teacher at the end of the following year. Geoffrey had arranged with the new

Minister to share the living at the Manse where Blodwin Williams was to look after both men in Norah's absence. Geoffrey was to go out as a locum to surrounding towns until Norah had obtained her degree then both would seek appointments and make a home together moving round the circuit every two years. Not a life Tansy envied at all.

It seemed an eternity to Tansy as the most important meal of the week was consumed, just Eva and Edward, Robert, James and Tansy. Norah and Geoffrey were eating at the Manse where Blodwen was roasting Welsh Lamb which pleased Geoffrey no end reminding him of his time at Merthyr; a dish new to Norah who never took much interest in food. As soon as Tansy had helped Eva clear and wash dishes the two women climbed the stairs to Eva's room with its space and large mirror. There Tansy opened the brown paper parcel and threw the taffeta across her parents' bed with a flourish. Eva gasped.

'My Tansy, whatever have you here?'

'Don't you think it beautiful, Mother? Can you make it up in time for my wedding day?' Eva took a deep breath and pronounced judgment.

'Tis indeed very beautiful but not very practical! Something you could wear up auver would have been better our Tansy! How much did it cost?' Tansy blushed but picked up the cloth and held it to her chin, whirled round the room then declared.

'I know tidden practical, Mother, but it is my wedding day. Just once in my life to have a gorgeous dress!' Tansy ignored the question of cost. 'No hand me downs just for once. Is it so much to ask?'

'Is it paid for?' Eva asked knowing taffeta of such quality must cost a pretty penny. 'Where did you get it?' Now Tansy began to get cross.

'For goodness sake Mother – just leave all that to me. Can you make it up in time or not? I'll do all the tacking and hemming'.

Now Eva laughed.

'My Tansy tacking! My Tansy hemming! That'll be the day.'

Then her face became serious. 'What style had you thought . . . let's get out Grandmother Thomas's pattern book and see – something simple would perhaps be best.' Moving to the wardrobe she brought out a worn and battered pattern book, sat down on the dressing stool and placed the book on the bed. She began to turn pages while Tansy hopped from one foot to the other in agitation dying to tell Eva what she wanted. Not an old pattern from her Grandmother Thomas's day but something fashionable, something new.

'Look Tansy, here's a simple dress, pity you haven't some lace for the neck' she paused deep in thought 'perhaps your Grandmother's lace . . .'

Now Tansy interrupted.

'No, no Mother – you're not to sacrifice Grandmother's lace – you should wear it in your own dress. What are you going to wear?' Her usual concern for others surfaced and Tansy sat beside her Mother feeling selfish at having bought so extravagantly for herself. Eva dismissed Tansy's concern and returned to the pattern book.

'Don't you worry yourself about Father and me. We shall wear our Sunday go-to-meeting clothes and our happiness will be to see our two daughters happily wed and on the same day too.'

'Mother I've thought of the sort of dress I want' she hesitated 'ankle length – the new length – with a small bustle and leg-of-mutton sleeves!!' Eva gasped and stared at Tansy in disbelief.

'And you want me to make this for you? Why I'm not sure if I can. Bustles would be difficult and those sleeves. Really, Tansy you need a proper dressmaker for a job like that!!'

A silence fell while Tansy pictured the Turquoise taffeta finished and ready for her to step into and Eva thought of the terror of cutting and sewing such expensive (for it surely must have cost a year's wages) material. Thought of the hours it would take to make. Then suddenly a yearning began, a yearning to do her daughter proud. To make the dress Tansy hankered after – Tansy the younger daughter, always dressed in second best, Norah's hand-me-downs, the old green suit of her Mother's now shabby. Surely she was entitled to what she wanted for once. Eva thought of the sacrifice Tansy had made with such good grace – going into service so that Norah could go to Goldsmith's College and train to be a teacher. Yes, she and Edward had promised that when Norah had finished her training, she, Tansy, would have a chance to do something in the way of training for a career. Now that that plan had been overruled by Tansy's decision to marry Martin Webber and become a sheep farmer's wife on Dartmoor things had changed. Suddenly she snapped shut the book and smiled at her youngest daughter.

'Very well, Tansy. I'll do my best if you will stay and help with the cooking and washing while I cut and sew. I can take patterns from your old dresses but I will need you to be here at home to try on the dress as it grows. Are you prepared to do that?' For answer Tansy grabbed her Mother around the waist and whirled her round and round until both fell on to the bed sending the Turquoise taffeta sliding on to the floor. Again Eva worried about the cost?

'Tell me how much you paid, Tansy? Perhaps your Father and I can give . . .'

But Tansy placed a finger on her Mother's lips and shook her head.

'No, Mother. Not another word. If you can make it up for me that will be all the wedding gift I want. Tomorrow' she said 'I have to call on the Vallances, collect my spare clothes and books.

Do you know who is lady's maiding for Emma and Caroline?' Eva shook her head.

'Now you'm not at 'Courtenay House' there's no-one to bring news. Blodwen used to call on her way home but now she's at the Manse . . .' she left the sentence unfinished and Tansy, tired suddenly from all the excitement of the last few days left her Mother's room to fall asleep on the bed in her and Norah's old room. Slept until Robert called her down to a supper of cold ham, potatoes and pickled onions followed by stewed fruit. Afterwards she read to her young brothers by the fire and felt such a sense of belonging that she thought with some apprehension of the future which lay ahead. Thought of the barren farm house on the moor; wondered how long it would take her to make it into a home for Martin and perhaps children. These thoughts reminded her that her friend Avril Moore was expecting a child and she asked her Mother.

'How is Avril Moore, Mother?' Eva shook her head.

'Hasn't been coming to Chapel this last few months. Dr. Jones told her twas time to stop their family after Eleanor died but ever since Avril has wanted a little girl to replace her. Tom is very worried.'

'Do you think she'll be alright?' Tansy asked. When Eva again shook her head Tansy decided to go and see her friend while she was here in Newton. 'I think I'll call on Avril while I'm here Mother' but first she had to go to 'Courtenay House' and she decided that this she would do on the very next day.

Edward Drewe gazed at his daughter across the breakfast porridge next day.

'Mother tells me she is to make your wedding dress our Tansy?'

'Yes Father. Tis to be kept a secret – no-one's to see it before the day – especially not Martin.'

Edward smiled, trust Tansy to be positive about this as she was about most things. Tansy went on.

'Unlucky to see the bride in her dress before they'm wed so tis said.'

'Luck seems to be with you now my maid.' He nodded his head, wiped his mouth and prepared to make his way to the Post Office counter. 'Just see you don't do anything to let it run out of the window. A fine young man Martin Webber. Needs a strong woman to support him and work with him in this new venture Your Mother and I believe you to be capable of achieving whatever you'm set on Tansy. Don't let us down!'

His words left Tansy feeling solemn and suddenly unsure. Could she really become a farmer's wife? Cook for her man when, although watching her Mother and Cook at 'Courtenay House' had had little opportunity to put what she'd seen into practice. But then again she could learn, couldn't she? She shrugged her shoulders began to clear away the porridge bowls and wash them in the scullery sink.

'Mother, I'm off to 'Courtenay House' – then I'll go down to see Avril Moore.'

'Alright Tansy but be back in time to help with dinner. By then I'll have the dress cut out – just hope your figure hasn't changed since last time I made you a dress!' Eva's last words fell on empty air because Tansy had already left the Post Office and was climbing 148 steps to reach the top of Wolborough Hill. At the top she hesitated for a moment then turned left to follow the road to 'Courtenay House' and by sheer force of habit take the path leading to the servants' entrance at the back of the house.

Familiar sounds met her as she pushed open the outer door familiar voices – Seth's deep bass interspersed with Cook's rosy tones. Suddenly she was in the Kitchen with its warmth and cooking smells and Cook was coming toward her arms outstretched in welcome.

'Why, tis Tansy. Bless my soul. Who would have thought it! After her leaving all of a sudden and us not knowing where she be to!'

Tansy blushed with pleasure and guilt at leaving the Vallances in the lurch, guilty at not giving a thought to the result of her absconding on the servants.

Seth too wanted to give her a hug but not before he'd wiped bloody hands on his apron and laid down his skinning knife.

42

'Well now Tansy have ee come back for good this time or have ee some other adventure waiting?'

'No, I'm not come to stay' then she added in a rush 'but tis so good to see you both.' She hesitated trying to find an easy way to break her news. 'I'm come to collect my wages and my books and clothes.'

Cook and Seth stood waiting for her to tell them what she had planned after the announcement that she was not coming back. She took a deep breath and plunged on.

'I'm to be married come Harvest Festival?' Again she paused while Cook clucked in delight and Seth's deeply tanned face split into a beaming smile but again both waited for more. Tansy hesitated till Cook pressed her.

'Bain't ee going to tell us who the lucky man is then or are we to guess?' When Tansy still stayed silent Cook went on.

'If it bain't Methody preacher from Wales?' here she waited for Tansy to confirm or deny. Tansy shook her head 'Then must be that young farmer from Lustleigh – what was his name?'

The worst over Tansy smiled at last and confirmed that it was Martin Webber she was to wed. She brushed away a tear at the suggestion that it might have been Geoffrey she was to marry – if only.

Cook sensing her distress took pity on her.

'You'd best go round front if you want to see Missis' Cook said 'being as how you'm not working here no more.' With further hugs from Cook and Seth, Tansy left the kitchen for the last time and walked round to the front door. Her heart began a slow pounding as she pulled the handle of the door bell and waited until she heard footsteps crossing the Hall. The door opened and there was Hetty Westcott who promptly rushed out to hug Tansy and exchange news.

'How is Jack?' Tansy wanted to know how Hetty's man who had had such a hard time when he returned from the Boer War was faring.

'Got a job at the Railway Yard now Tansy,' she

paused 'You coming back Tansy?' Tansy shook her head.

'Have come to see the Missis Hetty. Is she at home?' Who should appear now but Caroline Vallance herself looking elegant in a grey morning dress, hair piled in plaited coils and ringlets tight to her forehead. She stopped at sight of Tansy. She looked coldly at her and raised an enquiring eyebrow.

'Well Drewe, what are you doing here?'

'If you please ma'am' here Tansy gave a bob 'I'm come to collect my things' she hesitated 'and to say how sorry I am to have let you down . . .' her voice trailed off.

'I should think so! Sorry indeed . . . after Mr Vallance and I gave you a fresh start and a room of your own.'

Now Tansy flushed with anger as she remembered the raising of her status from kitchen to lady's maid had been the outcome of the Vallances' wrongful accusation that she had stolen Emma Vallance's birthday watch. She bit her lips forcing back the words that rose in her throat. She swallowed these bitter words and taking courage carried on.

'I've also come to say that I'm to be married at Harvest Festival and need my wages.'

Now Caroline's face flushed a deep angry red. She turned her back on Tansy and crossed the hall into the Morning Room. Tansy hurried after her and stood waiting for her past mistress' response. Ignoring her Caroline Vallance took her seat at the table and began looking at the day's menu. She kept Tansy waiting a full five minutes before she looked up.

'Still here, Drewe. What was it you wanted?'

'My books and clothes, ma'am, and if you please the wages I earned up to the time I left Newton Abbot.'

Caroline tapped on the table with a pen, wishing Charles was at home; he would have known how to handle this situation. Was Tansy Drewe entitled to wages even though she had left without giving notice?

'You realise you caused us great inconvenience? Just

44

at the time of the Summer Ball too!' She paused then opening a drawer withdrew an envelope which Tansy noted carried her name. Caroline continued. 'Unfortunately my husband deals with staff and wages and although he appears to have set aside wages for you to the end of September I'm not sure you are entitled in the light of your so precipitate departure without notice. I will speak to him about it but you may collect your things.'

'Thank you, ma'am.' There was nothing more Tansy could say although her naturally warm heart made her enquire.

'How is Miss Emma? And Master Harry – how is he?'

At this Caroline had the grace to smile and nod.

'Well, they're both fine – Emma is to announce her engagement to Christopher Westaway soon and Harry is learning to ride now.' She cut short Tansy's congratulations and waved a hand in dismissal.

'Off you go now.'

There seemed to be nothing more she could say so Tansy climbed the two flights of stairs to her old room and without pausing opened the door and walked in. She froze in horror at the sight of Janet Luscombe sitting sewing a striped skirt on the machine Tansy had used when she had been lady's maid to Emma and Caroline. At the sound of the door opening, the sharp intake of breath, her old enemy looked up. Her face equally startled now bore a look of triumph.

'What be doin here then Tansy Drewe? Come to ask for your old job back? Didn't Missis tell you I'm back where I belongs?' Tansy moved swiftly across the small room – her one thought to collect her things and leave. Janet had other thoughts and jumped up to bar Tansy's way. Tansy's hand flew to the scar on her cheek placed there by Janet in a past clash – would her enemy become violent on this occasion? They glared at one another until Emma Vallance hearing that Tansy was in the house burst into the room.

'Tansy how good to see you. Have you heard I'm to

45

be married next Spring?' Tansy laughed at the girl who stood, cheeks pink, looking so pleased to see her. 'Cook tells me you'm to be married too and in a few weeks time?'

Seizing the opportunity afforded by Emma Vallance's presence Tansy pushed past Janet Luscombe to open drawers and seize her underwear, take toilet things from the violet decorated wash-stand and sweep books from the tiny mantel shelf into her Mother's basket while Emma prattled on about the dress she was to wear. Finally she asked 'Are you coming back Drewe? Janet never does my hair like you used to?'

Tansy laughed and shook her head and with a triumphant glance at Janet she left the room to descend the stairs followed by Emma still pleading for her to return to 'Courtenay House'. She crossed the Hall and left the house relieved that she had achieved her purpose. She turned to wave to Emma Vallance who stood at the front door and hurried down the hill to the Post Office.

'What took you so long Tansy? I need you to set the table, your Father and the twins will be here any minute.' She smiled in answer to Tansy's enquiring look. 'Yes I've cut out the dress but there's not enough to make those full sleeves you wanted.' As Tansy's face fell Eva added. 'I'll pin it together this afternoon while you're out – you can try it on this evening and I can tack and sew it tomorrow and Wednesday but you must be here to try it on as I put it together.'

Tansy looked dubious thinking of Martin struggling to look after himself and the sheep. This wasn't what they had agreed, she had wanted to be at Teignhead learning to milk the cow and begin on the garden. Eva noticing the frown growing on her daughter's face now suggested.

'Why not send a post card to Martin – say I need you here for three days. If you write it now your Father can take it down with the mail to the main Post Office in time for the evening collection. Martin'll get it tomorrow.'

Now Tansy's frown was replaced by a smile and relieved that she could let Martin know what was happening she hurried to the desk, took a card from the compendium and sitting down chewed the end of the pen before writing.

'Dear Martin, Mother needs me here till Thursday. I'll be on the 5 o'clock train to Moreton. Please meet me. Tansy.'

'Now come along Tansy. There's potatoes to go into the dish and pickles to fetch while I carve the ham.' Edward was pleased to see Tansy.

'Tis good to have ee back home, our Tansy!' Now he looked serious 'though Vallance is not best pleased with ee I hear. Charles Vallance says they had problems replacing you in time for the Summer Ball!' Tansy nodded then burst out.

'Caroline Vallance wouldn't give me my wages when I went up to the house this morning.'

Eva clucked. 'Trust her, always the same, jumped up – trade background always tells.'

'Now now Eva' Edward shook his head 'You shouldn't speak so in front of the young folk.'

Eva continued. 'Forgotten when her family couldn't provide boots for school so's she and her brother couldn't attend. Full of airs and graces now she's changed her name from Hilda Widecombe to Caroline Vallance.' The expression on her face changed. 'Couldn't you have a word with Charles Vallance Edward? After all Tansy's entitled to her wages even if she didn't give proper notice.'

After a moment's thought Edward nodded and promised to speak to him next evening when the Elders held their weekly meeting. The meal continued in companionable silence, each deep in their own thoughts. Eva pondering the problem of fitting bustle into dress, Edward's the best moment to tackle Charles Vallance about Tansy's wages and Tansy's on what to

47

take to Avril Moore. With the many journeys back and forth from Teignhead to Newton her money was fast running out. As if her Father could read her thoughts he turned to her and asked.

'Without your wages you must be a little short our Tansy?' and when she blushed and nodded he drew five shillings from his waistcoat pocket and placed them beside Tansy's plate. 'Keep you going till us gets your wages, eh?'

Tansy rose and hugged him thinking how she would miss him and all the family when she moved out to Teignhead for good.

'You will come out and see us often?' she asked and both smiled and nodded at their youngest daughter.

'Of course we will' and Robert and James added their pleas, to be allowed to visit Teignhead Farm too.

'I should be very cross if you didn't!' Tansy said. Everyone laughed at this and Eva dismissed Tansy.

'Off you go to Avril. Take this and say we will be waiting for news.' Taking a jar of jam from the larder, Eva wrapped it in brown paper and Tansy holding it tight left the room and was gone.

5

DISASTERS

Tansy hurried downhill into town and at the Clock
Tower was about to turn into Moon Court when she
remembered the Moore family were no longer there.
After the Great Flood when baby Eleanor drowned
there Tom Moore had moved his family to Bradley
Lane where a terraced house opposite the Leat had
just become vacant. As she retraced her steps to Bank
Street a familiar figure emerged from the Globe Hotel,
hesitated for a moment, looking up and down the street
and Tansy realised it was her old adversary Jess Hallett.
Hoping to escape she pulled her hat down over her
face, quickened her pace but it was too late. Jess Hallett
had recognized her and now came after her calling out.

'Why, if tidn't Tansy Drewe! Minister's fancy woman!'
Tansy decided the best thing to do was ignore the
thickset figure, the so familiar billy cock hat, yellow
checked waistcoat and cord trousers and keep walking.
She was no match for the strong man who soon caught
up with her. As he drew level with her she could smell
his beery breath. The ginger hair needed cutting and
his cord trousers were plastered with clay.

'What be doing in Newton then my beauty!' he
demanded grasping her arm. Tansy tried to shake him
off but was dragged to a standstill. She clutched tight to
Avril Moore's jar of jam and prayed for deliverance.

'Living with a farmer on Moor I hear! Had enough of

Methody ways ave ee? Bit cold and lonely up there bain't it!' When Tansy didn't answer he swung her round to face him, his face pushed close to hers. 'I be working down clay pits now! Earning good money! Enough to keep a wife. What say, Tansy Drewe – now Mother's gone there be plenty of room. Warmer in a brick cottage near town than up auver Dartymoor!'

Each time Jess Hallett embarked on a new sentence Tansy pulled back from the fetid breath, the red face but couldn't free herself from his hold.

'I want nothing to do with ee Jess Hallett – go and cause mischief somewheres else! Whoever employs you must be mad and your Mother must bless the day she was freed from her ugly son. God rest her soul!'

Now Jess Hallett lost his temper and pulling her closer began to reach for her breasts and force his lips on hers in repetition of his behaviour on the day she had gone to the opening of the Penny Arcade. She was near to fainting when the door of the Hotel opened and Charles Vallance came out. Immediately he sized up the situation and began to belabour Jess Hallett about the head and shoulders with his gold knobbed cane. Hitting with such force that the younger man let Tansy go and howling in pain covering his head with his hands crouched away from Charles Vallance's blows.

'Run my dear. Go on your way – I'll see to this varmint.' Tansy clutching her jar of jam, thanked her past employer and hurried on to Avril Moore's house secure in the knowledge that Jess Hallett had learnt his lesson and would give up his pursuit of her.

Avril was horrified at the sight of her friend, drew her inside and made her sit and recover while she brewed tea. Her movements were slow as she tended her friend and listened to the account of the attack by Jess Hallett. Now it was Tansy's turn to ask for news.

'Not long to go now' Avril said with pride. 'Dr Jones didn't think I could go my time but see . . .' here she pulled aside her skirt to show Tansy her swollen belly.

Tansy smiled and laid a hand on her friend's stomach.

'I can feel the baby kicking Avril. Have you thought what you will call it?' Now Avril's face lit up.

'Tis to be Thomasin!'

'And what if tis a boy?' Tansy wanted to know. Avril shook her head. 'Tis a girl – I do know for sartin Tansy. Just the same feel as Eleanor – same movements – Tom keeps saying 'Don't be disappointed if tis a boy but I'm sure'. She laid a hand on Tansy's arm.

'You'm the only real woman friend I have – I'll never forget the night of the flood, the days after when you helped me to accept Eleanor was gone. This time would you promise to do something for me if anything should go wrong?' Tansy took the older woman's hands in hers.

'Of course I will – but nothing's going to go wrong!' She waited to hear what was on Avril's mind.

'If anything should happen to me' she paused then rushed on 'will you bring up my baby? My Thomasin?'

Tansy was taken aback, she hesitated, wanting to reassure Avril but unwilling to make such a promise.

'I know nothing about bringing up bairns Avril. I am to be married at Harvest Festival!'

Avril exclaimed and showed such pleasure that she continued 'I'm promised to Martin Webber, going to be a farmer's wife. Have to learn to milk cow, make cream and plant a garden . . .' She stopped seeing the disappointment growing on her friend's face. 'Why, of course, I'll look after your baby, Avril. I'm sure all will be well – you'll have your Thomasin before the week's out.' Relieved at receiving Tansy's promise Avril eased her back, slipped off shoes to stretch swollen feet towards the fire.

'Do you remember coming to see me in the Spring, Tansy? Asking me about monthlies?'

Tansy did indeed remember coming to see Avril when she was terrified she might be carrying Martin's child.

51

'I'm glad that nothing happened then Tansy. Now you can start your family the proper way with a Church blessing. This time next year you will be bringing a bairn of your own to see Thomasin.' This speech frightened Tansy who hadn't thought children came so quickly after marriage. Thought of Norah and Geoffrey; Norah set on becoming a teacher. What if she had a child while she was still at College. What would Norah do then?'

She heard Avril draw her breath in sharply, both hands flying to her stomach.

'Is Tom still working at Vitifer?' Tansy enquired not liking the look of Avril's face now turning pale, sweat breaking out on her forehead. Again Avril gasped.

'Do you want me to fetch someone?'

'No, tis too soon, just get me some water Tansy? My neighbour will fetch Dr Jones when tis time and the boys are big enough to go to Almshouses where Tom's parents are. I'll be fine. Off you go, Tansy, be happy.'

Reluctantly Tansy left Avril Moore and made her way home avoiding Bank Street and keeping a sharp look out in case Jess Hallett should still be about. Deep in thought Tansy now worried over two subjects – the first how she could possibly keep such a promise as Avril had extracted from her. She had helped her mother when the twins had been born but only to fetch and carry. Her other worry was at the confident forecast Avril had made that she Tansy would be bringing a baby to see her Thomasin the following year. Did it really happen so quickly.

Eva thought Tansy looked withdrawn and thoughtful when she came into the Sitting Room where she had laid the dress on the table.

'How is Avril?'

'Near her time I think. But she wouldn't let me call for help – said it was too soon.'

Eva nodded 'After all those boys she will know when this one's coming. Hoping for a girl is she?'

Tansy nodded then turned to the dress which fitted

very well, clinging to hips and tiny waist and needing only small adjustment. Tansy turned this way and that before the glass to see the effect of the bustle and hugged her Mother who complained when pins began to fall from the half finished gown. Delighted with her wedding dress Tansy's thoughts returned to babies.

'How soon was it before Norah was born?' She asked and when Eva looked puzzled added 'You know was she born in the first year you and Father were wed?'

Eva quickly realised what lay behind the question, smiled and adopted a vague expression.

'Let me see' she said 'perhaps it was toward the end of the first year – I can't really remember – perhaps it was early in the second year.' Then taking pity on Tansy added 'Children don't always come when we wants them – sometimes us has to wait a year or two.'

Tansy, slightly comforted, had to be content with that.

When Tansy stepped down from the train at Moreton there was no sign of Martin. Disappointed and feeling end of day tiredness she prepared to walk to Teignhead. However on leaving the Station there was Martin, shoulder in a sling, holding Lucifer by his bridle.

'Why Martin whatever have you done?' she exclaimed and Martin gave an imitation of a shrug which caused his face to crease in pain.

'Had a fall out with this varmint'. He indicated the horse who now began to paw the ground and whinney at sight of Tansy. She approached and rubbed his nose, feeling in her pocket for the sugar lumps she had stolen from Cook's kitchen at 'Courtenay House' against her next meeting with the cob.

'Tell me what Lucifer's done and what has happened to warrant putting your arm in a sling?'

'You'd best climb up – I can't ride yet Doctor says – not till my shoulder's mended. So you ride while I lead.'

This was a novel experience as Tansy, used to sitting

up front of Martin, now sat astride Lucifer – her legs too short for the stirrups. She clung to the saddle and swayed from side to side as Lucifer walked the road to Chagford, turned off on to the track past Thornworhthy and on over the bridge to Fernworthy Farm. Neither Farm produced a welcome or indeed any sight of soul or animal.

'They'm all inside having supper' Martin answered her unspoken question.

He went on to tell how he had fallen off when Lucifer reared up at the sudden flight of a grouse from beneath the cob's feet throwing him on to a granite boulder.

'Heard a crack and felt a sharp pain. Now I can't lift myself up on to Lucifer's back so he be getting fresher every day and I be getting farther and farther behind with all the jobs I must get done avore winter.'

'How long did Doctor say twould take to heal?' Again Martin tried to shrug, the spasm of pain again crossing his countenance.

'Six weeks or so. Sleeping's worst – can't get set any ways.' Now Tansy counted ahead – just over two weeks to the wedding!!

She began to think, think how to manage things for Martin. Someone must be asked to come and help. There was the peat – a winter's supply to get in, bracken for bedding for the cob. The newtake wall was far from finished. Confining sheep was a priority and Martin had promised to buy some chickens and build a secure house. The Barn wasn't weatherproof and needed filling with hay for fodder – then there was the oven Martin had promised to build. Leaving Fernworthy to cross the open moor Tansy looked ahead, looking for the ford and clapper bridge. One had to take one or the other to reach Teignhead Farm and she felt a surge of unexpected pleasure at the familiar scene. Back at the Post Office she had experienced such warmth and comfort that she had begun to dread returning to the basic life of Teignhead at the same time afraid to stay longer for fear her decision to make her future there would wither away.

'Don't ee fret Martin. Us'll get all done – there must be someone as'll come and help'. Martin looked doubtful. She added.

'Tis no time to be proud but now we must make up a bed for ee to sleep on – indoors – no more sleeping in the linhay among the straw.' With this positive tone Martin looked comforted and allowed Tansy to take the bridle and lead Lucifer into the stable, see him fed and turned out. Next she and Martin ate pasties her Mother had made earlier in the day, brewed tea and looked around for some way to make Martin a place to sleep.

'I'd a come straight away if I'd a knowed you was in such a pickle'. Tansy said.

'Not the sort of homecoming you was expecting Tansy Drewe? There's no need to make a fuss – I've sat up two nights I kin do same tonight.'

Deep in thought Tansy remembered how Martin had brought her here the night of the storm, the night she had fled Newton Abbot after Geoffrey Llewellyn's trial, the night she had learnt for the first time that Geoffrey and Norah were sweethearts. Remembered how Norsworthy's pony Fairy had cat jumped into the bog at the flash of lightning and clap of thunder and Martin had pulled them both out and brought her here on a sled. She turned to Martin.

'Wait here – I've an idea!'

Propping open the heavy door into the porch she hurried to the linhay, hauled out the sled and dragged it across the courtyard and through into the kitchen.

'Tansy, whatever be doin?'

Martin crossed the room to help her as she tried to place the sled close by the fire. Next she fetched the sheepskin and lay it the length of the sled, making a soft lining, adding a pillow.

'There you are; bed fit for a King.'

She helped him remove his clothes then with a sigh Martin sat on the sled, then lay back with Tansy's help until the sled formed a support for his body. He sighed with relief.

'That's so good – my shoulder is comfortable at last. Thank ee my maid'.

Tansy covered him with a blanket and soon was rewarded by the sound of his gentle breathing as he fell into the deep sleep of exhaustion caused by pain and lack of rest.

Next day they talked of getting help.

'Who looked out for the sheep when you came down for the Chapel Outing in the summer?'

'Twas Tom Osborne but he's working at Vitifer Mine Monday to Friday; only comes home weekends for change of clothes and vittles.

'So Wilmot Osborne's his wife then?' Martin nodded.

'Wilmot's been coming up to milk cow each day – they've no animals to see to at Fernworthy. Managed to persuade her to take what milk she needed.'

'What happened to their farm, Martin. It looks so neglected.'

'Tis a long story.'

'What about the folk at Thornworthy then? I bought lamp wicks for the farmer's wife the other day when I went to Chagford'.

'Would rather get the devil hisself than ask there. Don't call there again Tansy. No, best get Adam to come out if Feyther can spare un for a few days. Do you think you could go to Staddens tomorrow?'

'Why don't I ride Lucifer – be quicker than walking to Chagford.' Alarm filled Martin's face.

'You've seen what can happen – don't want you coming a cropper – that would be no good to anyone. No, you go to Chagford and take the Post Van to Moreton and train to Lustleigh.' Sarah Webber was surprised to see Tansy so soon after she and Martin's visit ten days before but agreed readily enough that Adam should return to Teignhead with Tansy and see to things.

'Perhaps I can help with the cow?' Fanny was at Adam's side smirking at Tansy pleased that she was

56

having to ask for help. Sarah thought on this idea for a moment or two, then, to Tansy's surprise, nodded in agreement.

'Twould be good sure enuff. Stay till Sunday – that should get some of the work done.' She turned to a cupboard opened it to take out 2 bottles. 'Take these Tansy – the Lavender Oil will ease Martin's muscles and the Arnica will bring out any bruising. Rub both in gently – the Arnica is good for shock too.' Now Fanny began to giggle with excitement at the thought of going on a jaunt with Adam away from her daily employment at 'Staddens'.

Sarah turned to her and spoke sharply.

'You're to help Tansy with the milking, show her how to make cream. You and Tansy can share the tallet – take some blankets with you. Adam pick up a small coop and take a couple of our best laying hens and corn to feed them.'

Adam left to harness the pony, Tom, and place him in the trap while Fanny went to catch the hens and place corn into a sack, Sarah fetched blankets and Tansy tried to quell her feelings of alarm at the thought of spending time with Fanny Luscombe, remembering how they had come to blows on the Granary steps here at 'Staddens' when Fanny discovered it was Tansy who worked at 'Courtenay House' with her sister Janet. Fanny had apparently come to terms with the fact that Martin was to wed Tansy and was now setting her cap at Adam. Already she made plans – Adam could sleep in the kitchen with Martin – use the truckle bed while she and Fanny could make beds of bracken in the tallet above. It would be rough comfort but at least she could learn dairy skills from Fanny and Adam could do the outside work.

Martin was cheered by the sight of Adam and Fanny and made a jolly meal of Licky Stew to which Tansy had added Hog's Pudding. Sarah had added a Fruit Cake and Butter to the parcels and this with a glass or two of Cider left them all in high good humour. Fanny asked

57

about the forthcoming wedding to which she assumed she would be invited.

'Us'll soon be family' she giggled and simpered at Adam from beneath huge blue eyes framed by long moth lashes, adding 'What be wearing then Tansy Drewe?' Martin spoke up for Tansy who sat looking embarrassed and shy.

'Tis a secret, none of us is to know until 29th September. That's right an't it Tansy?' Fanny had to be content with that.

Fanny turned her attention to Martin.

'Where be goin' honeymooning then Martin?'

Now it was Martin's turn to look awkward – he glanced at Tansy who spoke up boldly.

'Honeymoon be goin' to be right here! Why should us want to go away when us've just arrived. Gonna make a good home avore winter do come!'

Fanny looked round the almost empty room and, with a sneer on her face, back at the couple.

'Fair bit to do an't ee? Not even a stove to bake bread! Wouldn't suit me!' She sniffed and Martin who was outraged by Fanny's comments spoke up in defence of his place.

'Nobody asked you if it suited. Tidn't you as has to live up auver, takes special folk to make a good place on Moor. Keep your tongue pie to yourself!'

Adam sensing more trouble the longer they sat at table rose and pulled Fanny from her chair.

'Come Fanny let's go get cow in – show Tansy how to milk!' With a toss of her head Fanny followed him out through the porch while Tansy, still smarting from Fanny's remarks, busied herself clearing and washing dishes and Martin retired to seek comfort on the sled. She rubbed in the oil his Mother had sent while neither spoke, each deep in thought – Martin about the hard work which lay ahead in the months before days grew short and weather cold. Tansy thinking of the wedding to be got through with Norah and Geoffrey in the Methodist Church at Newton. She smiled as she thought of the wedding dress now nearly finished and Martin of the gold wedding ring he had hidden away against the day when Tansy would at last be his. The sweet smell of Lavender Oil filled the room and stirred his senses so that as Tansy passed him on her way to the Porch he reached out and caught her hand.

'Take no notice of Fanny – she's only young and silly.' She paused to squeeze his hand in return.

'Not long now my maid!' he said pulling Tansy down to kiss her on the mouth. A familiar warmth spread through Tansy's body and she reached for a blanket and with great tenderness tucked it around Martin.

'Not long.' she affirmed 'now my first lesson – milking the cow!' She laughed and was gone leaving Martin feeling more confident in their future together than he had done before. Tansy, crossing the courtyard, found Adam had tied the cow to a post in the linhay, Fanny was seated on a stool a pail placed beneath the cow's udders, gripped between her knees and the sharp almost musical sound of milk hitting the sides of the pail filling the linhay. Adam watched Fanny as he leant against the linhay wall and smoked a cigarette.

'Oh, it looks so easy!' Tansy said impatient to begin. 'Let me try, Fanny.' She began to stroke the cow's warm brown back and immediately Fanny rose and handed the pail to her. She smirked at Adam. 'Let's see you have a go then Miss know-it-all.'

'What's her name, Fanny?' The couple watched in amusement as Tansy sat on the stool and placed the half full pail beneath the cow. 'If I'm to get to know this cow I wants to know what she be called?' she appealed to the couple.

'Hortense, named by Mrs Webber on account of her being right awkward from the day she was born. Mrs Webber hand reared her on account of her mother dying when er was born. Only one that can milk her – why that be me! – That's right an't it, Adam?'

Adam nodded his head and threw his finished cigarette butt out into the courtyard.

The challenge made Tansy gritted her teeth and began to pull at the cow's udders but not s single drop of milk was forthcoming. Fanny and Adam stood watching laughing at Tansy's inexperience. Now she pulled harder urging Hortense 'Come on gal, give us your milk.' Suddenly the cow lifted her hind leg and kicked out sending Tansy, stool and pail flying. Milk drenched her legs and feet spilling most of the milk on to the linhay floor. Tansy spoke reproachfully to the cow while Adam and Fanny exchanged triumphant looks.

'What have I done to deserve that? Now my beauty you might as well get used to me seeing as I'm going to be milking ee every day from now on.'

Tansy stood to stroke the cow's neck and croon a lullaby. Gradually the cow's tail stopped swishing and Tansy took her seat once more, began to stroke the cow's udders more gently, squeezed them and after a moment or two milk was hissing against the sides of the pail. Tansy crooned her thanks as the pail filled with frothy white liquid.

'Good girl, Hortense. Good girl.'

Fanny disappointed at this turn about tugged at Adam's hand and together they left the Farm and didn't return until the sun had dropped behind Kes Tor and darkness filled the valley. When Tansy showed Martin the pail full of milk he was surprised and pleased with her success.

'Ee must strain it through muslin to get rid of the grass, then place it on the cold slab in the Dairy. You've done well – cows often don't let down their milk until they get to know the feel of strange hands. Where be Fanny and Adam to?'

Tansy shrugged feeling slightly guilty that their departure had gone unnoticed due to her excitement at winning over Hortense. She lit candles before answering Martin.

'What do ee think of Adam marrying Fanny then? Tis obvious they'm sweethearts!' Martin frowned and after a moment's thought commented.

'They'm as silly as one another – still they'm only young and will learn – Mother says she'll insist they live at the farm especially if Adam is to come into the farm when Feyther be done with it.' Tansy pursed her lips.

'A fly by night like Fanny won't want to be under your Mother's eye all day!'

Discussion now ceased as the lovers returned and Tansy judged it time to be off to bed; candlelit shadows danced about the walls of the room and Adam spoke up after a nudging from Fanny.

'Why don't Tansy have the truckle bed – t'would be more comfortable don't ee think our Martin?' Tansy was swift to scotch this idea.

'What and leave you and Fanny to climb into the tallet. I don't think so! You can get some bracken and make a bed up there for Fanny and me. When that's done you Fanny can put blankets on top and us'll be right cosy!' She gave Fanny a fiercely determined look which meant

'I'm taking no nonsense from ee Fanny Luscombe!' The young girl gave in and after many lingering looks in Adam's direction climbed the stairs and after removing her cotton dress settled down on the make shift bed and waited for Tansy to join her. When she showed signs of beginning a conversation Tansy shut her up immediately.

'We'll be up early Fanny. You've to show me how to make cream. Morning comes early up auver. Gonna be like a holiday for ee an't it Fanny so make the most of it but remember I'll be watching ee. No larking with Adam mind or Mrs Webber'll know it.' With such a threat Fanny gave in and was soon snoring gently while Tansy thought of the ill luck that had sent that grouse rising under Lucifer's feet. She wondered what a grouse looked like and sighed as she realised how much she had to learn about the Moor and the life she had chosen. It had been a long day and soon Tansy's breasts were rising and falling in deep slumber.

6

HUSBANDRY

As soon as Tansy heard the sound of cock crow coming across the valley – a new sound for her but one Fanny must hear every morning at 'Staddens' – she rose, brushed bracken from her chemise and taking her cotton dress stole silently down the steps from the tallet, leaving Fanny still asleep. The brothers lay still and she went outside to fetch water from the potwell and bring it inside to douse her face with the freezing water. Next she filled the skillet and stirring up the peat fire set it to heat. By the time Adam and Martin were awake she had let the hens out from the coop, thrown corn down for them, milked Hortense and, satisfied with her achievements, went inside where Adam was washing at the sink and Martin was trying to dress with the help of Fanny. After a breakfast of porridge, ham and eggs both men talked of all that needed to be done and Tansy turned to Fanny.

'Now you can show me how to make cream.'

'Where's the dairy then, Tansy?'

Martin showed them a door out of the kitchen, hinges rusty, stuck fast until he found an oil can and the door swung inward with a great creaking sound. Tansy almost fell down the deep stone steps on to the lower floor of the dark narrow extension to the farmhouse. She exclaimed in horror at the festoons of spider webs hanging from ceiling and wall. Both young women retreated to fetch besom, brushes and cloths to cover their heads and set about cleaning the room. It took them a couple of hours to clean then wash all the surfaces including the marble slab before Fanny was satisfied the dairy was clean enough for cream making. With the men gone to work on newtake walls they set about starting on the slow process with Fanny firmly in charge. Taking down a large saucepan she instructed Tansy.

'Put two pints of milk in this to stand till the cream rises. Then us'll put it over the fire to scald. After that cream will begin to form a ring around the edge and then slowly grow till tis all over the top.' Tansy listened then asked.

'What do we do after that?'

'Move it away from fire, don't let cream break up and leave in a cool place till tomorrow!'

'Takes a long time, don't it?' Tansy exclaimed, patience not being one of her virtues 'When is it ready to eat?'

'Soon as you can skim it off from the milk. Next day usually. Tis easy once you know how!' Fanny looked proud of the skill taught her by Sarah Webber. Once they'd set the saucepan of milk covered it with muslin and put it on the marble slab in the Dairy Tansy took two cans and, giving one to Fanny, set off across the Moor to pick wortleberries.

September sun warmed their backs as they picked lush purple fruit from among granite outcrops, disturbing grazing rabbits which to Tansy were pretty creatures but to Fanny, trained in country ways, were vermin.

'Martin'll have to put out traps if ee's gonna grow vegetables!'

Tansy's thoughts flew to her plans for making a garden like Sarah Webber's. There would be a stone path down the middle with vegetables one side and flowers and herbs the other.

'Tomorrow us'll start on the garden – tis right over-grown!' Fanny had enjoyed gathering her pail of berries; she nodded and smiled liking this change of scene free from Sarah Webber's keen eye which of late had been closely on her, missing nothing.

Hoping to catch Tansy off guard she asked.

'White, your wedding dress then?' but Tansy was not to be caught and only smiled and shook her head. Fanny went on 'When me and Adam marry tis white muslin I be gonna wear, roses in my hair and afterwards a honeymoon in Torquay.'

Tansy looked at the younger woman, noted her flushed cheeks, curly brown hair escaping it's pins, blue eyes shining.

'You seem very sure of yourself Miss. Has Adam asked ee then?' Fanny tossed her head.

'Not yet but tis only a matter of time before he do – then' she added looking determined 'with Martin up auver and out the way why one day I'll be mistress at "Staddens".'

Tansy couldn't help but laugh at the young woman's confidence but felt it wise to issue a warning.

'Take care Fanny that he hasn't his eye on another young maid. Remember how sure you were of Martin back along!' Fanny had the grace now to blush and stammer.

'That were then but this be now – anyways I always liked Adam best.'

She picked up her pail and began to run across the moor towards Teignhead Farm. A figure grew in the distance heading from Fernworthy toward the clapper and Tansy hurried after Fanny anxious to see who it could be. By the time the women had reached the farmhouse door Thomas, the assistant from Blackstone's Emporium, was waiting for them. In his hands he held a small neat parcel which he quickly presented to Tansy who at once offered him a glass of cider after his long walk. Draining the glass he wiped his mouth on his sleeve and left. Tansy hurried out to call after him.

'There must be some mistake, Thomas – I haven't ordered anything. Is it for Martin?'

Thomas kept moving away from Tansy, calling back to her.

'Mr Blackstone said I was not to take 'No' for an answer -bring parcel back and I lose my job!'

Kind hearted as ever Tansy gave up the chase and gave in to Fanny's demands to at least see what was in the parcel. She removed the brown paper wrapper to disclose two boxes tied together. One a shoe box, the other held gloves – she opened both under the inquisitive eyes of Fanny to reveal the grey suede gloves and boots she had tried on in the Shop at Chagford.

'Ooh, Tansy' Fanny exclaimed 'they'm beautiful! Try them on do!'

Tansy knowing all too well that both boots and gloves would fit perfectly thrust them back into their boxes, re-wrapped them with the paper and ran upstairs to hide them in the tallet.

'Bet Martin don't know about they!' Fanny exclaimed greeting Tansy with a malicious smile on her face.

'Don't tell him Fanny – tis a mistake – I'll be taking them back to Chagford next market day but tis best Martin doesn't know – he's too much to worry about just now.'

Fanny nodded but smiled to herself at the knowledge that she held a secret, a secret that Tansy didn't want known. Meanwhile Tansy, knowing she could afford neither boots or gloves wondered what Jacob Blackstone was thinking of. She didn't yet know how she was to pay for the dress material – her wages would go some way to meet the cost but not the whole £8. How long would it take her to learn to make enough cream to sell? How many eggs would two hens lay; they ate eggs every day but there were often a few left over. Perhaps Martin's plan of making a rabbit warren would be needed after all. She shuddered at the thought of trapping the wild creatures she and Fanny had seen springing from beneath their feet as they moved over the grass gathering berries earlier in the day. She sighed – she had so much to learn but now Fanny was calling her.

'Time to take vittles to the men Tansy. I've sliced some of Mrs Webber's ham; there's bread and we'll need to take cider and mugs. Come on.' Fanny handed her the cider jug, picked up the basket and was gone.

They found Martin and Adam among a pile of rubble as wall building went ahead. Adam placed the large anchor stones and Martin one handed filled in with smaller stones till the wall was locked in place. Both stopped work at the approach of the women, looked pleased and made seats among the rocks for them.

'Should you be doing that Martin?' Tansy wanted to know, but said nothing more knowing this man of action would find it impossible to watch others work. Bread and ham was soon consumed followed by mugs of cider making them drowsy as bees collected pollen from late flowering heather and Martin broached the subject of keeping bees.

'Don't bees sting?' Tansy wanted to know and the others laughed at her.

'There's a bee bole on the end of the house – just put the bee skeps in and the bees will do the rest. Skeps is straw hives' Martin explained to Tansy.

'Heather honey is good and would sell at Chagford Market -job for you Tansy!' Adam added his penny-worth and she became cross at all these new skills she was supposed to acquire and seemingly at once! She rose, collected basket and empty cider jug and set off back to the house to peer at the saucepan of milk, how was she supposed to tell when it was ready to scald over the fire?

Where was Fanny when she needed her? Fanny, however, didn't appear and instead Hortense came mooing at the courtyard gate and it was time for milking which Tansy found got easier each time. She put down linseed oil cake for the cow and looked up to greet Martin now looking tired but content.

'Good work done today, our Adam has made a good job and the wall is mended.'

'Where are they?' Tansy wanted to know and Martin looked surprised.

'Fanny said she was wanted to set cream.'

'And Adam?'

'He was going to sharpen peat cutters for tomorrow – why haven't you seen either of them?'

She shook her head and Martin looking cross set off to find the lovers. He hadn't far to look, discovering them in the linhay among the straw but, with memories of his own courtship of Tansy the Spring before, he made loud coughing noises and left them to come to the Kitchen in their own good time. Tansy stood at the courtyard gate watching the sun slowly slipping beyond Varracombe Hill spreading shadows across the moorland telling her it was time to make supper. Tomorrow she would learn another skill – make a garden. She had to be sure Martin left her the right tools to dig up the soil.

Sun's warmth gone the kitchen seemed cold and dark and Tansy lit the oil lamp, stirred up the fire and set about preparing their main meal of the day, remembering all too late her promise to Sarah Webber to keep the young ones out of trouble.

Tom Osborne had left out tools for Adam to pick up on his way to Teignhead, the budding iron, the long knife and turf iron. After supper Adam honed these tools by the fire while Tansy asked where they were going next day.

'Each Farm has its own turf tie' Martin explained 'Ours is at Whitehorse Hill, anywhere that's called 'White . . .' means peat is there. Tis hard work the cutting, the deeper the peat the better the quality. Then it must be left to dry before us can bring it home.'

'Do let me come.' Tansy exclaimed but Martin just shook his head, declaring 'It be too hard for a maid – in any case there be plenty for you to do here!' When she pouted he promised to take her there one day and then on to Cranmere Pool. Slightly appeased Tansy then pressed for a picnic and a swim in this famous pool. Now the brothers burst out laughing and shaking heads gathered up tools, bread, cheese and cider and prepared to leave announced they would not be back till nightfall. Tansy extracted a promise from Martin that he would leave the peat cutting to Adam, who fetched Lucifer harnessed him to the sled and settled Martin there with tools and vittles while he put his foot in the stirrup and swung up onto the cob's back. Fanny waved the men off blowing kisses to Adam with many promises to see him that evening on their return from Peat Passes. After attending to the cream Tansy led the way through the gate into the garden. Handing a fork to Fanny she took the spade and began to break up the rock hard ground, ground left untilled for a season and soon Tansy had worn blisters on both hands. Fanny worked beside her and by supper time the square of earth was broken up and cleared of stones which formed a rough path down the middle. Exhausted the women sat in the Kitchen drinking tea and talking of harder times just to console themselves that today hadn't been the worst work they had ever known.

'Haymaking – that be harder' Fanny declared 'all the turning and turning till the hay be dried, then throwing it up on to wagon or hayrick – but when the threshing machine do come.' Here her face shone with excitement 'that be best time – just taking round the cider and feeding the men. Then the harvest home when after the meal there be dancing till midnight.'

Now it was Tansy's turn and she related the visits of The Holy Terror to 'Courtenay House' where she had worn up similar blisters scrubbing floors and waxing furniture and stair rails.

Martin's face filled with pity when late in the day he saw the blisters and a tenderness filled his heart when

68

she showed him the hard work that had been done in his absence while Adam's darkened with passion and neither Martin nor Tansy could find it in their hearts to stop them when the lovers stole off after supper and didn't return till the moon and stars were up.

7

HARVEST FESTIVAL
29th SEPTEMBER

The 29th September arrived seeing the barn roof
mended, peat cut, dried and stacked for winter, and
under the laws of the ancient forest of Dartmoor eight
acres of moorland enclosed by Martin the new tenant
of Teignhead all with the help of Adam. He spoke of
making potato and carrot clamps to keep them supplied
till Spring.

'Mother will start you off with herbs, Tansy. Just ask
her next time we go home for dinner.'

Now Tansy fiercely retorted that this was 'home'
from now on and that he should not forget it. Adam
and Fanny had returned to 'Staddens' and Martin's
shoulder was mending well. Soon after sunrise Martin
and Tansy set off for 'Staddens'; Tansy carrying two
small boxes in a basket, a pail of wortleberries, now
topped, tailed and washed ready for Sarah Webber to
turn into jelly and a dish of clotted cream. At 'Staddens'
they left Lucifer and took Tom and the trap and set off
for Newton Abbot where Tansy changed clothes and
joined by both families set off downhill for Chapel
where Martin had already taken his place beside
Geoffrey in the front pew.

There was a gasp from the congregation when Tansy
walked into the building on Edward Drewe's arm and
Norah, dressed soberly in grey took his other arm. The

three processed slowly up the aisle to the organ strains of 'Lead us heavenly Father lead us'. Geoffrey, responding to the communal gasp, turned round to look at the three figures; his heart missed a beat at sight of Tansy in her brilliant turquoise dress and cloche hat. Geoffrey Llewellyn thought Tansy looked adorable, thought of all that could have been had their temperaments differed; he saw Norah looking at him, a question in her eyes. He smiled at Norah reassured that this calm girl was all he needed – not the excitement that would have been his life with Tansy. Geoffrey turned back to face the front of the Chapel aware of Martin's presence. Martin the mirror of Norah – calm and responsible; just the man for Tansy. Noted the look of surprise and pleasure as he too saw the turquoise dress, the flame coloured curls under the dashing set of cloche hat and to cap it all grey gloves and button boots which Martin knew hid blistered hands and tired feet; the baptism Tansy had experienced into the hard life of a Moorman's wife. Norah and Tansy continued steadily up the long aisle, Norah noticing the reaction of the congregation to Tansy's wedding dress and smiling until she saw Geoffrey's face with – the admiration plainly there; the long moment before his gaze shifted to her. Norah positive that Geoffrey was the man for her but was he sure she was the woman for him?

Meanwhile Tansy couldn't take her eyes off Geoffrey – tall, slim his auburn hair cut neatly to suit her sister's wishes. His green eyes looked into hers and she faltered. Conscious suddenly of her father's whispered 'Tansy!' she moved forward to Martin's side – Martin's not Geoffrey's. In a daze barely hearing the words spoken by the Minister as he read the service, until the question came.

'Who giveth these women to be married to these men?' Her Father's response

'I do'.

Tansy winced as Martin took her left hand in his and removed the grey glove from her blistered hand, a

71

small firm hand now with broken finger nails and rough skin. Geoffrey looked across from Norah's smooth pale hand, neat and whole from marking books and writing on blackboards to Tansy's and felt his throat constrict – he swallowed hard and began the response. 'I, Geoffrey, take thee Norah' followed by 'I, Martin, take thee Tansy' and Tansy felt as if someone had struck her.

The wedding breakfast had been laid out in the Post room, laid on a borrowed trestle table flanked by benches from Chapel. Eva had covered this table with Grandmother Thomas' best white linen tablecloth over starched white sheets and in the centre placed a cake made and iced the week before.

'It would have been better kept for six months!' Eva protested but Bessie Brimmacombe comforted her.

'Twill be fair enough maid. Don't worry!'

Eva placed a sprig of white heather on the top of the cake and together they laid cutlery and glass borrowed from neighbours until twenty places had been set: Norah and Geoffrey at one end Tansy and Martin at the other.

Both brides were invited to decorate the table with their bouquets – Norah's an elegant florist's bouquet of white roses paid for by Geoffrey – Tansy's heather gathered by Martin the day before. A strange contrast to the simplicity of Norah's grey suit and Tansy's sophisticated dress.

Rosemary Brimmacombe, home from College, suffered mixed emotions. She doubted Tansy loved Martin enough to be his wife but smiled across at her friend. The visiting minister, who had carried out the nuptials, now gave a blessing and the party relaxed after the serious business of the day.

Norah, relieved that Geoffrey was indeed now hers, held his hand until the toasts were made, glasses raised and both couples had responded. Hungry after such an early start they and the party ate until all that remained of the huge ham was the bone; salad bowls were empty, flummeries, jellies and tipsy cake gone washed down by cider and madeira. Robert and James had crawled beneath the table to recover from too much jelly and it was Martin who rose to thank Eva and Edward for the wedding breakfast, seconded by Geoffrey. Then Martin held out his hand to Tansy.

'Come' he paused blushing 'Mrs Webber' (at which the wedding party raised a cheer) ''tis time to go' and Tansy rose as if in a dream and, after being hugged and kissed by everyone but Norah and Geoffrey, it was she who issued an invitation to one and all to come and visit them at Teignhead as soon as they could manage. Outside the Post Office the trap was filled with presents topped by a cage of hens and a bag of corn. Tansy sat on a cider barrel and for once didn't insist on driving. It took a long time to reach Teignhead during which she uttered not a word. Martin looked anxiously at her from time to time, surprised that she wasn't full of chatter after such an amazing day. When he asked her how she thought the ceremony had gone, gave compliments on her dress and hat, and got no response he concentrated on driving Tom up the Wrey Valley, through Moreton to Chagford and on through the lanes past Thornworthy then over the bridge to Fernworthy Farm to pass the stone circle on to the open moor. At last they reached the stone clapper where Tom's hoofs clattered across and up the stroll to Teignhead. Martin helped Tansy down and together they unloaded all the parcels and boxes and took them into the house. Martin unhitched the pony from the borrowed trap, removed his harness, led him to the stable where he was fed then set free to enter one of the many walled enclosures surrounding the farm. The sun set over Sittaford Tor and at last Tansy and Martin were alone – facing one another across the pile of wedding presents. Martin noticed how pale her cheeks were,how shadowed her green eyes as without a word she began to lay sheets on the truckle bed – too narrow for a wedded couple but, with no alternative, she added the herb scented pillow given by Avril and Tom Moore and began to undress.

Martin, tired too but intensely happy, mirrored her movements and their clothes dropped piece by piece on to the flagstone floor until both stood naked and there was at last no barrier between them. Martin took Tansy in his arms and together they slid down on to the clean sheets, the narrowness of the bed bringing them even closer and they succombed to embrace and kiss until their bodies responded in a rush of emotion long held in abeyance from the time Tansy had fled from Newton to seek refuge with Martin at Teignhead. Emotions on hold now found a natural release in their coming together when nothing stood in the way and the lure of bodies became irresistible. Tansy gave in to his demands and time passed until, all needs satisfied, they lay replete and Tansy, half asleep, whispered 'I love you Geoffrey' and Martin startled into wakefulness responded 'Not Geoffrey – Martin!' Tansy opened her eyes as if seeing him for the first time that day smiled and responded.

'Of course, tis my Martin – not Geoffrey.'

Still fearful of losing her, Martin locked his arms about her naked body, buried his face in her mass of red hair, covered her face with kisses to remind himself that it was he and not Geoffrey who lay with Tansy, he who had married her and not Geoffrey but a chill cooled his spirits and struck at his heart and it was sometime before he fell into an uneasy sleep.

Both slept late and it was the hens' clamour that woke them. The sun lower now with the onset of autumn lit up the stones of the courtyard and Martin's boots rang as he crossed to the stable to feed Lucifer and turn him out while Tansy took the pail and milked Hortense, looking forward to making cream. Fanny had taught her well and confidently she poured off a measure of milk into a saucepan and set it on the marble slab in the dairy. Over breakfast they now planned their day as they were to do each day from now on. Tansy was for opening the wedding gifts but Martin showed impatience.

'They can wait – us mustn't waste the daylight hours – can do that evening times. First off I'll make a house and run for the chickens – it'll be your job to shut they in night times. They'm laying so there'll be eggs to collect.'

'What a wonderful present from your Mother and Father Martin. Six hens and the corn to feed them. Then the clock – most generous. Do let's put it on the mantel shelf – leastways it'll tell me when to expect you back for breakfast and dinner!'

Tansy sought out the square parcel she knew to hold the clock; Rosewood it was, with gilt decoration. Martin took it from her and set it down on the granite above the fire.

''Twill need winding every thirty hours, it chimes on the hour every hour. Yes, tis indeed a fine gift Tansy. Twas my Grandmother's – you know Mother's Mother.'

Martin smiled at Tansy's pleasure and left her listening to its ticking. Tansy began on the dishes, pausing when she heard steps outside – she opened the door to admit Wilmot Osborne.

'Did all go well yesterday? We heard you go by last night.' She asked and was surprised when Tansy's face suddenly crumpled and tears slid down her cheeks. Tansy swallowed hard and brushed away the tears.

'Why Tansy whatever's the matter?' Wilmot was alarmed, not at all the reaction she was expecting.

'Oh it went very well – tis just the excitement of it all. I expect I'm a little tired . . .' a confession never to have been uttered by Tansy in all her 19 years. She turned to the pile of gifts stacked up in the corner of the large bare room.

'So lucky us've been – just look at all the things us've been given.' Suddenly she made up her mind – why wait all day for Martin to come home. She turned to Wilmot.

'Will you help me open them, Wilmot?' The older woman remembered her own wedding and knew what pleasure had come from furnishing her first kitchen.

'Yes, of course, I'll help.' They set to and the first to be opened was Johnny Brimmacombe's carved wooden spoon.

'Only 16 the carver of this is – he's promised to make a settle when he do get suitable wood.' Wilmot ran her fingers over the flower carved handle then handed it back to Tansy who placed it on the mantel shelf by the clock. Wilmot said 'Tis a love spoon, Tansy – that's what that be!' Piece by piece the gifts were unwrapped, contents examined and admired. Charles & Caroline Vallance's boxed set of cutlery and carvers, Emma & Harry Vallance's pair of china dogs were set at each end of the mantel.

'Some things must be put outside' Tansy said laying Avril & Tom Moore's meat safe by the door.

'What did Martin give ee then?' Wilmot wanted to know and Tansy picked up a working apron and gardening gloves and put them on. Both Women laughed at the practical aspect of the bridegroom's gift.

'What did ee give Martin then?' There was a twinkle in Wilmot's eye and when Tansy pointed to Lucifer's feed bag both women laughed and laughed till the tears ran down their cheeks.

'Twas what he asked for and as we haven't money to spare for fancy things . . .' She paused remembering the cost of her wedding dress then continued. 'His brother Adam gave us a cider barrel -Martin's already put that in the pound house. Norah and Geoffrey's sheets are on the bed.'

Now at the mention of Geoffrey Tansy's face clouded and again she seemed about to cry. Wilmot hurried round the table to put her arms around the young woman.

'Takes a bit of getting used to – being married –

76

not what we expect – wonders if we've chosen right partner.' From her pocket Wilmot took a small package and laid it on the table saying. 'Come to Fernworthy whenever 'ee feels in need of some company' so saying she was gone.

Tansy opened the small package, puzzled at first at the contents, until she recognized the smell of it from her Mother's kitchen.

'Why, tis yeast that's what it be!'

Now she had the makings of bread with the flour she'd bought at Chagford and which now waited in the crock. But where was the bread oven. Surely the last farmer to live here would have made an oven for his wife. Martin had told her he had raised a herd of Devons then moved to Prince Hall Farm to supply the Prison. When Martin came back for his mid-day meal he laughed at the sight of the wedding gifts already arranged about the room. Eva and Edward Drewe's saucepans stood in a shiny row on the hearth. Rosemary and Bessie Brimmacombe's rose spattered teapot and set of three jugs on the table.

'Couldn't wait then Tansy Drewe' then stopped in confusion 'Tansy Webber, I means' finding the new surname strange on his tongue. They both laughed and she went on.

'Wilmot wanted to see what we'd had' She held out Wilmot's gift now re-wrapped and waited for Martin to respond. When he too seemed puzzled by the creamy lump she tossed her head.

'Brought us some yeast – could make bread now if'n we had oven to make it in.' She sniffed and Martin demanded.

'Where's the vittles then wife?' He sat at the table and picked up a knife and fork from the cutlery box. She whipped away the silver pieces placed them back in the box, getting out the worn ones from the kitchen drawer. Fetched plates and cheese and cider from the dairy. 'That be for best – this be good enough for everyday!'

So their life began and as the days went by a pattern emerged and Tansy learnt to fit milking Hortense now in calf with feeding hens and cockerel, gathering eggs, making cream both of which she planned to take to Chagford each Wednesday. Martin hired his father's ram to run with his sheep bringing them in at night to the shippen for fear they would be attacked by a fox he'd seen crossing the newtake. Unbeknownst to Tansy he set vermin traps and taking his gun whenever he left the house shot crows known for attacking sheep sometimes to the extent of pecking out their eyes. He brought home rabbits but had to skin them as Tansy felt too squeamish for the job. Patiently he waited for hunger to do its work.

Tansy worked on her garden, planted the herbs Sarah Webber had given her, walked the four miles to Chagford for bread and meat avoiding Blackstone's Emporium until a month had passed since she had put down the deposit on the turquoise taffeta. Then taking a deep breath, she plunged into the shop with two pounds clutched in her hand. The two pounds she had saved from her wages at 'Courtenay House'. Thomas worked on rolls of winter cloth, stacking them in place of summer cottons now stowed out of sight. He looked up, smiled when he saw who it was.

'I've come to pay the month's instalment' she breathed holding out the money in her work roughened hand for, however many times she donned her work gloves there were as many when she forgot.

'That and the two pounds I put down last month leaves another four pounds to pay – that's without the boots and gloves.' Thomas nodded entering Tansy's payment in a big ledger.

'Master's out' he said 'but I'll tell him you've paid.' Tansy hurried from the shop relieved that Jacob Blackstone hadn't been there to witness her embarrassment. Martin unaware of the debt hadn't asked about her wedding dress. Perhaps, thought Tansy, he assumed her parents had paid for the material and was unaware of the money she hid on the shelf high in the dairy roof. She sold her basket of eggs to the Grocer and cream to the Dairy. Proud of herself she mused – if only she had a bread oven she could make and sell bread. Both she and Martin looked forward to having the proceeds from the sheep fleeces; though each had different plans for its disposal. At the end of each day both were too tired to stay awake long enough to make love and, the truckle bed not large enough for both of them, Martin slept on the floor on a sheep fleece and was gone in the morning by the time Tansy awoke and began her chores.

Tansy raged each time Martin saddled up Lucifer and was gone – every day there was a reason for his absence. This time.

'The drift needs every man that can be spared from his farm!'

'But I can't spare you; want help with limewashing the walls!' Tansy wailed.

'When us has a herd of cattle and ponies well then I can call on moormen to help round they up – get scattered over the Moor. Drift means at the end of the day us can sort out our own and bring them back.'

'How do you know which are yours if there's so many?'

'Brand em!'

'What burn them? Oh, no!'

'Us just burn's into the flesh with our own mark – only hurts for a moment! Sheep we mark with coloured dye.' Seeing the look of horror on Tansy's face he added. 'If you'm to be a farmer's wife ee'll have to get used to treating animals differently. They are our means of livelihood – pigs have to have a ring put through their noses – else they dig under fences. Up here with walls they might not need it.'

There seems to be a lot of cruelty in this farming Tansy thought. 'Where is today's drift taking place' she demanded.

'Horse Ford over beyond Combestone Tor – we will meet at Huccaby Bridge and drive up auver.'

'Do ee want vittles?' Tansy offered.

'End of day those without animals to drive home 'ul share cider and pasties at Forest Inn, Hexworthy.'

'So tidden all work then!' Tansy exclaimed laughing.

'You'll soon learn ways of moor – neighbours is life savers when trouble comes. You'll learn!'

8

SECRETS

As autumn gave way to winter the valley changed colour, the almost white grasses turning to a deep gold interlaced with purple. Rains fell swelling the Manga until the noise of its descent roared over granite boulders and flooded the clapper below the Farm. Tansy leapt from tuft to tuft to cross the Great Mire each time she wished to visit Sittaford Tor until it became impassable and she changed her route to the higher ford to walk the Postbridge track. From the Tor she could see Postbridge and she planned to follow the river down to the village one day. Each Sunday Tansy and Martin rode Lucifer to Chapel at Chagford then continued to 'Staddens' where news was exchanged over a large roast dinner cooked in Sarah Webber's iron range and consumed by Amos, Sarah, Adam, Fanny, Martin and Tansy who thought Fanny looked pale and had nothing to say at table. After the meal she and Adam hurried out while Tansy helped Sarah wash dishes,

'Do you know Wilmot and Tom Osborne?' Tansy asked Sarah who paused in her clearing and stacking.

'Something happened between the Osbornes and the farmer at Thornworthy – Martin will never say what 'twas – says Tom Osbornes sworn him to secrecy. I only know that the Osbornes suddenly lost all their stock and horses; now Tom works at Vitifer Mine and that is indeed a hard life. Now there's bitter feelings between the farmer at Thornworthy and Tom and Wilmot Osborne.'

'That explains why Martin won't answer my questions on the subject and has forbidden me to call there ever again.' Sarah shook her head and said.

'Best leave it be, 'twill sort itself out betimes I reckon.'

'When be coining out to see us? Martin would be so pleased if his Feyther would come too.' Tansy asked.

'Perhaps if you was to ask un,Tansy, he might be persuaded. He still won't accept Martin's gone for good – even now you'm wed and settled. Go and see him – he's out in the shippen as like as not.' Amos's answer was curt.

'No, us shan't come till the winter when I'll fetch ee down off Moor. Tis a hard life you'm set on Tansy – a life I wouldn't wish on my own daughter! Stubborn is our Martin, allus has been as you'll find out afore long.' Tansy protested.

'But you have Adam to take on the farm when you'm retired. He and Fanny look to be courtin' and soon they'll be set on making a life here together.' Amos just shook his head.

'Not of the same mettle as Martin – our Adam, why he'll fritter away the farm and that Fanny isn't strong enough to keep un on the straight and narrow. You mark my words – no good can come of that partnership!!'

Tansy's arguments set aside, she could do nothing but return to Sarah and beg her to come as soon as she could manage. She had a visitor the following Saturday but it wasn't Sarah but Fanny.

'Why Fanny what a surprise to see you.'

Tansy up to her arms in flour and suet was making dumplings for supper, hoping that this time the round lumps would rise like her Mother's and not stay small and hard like stones. 'What brings you here?' she asked. Fanny blushed and put down a basket on the table. 'Brought a few things from Mrs Webber.' However,

82

when Tansy looked beneath the cloth she doubted Sarah Webber had had anything to do with the contents. There was a paper screw which when opened revealed mixed boilings, a fancy cake with icing and angelica on top and a bottle of liquid she didn't recognize. She looked up sharply at the girl who stood blushing and twisting her hands together, obviously in some distress.

'Mrs Webber didn't send these things did she Fanny?' Fanny shook her head looking nervously round.

'Is Martin here?' she asked.

'Is it Martin you've come to see?' Tansy asked and wasn't surprised when Fanny shook her head and sat down suddenly on the bench by the table.

'He's gone to look at sheep over to Moreton – won't be back till late.' Now she took pity on the girl. 'What is it Fanny? What's wrong?' Fanny kept her eyes down and muttered.

'Haven't had my monthlies – not last month nor this – what am I going to do Tansy?'

All now became clear to Tansy – the presents, the bottle of what was it? She had heard how unwanted babies could be got rid of by taking gin, soaking in a scalding hot bath or taking penny royal. She didn't know if any of these measures worked but did know the terror of missed monthlies. Remembered when after months without a show the relief when the flow of blood came between her legs.

'Have you been lying with Adam then?' Not surprised when the young girl nodded her head.

'He said it would be alright if he withdrew at the last minute but he didn't always . . . What will Mrs Webber say? Will I lose my place?'

Tansy looked at Fanny's huge blue eyes, eyes now brimming over with tears and felt anger rise that Adam had taken advantage of Fanny's willingness. Then remembered how Martin had taken the same path with her when she and Sarah had visited Teign-head the previous Spring only stopping his love making when she had protested. It wasn't fair! So she promised.

'I'll see what I can do Fanny. Don't say anything till I've spoken to Martin.'

Now Fanny became extremely agitated, wringing her hands and jumping up from her seat at the table.

'No, no, you mustn't tell Martin – he'll be angry with Adam and tell Mrs Webber! No, no, Tansy, you mustn't tell anyone. Just tell me what to do.'

Tansy thought hard – who could she ask for help – she hardly knew Wilmot Osborne. No, the only woman she felt close enough to approach was Avril Moore but she was at Newton and Newton was a long way away. How could she Tansy take Fanny to Newton without arousing suspicion. Not known for liking one another Tansy and Fanny were now locked together in a problem that wasn't going to go away. Had to be solved one way or another.

'Do you love Adam?' Tansy wanted to be sure of her ground.

'Oh, yes, Tansy I do.'

'Then you want to marry him?' Fanny blushed and nodded.

'Perhaps we should tell Mrs Webber – she'll make Adam do the right thing.'

'No, no – she might not. In any case I doesn't want to be married feeling so sick as I do. There's my Feyther too – he would take the strap to me if he found out. I can't tell Janet either – she always told me not to let anyone – you know!' Now she rushed on 'but I couldn't stop him, Tansy – just couldn't and truth be told I didn't want un to stop!'

At a loss what to say or do both young women sat, Fanny miserable but relieved that she had told someone. Tansy, angry with Adam, sorry for Fanny not knowing what to do next and the sound of footsteps outside followed by a knocking on the porch door came as a relief to both.

Tansy opened the door to two men, one large with side whiskers wearing a plaid coat caped around the shoulders. His companion even taller with a hawk like face topped by a felt hat and beneath a dark suit, the coat with tails. Both smiled at her and she found herself curtseying, as she would have done had she been opening the door to visitors at 'Courtenay House'.

'Can I help you, Sir?' she addressed the most imposing of the pair who at once produced a square parcel from a pocket inside the plaid coat and held it out.

'I had heard there were new tenants at Teignhead. I took this photograph last Spring and made a copy. Thought you might like to have it.' He smiled and went on 'I assume you are the new tenant?'

Tansy drew herself up to her full height and for the first time experienced pride at being thus addressed.

'I'm Mrs Webber, sir. Martin Webber is my husband and he has been farming here since the Spring of this year.'

Remembering her manners she invited both men into the house, both so tall that they had to stoop to pass through the Porch and under the house lintel.

'I should introduce myself, Mrs Webber – I am Robert Burnard and I live at Huccaby and this is the Reverend Sabine Baring-Gould from Lew Trenchard near Okehampton. We've been to look at the Grey Wethers – often pass this way when we're looking at the stones'.

Tansy showed real excitement as she took the parcel from Robert Burnard and turned to the other man.

'Are you the gentleman who wrote 'Onward Christian soldiers?' she demanded and when he nodded and smiled she rushed on. 'The hymn we sang as we marched from Newton to the Puritan Pit with Geoffrey Llewellyn our Minister. Her hand flew to her mouth as she remembered her manners and now indicated the benches at the table.

'I'm forgetting myself – please do sit, sirs,and take some cider or tea?'

Fanny hovered in the background her own problem

quite forgotten in this unexpected visit from such elevated company.

'Thank you Mrs Webber – it's most kind of you but we must be on our way. We've a call to make at Moreton and have left our trap at Fernworthy Farm. The nights are beginning to draw in aren't they?' Still they lingered and Tansy realised they were waiting for her to open the parcel and immediately she tore off the brown paper to reveal the photo.

'Tis very good – Martin will be so pleased with it – it shall be placed over the fire when he gets home.'

Both men rose to leave but as they turned to go looked enquiringly at Fanny.'

'This is Fanny Luscombe – she's dairymaid at 'Staddens' – a farm at Lustleigh.' She paused while Fanny made her curtseys, blushing and twisting her hands together.

'Are you staying here Miss Luscombe'. The reverend gentleman asked and when Fanny hesitated and looked to Tansy the latter explained.

'No, she's just come to visit and has to go back tonight', She looked appealingly at the men who responded at once.

'We should be pleased to take Miss Luscombe as far as Moreton if she doesn't mind walking to Fernworthy Farm?'

Now quite alarmed Fanny again appealed to Tansy for a decision and this was swift in coming.

'That would be most kind, Sir. Come Fanny I'll walk so far as Fernworthy with you then with this gentleman's help you will be back at 'Staddens' before tis dark.'

She took down her jacket and hat, quickly emptied the basket and gave it back to Fanny. The four set off and Tansy learnt much that was to prove of interest to her about the stones lying in such profusion about the Moor. She saw Fanny seated comfortably in the trap, waved till it was out of sight then hurried back to gaze proudly at the photograph now propped up on the granite mantel. Just wait till she told Martin that the famous Sabine Baring Gould had been here in their home. She hadn't heard of the other man Robert Burnard but when she told Martin the names of their visitor he was visibly impressed.

'Robert Burnard I believe to be a photographer – he and Baring Gould be called 'the History Men'. What were they doing over here I wonder?'

'Visiting 'Grey Wethers' whatever they be.'

Martin now gazed long and hard at the photograph – Looks as if thatch is finished. Must speak to the Duchy's agent ask for slate. Rent is too high for a building with such a poor roof!' Tansy asked what the rent was.

'Sixty pound a year. Thatch is only reed and leaks when the storms come.' Tansy was horrified.

'Sixty pounds why that's a scandal. That's more than a year' wages, more than I earned at 'Courtenay house'.

'Some years sheep wool only fetches threepence a pound; us'll need a lot of fleeces to pay the rent alone.' He paused pondering on the question then looked cheered at his thoughts. 'Has been fetching as much as four shillin' and sixpence a pound since the War so we must pray Boers don't give in too soon.' Tansy exclaimed.

'Men've been killed out there. You wouldn't want War to go on just so's we can get rich?' Martin laughed bitterly.

'Rich is something we won't be for a long time to come!' Tansy now offered a solution of her own.

'Got ten shillings an ounce for my hair when I went to London after Janet Luscombe told Mrs Vallance that I'd stolen Miss Emma's watch. Could always sell my hair, Martin!' His face darkened.

'No-one's going to accuse you of theft out here. We would have to be destitute before I'd agree to your selling your hair. You'll find life is hard and whichever way money comes in we've to be grateful.'

He sought to lighten their mood which had come with talk of War and leaking roofs.

'I'll tell ee a story of a sheep farmer, stranger to these parts, who stopped for a drink at Warren House. Well, ee was talked into buying a flock of grey wethers just below Sittaford only to find – well, you've seen the stone circles for yourself!'

'What a dirty trick!' Tansy exclaimed, then asked 'What are wethers?'

'Castrated lambs!'

Still not understanding she watched as Martin downed his cider and laughed and laughed till Tansy protested.

'That's shameful – to play such a trick – did the farmer get his money back?'

Martin shook his head and shrugged – realised Tansy didn't see the joke. Sighed realising how different was the thinking between men and women. Fetching a hammer he nailed the hanger of Robert Burnard's photograph to the wall above his Grandmother's clock.

Meanwhile Tansy's thoughts went back to the problem of Fanny – perhaps Wilmot Osborne would have some ideas. She had said 'Come whenever you need company' and this invitation cheered her. She had hidden the sweets, cake and bottle of gin Fanny had brought high up on the shelf in the Dairy and resolved next time Martin went farther afield she would go to Fernworthy.

Martin had made a good bargain with the Farmer at Moreton, had driven the sheep home along the road towards Postbridge, brought them across Meripit Hill to Teignhead. Not in the best condition but Martin was confident he could improve this and was proud of his growing flock. Adam was bringing over 'Staddens' ram to run with the ewes in a week or two; the lambs would be born late April when the new grass was growing and the weather warm. The ewes could be shorn in July and the wool sold at Chagford Market. Martin wanted to celebrate and Tansy opened Bessy Brimmacombe's wedding gift of Madeira wine which led to a sharing of the truckle bed in a sudden mood of happiness. The depths of the night saw Tansy waking to the sounds of a ruckus outside. Hens squawking, followed by shots and curses in Martin's broad dialect.

'You vermin – just ee wait till I catches ee!!'

Suddenly the door banged and Martin was standing over her. In his hand he held a handful of feathers and a chicken head which dripped blood on to Tansy's face. This was followed by the handful of feathers until she screamed at him.

'Whatever's happened – what be shooting this time of night. She sat up, trying to rub the sticky blood and feathers from her face.

'You may well ask my maid. Shooting at fox – got one of the hens he have cause someone didn't shut them in the henhouse!'

'Oh, I didn't remember hens – what with the History Men's visit and you being so pleased with the sheep' she almost added 'and Fanny's visit' but stopped herself just in time. Martin looked grim.

'Tisn't enough to shut hens in when us feels like it! Has to be done every night – 365 nights of the year – and if you'm not here then ee must find someone to do it for ee!!' Tansy bit her tongue, picked up the feathers and washed her face at the sink. Knowing the better part of defence is always to attack now faced Martin.

'Fanny suggested we put down vermin traps. Would that be a good idea.' Martin, however, wasn't to be diverted from his determination to drum it into Tansy's brain that traps were no substitute for the discipline of shutting hens up each and every night.

'Once Mr. Reynard tastes blood he'll be back so don't let it happen again!'

Light began to creep through the window and now both, wide awake and cross with one another dressed and Tansy stirred up the fire and fetched water from the well and made tea. Seeking to appease him Tansy asked what he was to do this day.

'Want to put new ewes through sheep wash but I must clean it out first. Then us'll need to keep un in shippen because Long Wools are daft sheep but not daft enough that they can't find their way back home. I'll need you to help douse them. Moss will guard one side while you prod ewes into water and I haul them out t'other. We'll feed them inside for a few days until they'm used to their new home then we can let them out into the newtake.'

'Won't they just jump over the wall?' Tansy wanted to know and Martin shrugged.

'Not if we give them good feed!'

Tansy put the dishes to soak in the sink thinking again of Fanny wondering how long she would be able to keep her secret from Mrs Webber and Adam. If opportunity didn't arise sooner she planned to call on Wilmot the following market day when she took cream and eggs to Chagford.

'Come on then Tansy if you'm coming!'

Martin, impatient to begin, stood in the Porch waiting for her Moss at his heels.

9

THE BLIZZARD

Christmas 1900 passed with visits to the Post Office and Staddens. Tansy begged her mother to arrange their own to coincide with Norah and Geoffrey's visit to friends in Kent. One day at each home was all they could spare from the animals and when the twins pressed Tansy that they be allowed to come and stay Eva, knowing the shortcomings of beds at Teignhead,told them they would be back at School in a day or two.

'We shall go soon – at Easter if not before – then we shall take train to Moreton, Coach to Chagford and walk from there. See all the things Tansy have told us about on the way – take fishing rods or jars for tadpoles!' Robert and James had to be content with that and they waved their goodbyes from the top of Beaumont Road, and were still there when Tansy and Martin turned into East Street, and hurried to catch the last train from Newton. January and February passed slowly, short days giving Tansy the opportunity to read the books she had received at Christmas. Norah and Geoffrey had presented her with a beautifully bound copy of 'Little Women' by Louisa May Alcott and Rosemary gave her Charles Kingsley's story of Tom the chimney sweep 'The Water Babies' which Tansy was anxious to begin. But first there was the mending, always the mending – this she tackled with the needles and thread from Martin's gift; a wooden box decorated with mother-of-pearl set in rosewood with compartments inside for everything a woman needed to keep her man and family well kept. So after supper they settled down in the soft light from the oil lamp – Martin mending vermin traps or harness, Tansy socks and shirts then for her the treat of a chapter or two of Rosemary's gift. Although she had opened 'Little Women' she hesitated to hold the book knowing that probably it was Geoffrey who had chosen it. Instead she replaced it on the shelf in the shell cupboard beside the hearth. Beside it was the bottle of 'Bradley Woods perfume' he had given her the Christmas before; half used now and the scent evaporated still she loved the bottle with its rose decorated lid. She still thought of Geoffrey and lied when Martin offered her 'a penny for your thoughts?'

Unusually dry for the time of year Martin grumbled that they needed rain for the 16 ewes now cropping beyond the newtake walls. Lucifer had cast a shoe and Tansy decided to go with Martin to the Blacksmith's at Chagford. A bitter north east wind had sprung up during the night and Martin asked Tansy.

'How much flour and tea have ee? Might be an idea to stock up at Blackstone's while we'm in Chagford.' This was the last thing Tansy wanted to do and she protested.

'Can't it wait until next time I comes?' Martin shook his head.

'Don't like the feel of the wind – north east winds mean snow like as not. We must get back up auver soon as we can.' Tansy tried to remember how much the bins held.'

'Porridge oats is low and sugar.'

Clouds built steadily as they led Lucifer over the now familiar track to Chagford and by the time Lucifer had been shod and Tansy had bought supplies from the other store to avoid any chance of an encounter with Jacob Blackstone it had begun to be difficult to stand in the freezing wind. Dampness fell which wasn't rain, just a dampness on the face.

'If only you'd let me bring Lucifer when I come in I could carry more vittles each time instead of having to buy things a bit at a time.'

'We need a pony and trap' Martin said but before that I must widen the stroll make it easier for us to drive up into Courtyard.'

Tansy was all for stopping at the Osbornes' but again Martin urged Lucifer on. Now the clouds filled the valley and turned to soft flakes of snow as they crossed the bridge at Fernworthy farm. By the time they passed the stone circle they could see but a few yards ahead. Martin relaxed his grip on the reins and let Lucifer's instinct for home guide them across the valley. They descended from the cob at the clapper where it became increasingly difficult to walk against the power of the wind and the swirling snow. During the short ride from Chagford to Teignhead the temperature had dropped – Tansy's ears ached with the cold and their clothes were saturated. Leaving Tansy to take in the stores Martin remounted Lucifer and set off to look for the sheep left out to graze beyond the newtake walls. Tansy stirred the peat into life with the bellows and filled a kettle with water from the pot well, shivering with the first freeze of the winter. She took off her wet clothes and put on her winter flannel nightdress, wrapped herself in the new shawl Sarah Webber had given her at Christmas. She heard Martin call Moss and the sound of harness jingle and hooves thudding on the snow lessened until all was quiet. The square window was soon covered in a pattern of snow flakes and Tansy drew close the fire to wait for Martin's return. As the evening wore on she opened the porch door but all she could see was a wall of white, all she could feel was the bitter wind, all she could hear was the eerie whining of the wind in the ash trees. To her call of 'Martin' there was no response and she removed the stew from the fire, and, worn out with cold and worry, eventually fell asleep only waking when the clock struck six. She saw only the empty room and again opened the door into the porch. It had stopped snowing and a strange yellow light filled the valley. Again she called 'Martin are you there?' thinking that perhaps he had returned during the night and not wanting to disturb her had stopped in the stable with Lucifer and Moss. She dressed quickly and taking a shovel from the pile of tools in the porch cleared a path through deep snow to the outbuildings which she searched one by one. No sound met her except the clucking of the fowls from the hen house. She trod across the courtyard to the stone gate post at the entrance to the nearest enclosure where Martin kept the sheep when he was from home, The gate stood open but was jammed back by several feet of snow. Nothing could tell her if Martin had ridden this way; any foot or hoof print obliterated by the heavy snowfall during the night. She decided to return to the warmth of the kitchen and hot up soup against their return but as the day passed and they did not return her anxiety grew, tinged with anger. How far had they gone in their search for the sheep? They should have come back long ago? She began to hate Martin's Grandmother's clock as it chimed the hours away. She tried to read but couldn't concentrate her thoughts on Tom's story. she milked Hortense and fed the fowls. As the pane of glass darkened and nightfall approached she fetched her shawl, lit the storm lantern and set out to look for the missing man, horse and dog.

After going to the slotted gate and waving the lantern and calling with no response she reasoned that Martin must have gone far afield and she slipped and slid down the stroll to the clapper; here the stream was frozen so she crossed the ford and turning toward Sittaford set off along its course stopping to regain her breath frozen outside but generating a fierce heat inside her body. The sky cleared and stars came out followed by a full moon which lit the moor and encouraged her to struggle toward the newtake wall.

Here she found the gate, again open and snowed back. Following the track she made her painful way up the Sittaford Track until moonlight made shadows to her left and she recognized the stones of Grey Wethers. The snow was deep but the wind had blown it away from the moor and piled it up against the two circles. She stopped to rest trying to decide whether to go back to Teignhead or make for the Postbridge Road. She had often sat on Sittaford Tor and looked down at the village of Postbridge, planning how she would follow the river down one day. Past journeys through Grey Wethers always took them to the Warren House Inn which she knew was beyond Whitehill and this lay ahead of her, and, making up her mind she struggled on, climbing up the hill and after an hour reaching the ridge. From here she could see lights and black figures and voices shouting. Her heart pounding she rested and waved the lantern to and fro in the hope of attracting the attention of the people clustered round a large black shape. She held her hands at the lamp which gave a little warmth – her legs shook and her breath left her mouth in a visible plume. Clouds began to build across the moon and dampness filled the air Knowing she must find shelter before the next snow storm Tansy struggled on until she could distinguish the black shape which turned into a coach surrounded by men all digging; among them Martin. When he saw her he came toward her, amazement on his face.

'Whatever possessed you to leave the farm?' he demanded and Tansy relieved to find him but angry to find him so far from home, shouted.

'Whatever possessed you to leave the farm and where are the sheep you went to find?' The passengers of the coach stood listening to this altercation resting on spades which had freed wheels from snow. Caught in the blizzard it had slid off Meripit Hill in the driver's haste to get to Postbridge before the road became impassable. Both passengers and Martin had struggled back to the Warren House Inn to shelter during the night and were now trying to extricate the coach before more snow covered it up again.

When Martin explained that he had been quite safe and that Tansy needn't have worried but should have stayed at Teignhead in the warm and dry Tansy grew even more furious.

'So you were safe and sound all night while I was worried out of my life for you and the sheep!' Now Martin's face darkened and showed dismay.

'I searched all the newtake walls between Teignhead and Fernworthy and Grey Wethers and Whitehill – from there I saw the coach come off the road and roll downhill till it fetched up here. Lucky no-one was killed.'

'Where's Lucifer and Moss?' Tansy demanded, somewhat pacified by this tale of disaster.

'They're at Warren House. Moss would've found sheep if they'd a been anywhere we was looking!'

Now the digging was resumed and the driver of the coach turned to Martin.

'You've a brave young woman there to be sure. Best take her to the Inn, we can manage now and thank ee kindly for your help.' Suddenly Tansy's legs couldn't hold her any more, crumpled beneath her and Martin gathered her up and struggled up the road to the Inn where he rubbed her hands and feet until they burned as feeling returned and unbidden tears came to Tansy's eyes. The landlord warmed wine by the fire and gave this to her with a platter of bread and cheese.

'You'd best stay the night!' he advised and so they did, sleeping on the settle by the fire wrapped in sheep fleeces.

Fresh snow had fallen in the night and Tansy's tracks were covered over and it was Moss who led the way home, disappearing from time to time when the depth of snow was more than his height and Martin hauled him out. Tansy sat on Lucifer's back and Martin led the cob slowly and with great care. After what seemed like hours they found the clapper and took the stroll up into the courtyard. After rubbing Lucifer down and feeding him and Hortense Martin and Moss came to thaw out by the fire and he and Tansy slept wrapped in fleeces, lulled to sleep by the sound of flurries of snow on the window and the whining of wind in the ash trees. They woke to fresh falls of snow piled deep against the house walls. Martin voiced his worries for the sheep now missing for 48 hours. 'Could be safe and just buried in the snow but with gaps made by rocks just big enough to allow them to breathe. That's our only hope unless' he added 'the Long Wools I bought sensed the snow was coming and made for their old home. I'll take Moss, some poles, a shovel and try again.'

'This time I be coming with you Martin. Not staying here worrying myself to death.' And Martin seemed glad to have her and made no demur.

Each day they set out to search another enclosure probing deep with poles into snowbanks close newtake walls but without success until Martin was full of dread.

'If us don't find them soon it'll be too late'.

Tansy thought of her promise to help Fanny which she couldn't deal with all the time snow fell each night. Peat smoked as they were forced to burn wet blocks after using great quantities of dried fuel from the Barn. Snow and cold crept through roof and walls at night and they huddled together too exhausted and worried to sleep.

'Let's try a different direction.' Martin said 'Go North to Peat Passes, tis the only place providing shelter within easy reach.'

So they climbed the Little Varracombe, now frozen, to Stats House an oval shelter built for the peat cutters. The ground normally a mire was frozen over thus enabling them to walk to the peat cuts. Now Moss became excited and ran to and fro barking and whining – Martin drove the pole into the peat until he felt the firmness and shape of bodies beneath. Both he and Tansy dug through the layer of ice and the shapes of sheep gradually appeared. They found 6 sheep frozen to death, just below the rim of the cut.

'Must have sought shelter here and perhaps fell asleep and became frozen in the night!'

Tansy felt desolate at the sight of the stiff corpses but where were the remaining 10 animals.

'I shall have to come back with the sled for these. We must keep searching – t'other ewes wouldn't be far away – keep close together as a rule. Let's try Sandy Hole Pass where there's a little shelter there.'

Now the sun came through the cloud and snow and ice began to melt making it harder to cover the ground. On reaching the track Moss again showed excitement and in a deep gulley leading off the path he began to scrabble with his paws. Confident that the dog had found again Martin began to dig, gently at first till the frozen snow was breached and they heard a faint bleating. After ten minutes digging sheep fleece appeared and Martin began to drag out the first of the remaining flock. There was no movement from the animals.

'What happened?' Tansy asked.

'They must have suffocated – couldn't breath under the snow. Sometimes if there are rocks with gaps clear of snow between a sheep can survive for days. Tidn't to be this time.' Now there was a faint sound and Martin stopped in his efforts to pull out the dead flock. The sound developed into a faint bleating and there between the wall and a single stone lay a lamb which eyed them in terror. Martin moved to lift it out of the Sheeps' grave but it shrank back into the hole which had provided protection and life saving air. Tansy stepped in front of Martin.

'Let me!'

Crouching in the hole she gathered the tiny creature to her, struggled up and taking off her shawl wrapped it about the tiny grey lamb which was all skin and bone.

'Tis a miracle – must have sucked from its' mother; sucked until she died.'

Martin was amazed at its survival but saddened at the loss of the ewes; wiped his eyes with the back of his hand shaking off Tansy's comforting hand.

'Let's get this creature back to the farm if we'm to save it then I'll set about paunching all the ones we found at Peat Passes. Now frozen so we might be able to sell them to the butcher at Chagford.' Now Tansy was horrified.

'Surely folks won't be able to eat dead sheep!' Martin shrugged.

'We've lost our spring crop of lambs and the fleece from the ewes. Best to cut our losses – frozen lamb will keep for a while if tis hung and we may get a good price for it. Tomorrow I'll take the sled and go back to peat passes before fox and buzzard find the corpses.'

It took Tansy a while to realise the magnitude of the disaster.

'How will we pay the rent?' she wanted to know. 'What about your idea of making rabbit warrens?' She quelled her dislike of the idea of making warrens to breed rabbits to sell.

'Twould take too long' Martin responded 'Us needs money coming in now'.

'I could go back to service – there's bound to be big houses at Chagford wanting kitchen maids!' Now Martin looked angry.

'I didn't marry you to have you go out scivvying. No, no, I'll be bread winner.' He paused thinking. 'There's another way to earn a living close by – mining black tin at Vitifer'.

'Mining – going down underground – surely that's dangerous?

'You know Tom Moore – Avril's husband – well he's been mining at Vitifer for over a year now. Comes out from Newton every Monday and works till mid-day Saturday. Other Tom – Osborne – Wilmot's husband –

he keeps his family on what he earns since he lost his animals.'

'Won't your clothes be ruined?'

Martin looked at Tansy quizzically – how much to tell – how much to leave unsaid. He tossed it off casually.

'There's flannel shirts and jackets called 'slops' made of canvas. Tis tough old stuff – then there's trousers too called rushin Ducks, and Yorks, like us farmers wears below knees – gaiters like. All kept in the Dry where miners change before and after each shift.'

'Then the miners don't have to buy their own? We could use money from sale of sheep to get what you need, couldn't we?'

'There's no need for you to worry. Tom Osborne can arrange stuff for us. In any case it'll only be for a while till I've earned enough to buy more ewes.'

'Whatever will your Father say?' Tansy wanted to know remembering Amos Webber's words about the harshness of life on the Moor. Martin gritted his teeth.

'Us'll not go to Staddens yet – the last thing us needs be Feyther's gibes. Tis a setback but us'll get over it.' Tansy thought of the money she owed Jacob Blackstone – wondered how she was to get to Chagford to pay the month's instalment now overdue. Distraction came with the needs of the rescued lamb, christened Storm, which Tansy fed through her garden gloves which she cut at the finger ends and filled with milk from Hortense. Soon the lamb grew strong enough to follow her everywhere. Meanwhile corn for the hens was running low and snow still came every night stopping at dawn when the sky cleared and the sun rose in a red ball behind the house, spreading its fire across the snow covered valley, melting the surfaces then disappearing as fresh snow clouds built, the temperature dropped below freezing and icicles hung from the eaves of the house. Every morning Martin broke ice in the potwell and Tansy boiled snow to water the fowls, Lucifer and Hortense.

Martin harnessed Lucifer to the sled, took the frozen sheep into Chagford, now cut off from the outside world. The streets had been cleared but were lined with banks of dirty snow. The price Martin got for his animals wasn't as good as he'd hoped for – he was not the only hill farmer trying to salvage what he could from their dead flocks.

He also stopped off at the Osbornes' to leave a message for Tom Osborne that he wanted to sign on at Vitifer Mine to begin the following Monday. Wilmot told him some miners had been unable to reach the Mine because of snowdrifts so there was work for the having. He also brought back oatmeal, flour, tea for he and Tansy and corn for the hens. From the butcher's he brought marrow bones for Moss as a reward for his hard work in finding the sheep and the dog spent hours sucking out the marrow, before trying to bury them among the peat blocks set to dry by the fire.

Tansy fretted about Fanny and asked Martin to take her to 'Staddens' but he just shook his head and said they must bide here and keep the animals and themselves alive against the end of the blizzard which must come soon. In fact it was five weeks before the snow melted and the Moor became a vast lake, rivers overflowed with melting snow and burst their banks flooding the in-country. News came that at Newton the Lemon had burst its banks and flooded part of the town. Meanwhile Martin left before dawn each day to walk to Vitifer and all the company Tansy had was the ewe lamb, Storm, and Moss who at first snapped at the little creature and tried to keep it away from Tansy. Eventually he came to find the little creature warm to lie near and once Tansy had finished milking Hortense and feeding Lucifer and the hens, he slunk to the fire and lay beside it and slept the day away. Martin forbad Tansy to leave the Farm.

'Tis dangerous – river's up over banks, bogs are deep and dangerous – twill soon pass.'

He came back exhausted from the mine, falling asleep over his meal then waking to sleep again. He rose at five o'clock before the sun and set off for Vitifer with its cold damp, its dangers from flood and dynamite. Tansy grew to hate the rosewood clock with its inexorable ticking and striking every hour. Sometimes the sound of the porch door shutting as Martin left was the first sound. Tansy heard and each day stretched out minute by minute and all she could do to pass the time was sit and read.

10

VITIFER MINE

The second week after the Great Blizzard ended a strong wind blew from the East drying tracks and bogs, Tansy, not wishing to put off her visit to Wilmot and Chagford a day longer, set off with her basket of eggs and cream for the Dairy She called in with her secret hoard of money at Blackstone's Emporium hoping to pay Thomas as she had on her last visit but this was not to be. Jacob Blackstone stood rocking back and forth outside the entrance to the shop and bowed as Tansy approached. He held open the door and ushered her in.

'How are you today Mrs Webber?' he asked and Tansy blushed and responded by holding out the money.

'Here you are Mr Blackstone Sir. Last month's instalment for the material.' She added hastily 'I hope to start paying for the hat, gloves and boots next month.' Blackstone however declined the payment with a shake of the head.

'I hear you have had trouble up at Teignhead. Tis six weeks since you paid – interest becomes payable for the two weeks you'm overdue. Dinna worry, we'll just add it on to the bill.' Tansy was stunned.

'You said nothing about interest when I bought the material; the boots and gloves you sent yourself although I insist on paying for those items too.'

Jacob Blackstone smiled his greasy smile and took the money Tansy still offered. He turned it over in his hands as if it was dirty.

'There's other ways of paying off a debt!' he smiled and twirled the ends of his moustache. Grabbing her arm he pulled her to the back of the shop and through a door and out of earshot of Thomas.

'I live here alone and need company from time to time' he said 'Each week I take a good dinner at the Three Crowns and it would be very pleasant if I could have the company of a lovely young woman like you. What do you say?'

Tansy was thoroughly alarmed and pulled away from his restraining hand, she moved toward the door and back into the shop.

'No thank you Sir. I am a married woman and do not wish to eat at the Three Crowns with you. Just take my money as it falls due – next month twill be two pounds then there will be but two left to pay. But I'll not pay interest – tidd'n fair – you never said ought about interest. The blizzard stopped me getting into Chagford as well you know.' Now Blackstone's face grew red.

'Didn't stop your man coming in to sell dead sheep, did it? Didn't stop him making money!' Now a sly look came over his face 'Not giving ee enough then?'

He paused as Tansy opened the door into the shop. 'Wonder if he knows about the money you owes me?' He sneered. 'Wonder what he'd say if'n he knew his woman owed money to Jacob Blackstone.'

A chill descended on Tansy, she knew how angry Martin would be to know she owed money, money pledged even before they were wed.

'You mustn't tell Martin' Tansy blurted out, then realised her mistake as Blackstone took advantage of her distress.

'Us'll see about that! Course if as I hear he be working at Vitifer and could give us the money then us'd say no more about it.' Tansy hesitated in the shop, fearful now that Blackstone intended telling Martin of her debt. He continued.

'Us would even forget about the debt altogether' and as her hopes rose he went on 'but that would depend on his woman coming to The Three Crowns with me next week – day time would be best when her man's at work?'

Tansy hopes, dashed once more, she shook her head and hurried from the shop to finish her purchases and leave Chagford to call in on Wilmot Osborne who sensed at once something was wrong. She made the young woman sit while she brewed tea before asking.

'You seem a little upset my dear. Can I help?'

Tansy hesitated not wishing to acquaint her new friend with the details of an affair not entirely in her favour. Instead she embarked on the news that Martin was now working at Vitifer with Wilmot's husband.

'Can ee tell me what tis like – this Mine work – he do come home so tired night times he can hardly eat, falls asleep over his vittles. He leaves so early, before I'm awake and not eating anything afore he goes.'

'Try and make him have a cup of tea and bread and cream -that keeps them going – or another thing is kettle broth.'

'Whatever's kettle broth?' Tansy demanded.

'Tis bread in a basin with hot water or tea poured over it with a lump of butter added.'

'After an eight hour shift underground in bad air and soaking wet they doesn't really need the long walk home. My Tom stays in the men's dormitory Monday to Saturday mid-day. Think on it, Tansy.'

'Couldn't he work above ground Wilmot?' Wilmot poured fresh tea for them both and nodded.

'Don't pay so much – underground's twenty six shilling a week he'll earn sheep money in a few months like as not.'

'Must say he got the job in the Mine so quick – was that due to Tom?'

Wilmot nodded.

Tom told mine captain Martin was experienced – didn't add what he was experienced in!!!' Both women laughed and Tansy remembered the real reason she had come to see Wilmot – a visit long overdue because of the blizzard.

'There's something else I wish to ask you.' She hesitated not sure how to put such a delicate question. The older woman smiled and when Tansy still hesitated she shushed the children from the room and gave her all her attention.

'Now you can speak freely and if I can help then surely I will.' Grey eyes friendly, pale face calm, air expectant all made it even harder for Tansy to broach Fanny's problem.

'I knows a young girl, just seventeen who has told me' here Tansy hesitated 'she hasn't had her monthlies for two months' she paused and remembered Fanny had broken her news before the blizzard 'p'raps tis three months, nearer four now – tis some time since she told me' again she hesitated and Wilmot sought to help her out.

'She is upset and wants to do something about it?' she asked. Relieved at her quick grasp of the situation Tansy nodded and waited to hear what advice her friend would give.

'Tis a little late for bringing it on' she said 'sometimes Penny Royal does the trick, sometimes lots of Gin and hot baths or, if she's really desperate' she hesitated 'I shouldn't advise this myself but they do say as jumping off a table can bring about a miscarriage – though that might cause worse than having the baby – even damage the child itself'. Wilmot paused then smiling encouragingly at Tansy said. 'Tisn't the end of the world my dear. There's always food for each mouth that comes. You shouldn't think of trying these tricks – why you will make a splended mother!'

Now Tansy realised Wilmot thought she was asking advice for herself and rushed in.

'No, no, Wilmot, tid'n for me, tis for someone I

promised to help but blizzard put a stop to my seeking help till, well, till now. I'm truly grateful Wilmot.'

She bade farewell to her friend and set off for Teignhead happy knowing what to tell Fanny when next she saw her but fearing it would be too late and indeed, before she had the opportunity to do just that news arrived with the postman who, after his long walk, stepped in for a drink of cider. Passing on such news as he thought of interest to each hamlet he now told her.

'Young maid as was here back in September putting up banns at Lustleigh I hear t'other day, Mrs Webber.' Tansy's ears flew open.

'Do you mean Fanny Luscombe?' The postman nodded.

'Sure 'nuff, wedding young master at 'Staddens' they do say.' Tansy sat down shocked but relieved at the news.

'Have they set a date do you know, Postee?' The man shook his head adding.

'Sooner than later I would guess judging by the size of her belly.' He finished his jar and was gone. Tansy sighed knowing her visit to Wilmot's earlier in the day had been in vain. What would Martin say if he knew Tansy had kept this a secret from him? She knew he would be angry with Adam? Never one to prevaricate she decided to tell Martin as soon as he came home on the Saturday.

'Told you they were a daft couple!' he exclaimed. 'Now they'll be beneath Mother and Feyther's feet for years.'

'Don't you think we should go to 'Staddens' Martin? See how things are? If there's to be a wedding . . .' Martin shrugged and agreed. 'Sunday us'll go! Hear the worst. Should be us breaking the news of a baby.' Suddenly he caught Tansy around the waist and brought her close. She looked into his face.

'Maybe we'm to blame Martin. Should've stopped them going off when they were here?'

'Forget about them Tansy – think about us!' He

closed her mouth with his and Tansy sensed the familiar response warming her body and opened her mouth to his – began the first lovemaking since the blizzard had killed his sheep, since he had gone to work at the mine. She sensed anger in his mood, surely not with her, as he ripped off her clothes and drew her down on to the fleece. Still she fought to tell him she had known Fanny's secret, each time she opened her mouth to speak, he closed it with his own, ran hands, hands rough with stone cutting, over her soft body, hurting her, attacking her as if she was an enemy. She felt her lips and breasts swelling until she longed for him to come – still he held himself above her then suddenly began to drive hard inside her, again and again. Took her hands in his and stretched her arms above her head until every part of their bodies touched. So they stayed until she whispered his name.

'Martin, what is it? Why are you so angry? What have I done?' Letting her go Martin's face was full of compassion.

'Forgive me my maid. Forgive me if I've hurt you. Twas the last thing I wanted to happen – your first winter on the Moor and to lose the sheep. Tis hard for you with me at the Mine.' She laid her cheek against his and comforted him.

'At least perhaps the worst is over – they do say twas the most harsh blizzard for years' Tansy said adding 'anything that comes after cannot be as bad!'

Martin somewhat consoled removed himself from the bed and fell asleep almost immediately on the floor. The clock struck five waking Tansy but still Martin slept; responding at last to her urging, it was only after he'd left for Vitifer that she found his food sack still lay where she'd placed it on the table. Tansy thought of the long day ahead for Martin without food; made up her mind. She would take it to Vitifer and taking down jacket and hat picked up the sack and passed out through the porch where she hesitated – twould be a long walk unless she rode Lucifer. The cob was grazing with the cow in the top enclosure. How long would it take her to catch and harness him? Martin's warning sounded in her ears.

'Don't ee try and ride Lucifer – he'm too bold for you to manage – throw you off soon as look at you.'

How long would it take to cross the valley floor to Grey Wethers, White Ridge to Warren House Inn then to cross the road and descend to the Mine. She made up her mind and entered the first enclosure, removed the bars from the slotted gateposts of the second. She called Lucifer who immediately pricked up his ears and ambled toward her. She spoke gently to him, caught hold his halter, led him down to the stable where she dragged down saddle and bridle, shortening stirrups to the length of her legs instead of Martin's. By dint of passing beneath the cob fastened all in place. Standing on a box she climbed onto his back then crouching low they passed out through the stable door, made their way down the stroll to the clapper and ventured out onto the open Moor.

Lucifer walked steadily until she clicked her tongue, squeezed his sides with her legs when he broke into a trot until the track passed through the outer newtake wall where she turned right to climb Sittaford. When she saw the Grey Wethers circles she rode between them and climbed Whitehill, mindful of the treacherous bog below. A whistling sound followed by the call of 'peewit' alerted her to a flock of black and white birds which rose from the moor in front of them and flew in a wheeling cloud above their heads. After climbing high this flock descended to settle and feed at a distance from them. Tansy was enchanted – she must ask Martin what these birds were. She drew in the reins, stopped Lucifer and she searched the undulating land, white tussocks, saw the touches of yellow that meant gorse had begun to blossom in this wilderness. Remembered Amos Webber's teasing her with his 'Kissing's in season when gorse is in bloom' and kissing reminded her of Martin and their love making the night before. Martin would not approve of her journey but she was determined not to let that thought spoil the day. She felt free and excited and urged Lucifer into a gallop across to the Postbridge road where she turned left to pass the Warren House Inn then descend the old spoil heaps to Vitifer Mine. It was hard work clinging to the saddle but when she arrived at the office building she felt proud of her achievement. She took the crib from the saddle bag and enquired of the Clerk for Martin Webber. She waited ten minutes or so until a man approached – a man she didn't recognize wearing dirt covered ducks and jacket, a hard hat with a candle stuck to the brim, a face covered with dust but, when he spoke, there was no doubt that the man inside this strange wear was indeed Martin.

'What be doin' here?' He demanded and before she could answer wanted to know. 'Did ee walk?'

Tansy motioned to Lucifer grazing nearby on the grass outside the Blacksmith's shop. Martin's mouth tightened his eyes became angry. 'Told ee not to ride un didn't I?'

She gave him his crib still proud of her achievement and asked.

'Can I see what you'm doing? Come all this way I have – Lucifer was as good as gold. Now I wants to see how Black Tin be got!'

'Tis men's work and no place for a woman!' Martin shouted at her. 'Best begone afore Lucifer gets cold. Where be Moss to?'

'Tied him up in the barn I did!' Now she pleaded 'Please Martin let's see where you be working all these long hours and so far from home.'

Furious Martin turned to go back to the adit when the door of a house opened and a man stepped out to see who had arrived.

'Just a moment Webber? Who might you be leaving your shift for?'

'Tis my wife Sir. Come to bring crib left behind this morning' he paused then answering the appeal in

110

Tansy's eyes added reluctantly 'wants to see down the mine.' He turned back to Tansy. 'This be Mine Captain – he's in charge here.' The man smiled at Tansy, impressed by this attractive young woman.

'Ridden from Teignhead Farm on this gurt beast have ee?' When Tansy nodded he agreed. 'If'n ee can manage that I don't see why ee shouldn't go down mine. Wait here.'

He fetched workman's jacket, trousers and hard hat from the Dry handed them to Tansy. 'Put these on young woman and come with me.' Captain Henry Wilson for this was his name, led the way followed by Tansy with Martin bringing up the rear. She felt rails beneath her feet, wet ran from the granite walls and the farther they progressed the harder it became to breathe, the harder it became to see in spite of the candles the Captain and Martin had lit on their hats. It wasn't cold which surprised her and in fact it became warmer the further in they went till they arrived at the shaft where Martin and Tom Osborne were working. Two other men worked from ladders – one holding a drill at the edge of a vertical seam of tin the other hammering it in. The tin looked dark against the surrounding granite and both men held clay pipes clenched between their teeth. This made Tansy gasp.

'I thought it dangerous to have naked lights down mines' she said and both Captain Wilson and the men laughed.

'There's no gas down here like there is in the Welsh coal mines. Tis quite safe; only dangers be from flooding when we reach water level, timbers sometimes fall from the roof or from explosions when we'm breaking into a new shaft!' Really alarmed now her face showed it and Martin sought to allay her fears.

'Fair warning be given and every man accounted for before fuses are lit!'

This had to satisfy Tansy and she watched as Martin took his place beside Tom Osborne and resumed work. Captain Wilson turned to Tansy.

'Best let them get on, tis a hard life but tis a living after all and pays well. Been going on since 1750 at Vitifer so there's no need for ee to worry my maid!' So saying Captain Wilson led Tansy up and out of the mine to be greeted by a large woman with a trail of children. Tansy turned to thank the Captain, his silver hair shining in the sunlight, his blue eyes filled with compassion for her. He led her to the Dry where she removed the heavy canvas trousers and coat, hanging them and the hat upon a peg and thanking him, tried to come to terms with the bare facts of the life Martin had adopted so that they could survive the loss of their sheep.

Now she had to leave him there in the bowels of the earth and go back to Teignhead. She pondered to herself, was she glad to know how he spent the long days away from home or shocked at the harsh reality of a miner's life. Her thoughts were interrupted when she reached the Blacksmith's shop and the waiting woman.

'Haven't you been down the mine?' Tansy asked in response to the woman's enquiry as to what she was doing here.

'No nor wish to.' Then her desire for female company got the better of her and she invited Tansy into the cottage next the Mine Captain's house; with the offer of tea after which she took her to see her vegetable plot.

'What are these?' Tansy wanted to know at sight of low bushes covered in dark green spiky leaves.

'Gooseberries my lover. Grows potatoes, cabbage and gooseberries which fruit in the summer and makes good pies which I cook for the men that stays in dormitories. Very fond of my gooseberry pies they be.' Now she showed Tansy the canteen beneath the men's sleeping quarters.

'Has a party here once a year. You should come – there's dancing and singing. Tis a happy time – the miners' families comes out with their children. Tis the owner pays for it all.' Now she was curious to know about Tansy. 'Mine Captain says you'm from Teignhead Farm?'

Tansy told the woman how she had recently married Martin Webber, who was working here at the Mine having lost their sheep in the Blizzard. The woman nodded in sympathy.

'Twas very bad – snow up to the bedroom windows here and half miners couldn't get here. Lots of ships were lost at sea when the hurricane struck! Us do have bad snowfalls most winters so tis best always to keep a sack of potatoes indoors with a bag of flour just in case. Baker calls here every week but sometimes he's so tipsy loaves are found floating in the stream. Elsie here gets milk from Headland Warren Farm every day – earns a penny every time her goes.'

Sensing Tansy who had told her she had brought her man's crib, had none for herself, she offered bread and cheese for which Tansy was indeed grateful. She gave Lucifer water and hay from the Blacksmith's shop and set off home. The surface workers gathered to watch her depart, and she sang as she went, joining the larks overhead. Reaching Teignhead she let Moss out of the Barn where he barked and jumped around them, pleased to see both woman and horse. She knew her decision to leave him here had been right – Martin would have been even angrier if she'd taken Moss down the shaft. She began the nightly ritual of milking, feeding the hens and Storm then went indoors to prepare Likky Stew and now she had mastered the knack a couple of dumplings against the imminent arrival of her man. She knew her instinct had not betrayed her when Moss rose whining from his place by the fire and ten minutes later the door opened to admit Martin who greeted Tansy with a mixture of impatience and admiration.

'Pleased with yourself no doubt my maid?' he said removing jacket and sitting down to await supper. She ignored him and busied herself with setting the table and ladling out stew; secretly delighted that she had

113

mastered Lucifer and, even more important, learnt what Martin had to do to earn the 26/- a week.

'Surprised to see me, no doubt?' was all she said and Martin gave in at last.

'You can say that! Men were mazed as I was but' he added seriously 'you won't need to do that again cause I've decided to sleep in the dormitory Monday to Saturday dinner time. Best to save energy for work – stead of walking cross Moor and back every day.' He looked at her a question in his eyes. 'Could you stay here on your own for so long?'

Tansy, shocked at first, swallowed hard then declared.

'No, no Martin 'tis best you stay – get money for ewes more quickly won't ee?'

However, as she cleared away their meal a feeling of anxiety crept over her at the thought of being here alone. Already aware that Martin was working at Vitifer, how long would it be before Jacob Blackstone knew Martin was sleeping there at night?' She scolded herself for being so foolish but it was long after Martin's snores filled the room, the wind got up and sounds of water tumbling down the stones of the Manga lulled her to sleep.

11

SETTLEMENT DAY

Now Tansy's long week from Monday when Martin left
for Vitifer, until Saturday mid-day, when he returned
awoke a longing in Tansy demonstrated by the pleasure
she got from preparing for his return. Always making
sure the fire was burning brightly, a good meat meal
was on the trivet and fresh bread and cake fetched
home from Chagford where she made sure to avoid
Jacob Blackstone's emporium. She achieved this by
entrusting Wilmot with her secret and getting her to
pay the next two instalments. Wilmot was happy to
carry out these errands but brought back a message
from Jacob to the effect that she still owed him interest,
accumulated when the snows came, plus extra for the
gloves and boots not yet paid for. Tansy bit her lips and
knew she would have to go and see him if she was to
settle these matters once and for all. She feared that he
had duped her from her very first visit when she
bought the material for her wedding dress, feared he
had told her the price was lower than it really had been.
She put this visit off and worked on her garden from
where, if she straightened her back, she had a good
view of the stroll down to the clapper and the track
across the Moor toward Fernworthy.

Not many days passed without a visitor coming along
the valley and the History men (as Martin called Robert
Burnard and Sabine Baring Gould) called again and

bought cream; telling her that they planned to excavate Grimspound – an early Bronze Age settlement this side of the long hump backed Hameldown Tor. Tansy, interested instantly, made them promise to tell her when they intended to begin.

In the meantime she worked hard on her garden, planted cabbage plants and earlies on one side the stone path, herbs and flowers from Sarah Webber's garden on the other. All were growing well including six gooseberry bushes, which looked very small and prickly, but these too were beginning to shoot. She longed for an oven so she could try and make bread, pies and cakes. The animals kept her busy and she avoided the temptation to ride Lucifer again. Wilmot told her about Cranmere Pool and she longed to visit it. Instead she climbed to the top of Sittaford Tor and looked down to Postbridge, dreaming of the day she would have money to spend on a meal at the East Dart Hotel.

The next time she was in Chagford she was forced to call at Blackstone's Emporium; the handle of the skillet had come away from the pan and refused to respond to Martin's attempts to mend it.

'Best get a new one' he advised 'get one next Wednesday.' In her attempts to avoid Blackstone's Tansy tried several of the blacksmiths but each shook his head explaining it was the mix of wood and metal which made it impossible to fix. So she stepped into the Emporium hoping against hope that Jacob would be about his business elsewhere. Thomas quickly found what she wanted but before she could pay Jacob Blackstone emerged from the back room dismissed Thomas at once and smiled greasily at Tansy, she proffered the coins toward him.

'I've finished my business here – if you will please take my money for the skillet I'll be off.'

Jacob however showed no signs of finishing the transaction but stood holding the skillet.

'I hear your man's working at Vitifer mine all week.

116

Must be lonely for a young 'oman out auver?' Tansy shook her head.

'There's plenty to do looking after animals and people are always calling in.'

She could have bitten her tongue the moment she had spoken these words as Jacob smiled and moved closer.

'Twould be no trouble to bring this skillet out – save you carrying un all that way. Might be something I could do for you while I be there?' Now Tansy felt really alarmed.

'Just give me my skillet – I need to use it tonight and cannot wait for it to be delivered another day.' At this Jacob's face turned an angry red and he could do nothing but wrap the utensil and hold it out to her. He took the money from her but in doing so caught her wrist.

'Still owes me interest young 'oman – when be goin' to pay that?'

'Next month'll see the end of it, Sir.' Tansy declared but Jacob showed no sign of letting go her wrist and now she began to struggle. Of Thomas there was no sign.

'Can't wait another month – needs that money and needs it now!!'

Tansy looked down away from the man who stood over her glaring and sweating. She noticed the lino of the shop floor, noticed how filthy it was; why, you couldn't even guess the colour and to destract Jacob Blackstone she remarked.

'Shop floor could do with a good clean. No time for Thomas to do that in addition to his other duties I reckon?' Now Jacob's face changed from angry red to furious purple as he experienced the rage of being criticised by Tansy. He jeered.

'P'raps ee'd like to clean it for us young oman?' Adding slyly. 'A 'course if ee'd like the job t'would be a way of paying off the money ee owes me.' He turned back to the counter, taking brown paper from a roll on the counter and wrapping the skillet while Tansy stood biting her tongue in despair. Was she ever going to get out of his clutches? Perhaps if she washed his filthy floor that would be the end of it. It was getting late – near the time when shops would begin closing and people making their way home. She sized up the floor – how long would it take her? Would he really cancel the outstanding debt if she did the work? She drew a deep breath and offered.

'Clean the floor for you but it has to be now and you have to give me a receipt for the money soon's I'm finished.' Jacob's eyes gleamed and he called Thomas, who appeared so quickly it was obvious he'd been waiting behind the door of the back room as instructed by his master no doubt.

'Thomas, fetch bucket of water, scrubbing brush and soap. Mrs Webber be going to clean floor for us – hurry up now!' Thomas looked at Tansy in amazement but did as he was told. 'You can get off home now . . .'

Thomas protested.

'But tidden seven o'clock yet Mr Blackstone.' Jacob grabbed him and pushed him towards the door.

'You do as I say Thomas or you'll be sorry.' He left immediately, grateful for this opportunity to gain an evening off. Tansy rolled up her sleeves, tested the water and straightened up, looked at Jacob levelly.

'Can't get rid of this much dirt without hotwater' she averred and refused to begin. 'Hot water it must be or I'm going!'

Jacob took the bucket and retreated to the back room while Tansy waited thinking herself not a little mad to be embarking on such a bargain with such a man. He reappeared with a steaming kettle and poured its contents into the bucket. Again she tested the temperature then asked for a kneeler. Once this was forthcoming she placed it by the open shop door and began to scrub ever conscious of Jacob's presence behind her until the red of the lino began to emerge from beneath the dirt. Tansy began to enjoy her work which reminded her of days at 'Courtenay House' when floors shone at all times and especially when Charles Vallance's mother was coming for one of her twice yearly visits. Steadily she worked her way across the shop, even beginning to hum a little with satisfaction at a job well done. Picking up the bucket of now filthy water she turned to find Jacob still watching her; he smiled when she offered him the bucket with the request for more water.

'Don't fetch water for skivvies – not after first bucket -now you'm on your own – plenty through the back room – stove to heat it too.' He took a half hunter watch from his pocket and looked at it.

'Pays a shillin an hour for cleaning!'

Now Tansy's temper rose at this trick. Immediately she began to roll down her sleeves, picking up the parcel and her shopping basket and preparing to leave. Wanting to keep her in the shop as long as possible Jacob amended his price.

'Didn't ask how much I paid did ee? Not so clever after all . . . said I'd cancel what you owes but didn't say how many times you'm to wash floor to earn that 3 pounds did I?' Quickly he moved across the clean lino to the shop door which he closed and locked, taking the key from the lock and placing it in his inside pocket. Tansy felt frightened – how was she to get away now? Why had he locked the door before his normal closing time of seven. To play for time she heated more water all the time conscious of Jacob close behind her. She continued scrubbing lino but now she felt far from happy; no longer sang or thought of 'Courtenay House'. The silence grew and the only sound were Jacob Blackstone's breathing as he watched her figure moving across the room and the occasional rattle of hooves as a horse and cart passed by outside. At last there was no more lino to scrub and after five buckets of water Tansy guessed she had spent nearly two hours at work. It was dark outside the shop and the lamplighter was setting his lantern to street lamps.

119

'Now that's much better – don't know how you could put up with such grime – can't be good for business!!' Tansy tried to keep her voice calm and even 'Now if you will give me a note cancelling the 8 pounds I'll be going.'

'I've a better idea, Mrs Webber' Jacob said 'Tis late now and I'm not happy to see a young 'oman like you walking across Moor when tis dark – take you home in my pony and trap and give ee docket when us gets there.'

Tansy froze; was she never to get rid of the varmint? He had the key to the shop door so she had to agree if she was to get out.

'That would be kind – tis a long walk back to Teignhead – thank you' she looked at him with determination 'but to guarantee the bargain give me your watch and when us gets there I'll give it back when ee gives me the receipt for the money!'

She heard Jacob's sharp intake of breath at her cunning. Quickly he unlocked the door of the shop and tried to usher her through but she wouldn't budge; stood without moving on the threshold.

'I'll scream if you don't do as I ask!'

He hesitated, looked up and down the street where the evening's imbibers were beginning to emerge from the town's terraces. Blacksmiths and shop assistants too all heading for The Three Crowns.

'Tis your choice Jacob Blackstone. Hand over your watch or I'll scream right now . . .' she opened her mouth filled her lungs and uttered a practice sound, soft but not soft enough for it not to be heard by a young man crossing the street close by. He looked over at Tansy, wondered what she was doing standing with Jacob Blackstone outside his shop. Tansy opened her mouth to emit a second scream when the shopkeeper placed his hand over her mouth, pulled her through the door and dragged her round to the back of the shop and out to the yard where he kept his pony and trap.

'You keep quiet if you wants your debt cancelled.' He quickly tacked up the pony put it between shafts and invited her to climb up but Tansy stood firm, holding out her hand for the pledge, refused to mount until Blackstone handed over his watch which she thrust deep into her bodice. Swearing Jacob whipped up the pony into a trot and flew out under the arch into the street. Lights glowed from cottage windows as they left the town, turning off at Waye Barton, trotting through the lanes past Hurston and Jurston past Frenchbeer and so to Fernworthy where they crossed the river by the bridge and Tansy tried to think of an excuse to stop at Wilmot's house where the dogs ran barking to greet them. No lights showed at the parlour window and no Wilmot appeared at the door as she did normally the moment the dogs barked.

'I need to stop and speak to Wilmot Osborne' She muttered but Jacob kept his hands firmly on the reins, urged the pony on across the open Moor to the Teignhead Clapper where he dismounted and taking the pony from the shafts lead him towards the house. Tansy protested that there was no need for him to come any further but he ignored her, a grim look on his face – taking hold her arm he dragged her and the pony up the stroll. At the farm he tied the pony to the hitching ring and waited for Tansy to open the door. He followed her inside where Moss rose growling from the fire to bark at Jacob's heels and was rewarded with a kick for his pains. The blow landed and Moss cowered away whimpering. As Jacob looked round at the simple room Tansy on the pretext of drawing cider from the butt in the corner, removed the watch and hid it behind the peat blocks. She stirred the fire into life patting Moss to comfort him and then placing a mug of cider before Jacob demanded.

'Tis time to exchange tokens – you give me receipt for money which I knows is in your inside pocket then I'll give ee watch. That's what we agreed! Then you best be on your way afore it gets too dark to see bog lying close

121

track. Fell into it myself one night pony frightened by night noises jumped sideways and sank dragging me in too. Lucky to escape I was.' Jacob Blackstone made no move to settle up but sneered.

'I don't scare easy, Madam. Your man not coming home tonight -us be all on our lonesome. Better I stay and keep you safe!!' Tansy felt cold inside, his meaning all too plain. Now all depended on Moss. Could she rely on him to spring to her defence?

'Now tis time to exchange receipt for watch then you be off or I'll report ee to the Constable at Chagford so I will. Not to mention my Martin when he comes home from Vitifer Saturday.' Jacob laughed,rose from his place at the table, swallowed the cider and came toward her – Moss growled and began to crawl across the floor toward him. Jacob seized a spade from the corner of the room and faced the dog who began to circle the man baring his teeth and growling low in his throat. Tansy relieved with the dog's protection didn't want a conclusion until she had the receipt safe in her hands. Didn't want all her hard work in the shop to go for nothing.

'Hand it over now Jacob Blackstone or I'll set Moss on you.' Now the man began to lay about him with the spade just missing the dog by inches but showing no sign of handing over the receipt till Tansy fearing he wasn't going to keep his side of the bargain seized Martin's gun from behind the door and aimed it at the man.

'Tis loaded – always loaded – Martin keeps it that way in case of foxes in the night. I can shoot – don't think I won't.' Faced with attacking dog and armed woman Jacob Blackstone at last gave in and, placing a slip of paper on the table, left the house but it was only when Tansy heard departing hooves that she lowered the gun, replaced it behind the door and hugged and patted Moss in gratitude and relief at her escape. Then it was she remembered that she still had Jacob's watch and removed it from behind the peat stack and hid it on the high shelf in the dairy and got ready for bed. It was only when she lay wrapped in the sheepskin that she began to shake and much longer before she fell into an uneasy sleep.

12

DANCING AT VITIFER

April's end brought an invitation for Tansy to attend
the dance at the Miners' lodgings at Vitifer. Martin
delivered this with great reluctance; he preferred to
spend his Saturday nights at Teignhead, glad to get
away from the Mine where he laboured so hard each
week. However, knowing Tansy's fondness for dancing
and knowing how cross she would be if she heard a
Dance had taken place without her, he passed the
invitation on. Wilmot and her children were going so it
was arranged that all of them would go together.

A disagreement grew between Martin and Tansy who
wanted to wear her wedding gown; Martin said it would
be too fancy for the party where miners' wives
would have had to walk some miles and would be
wearing plain every day dress.

'Whenever shall I wear it again?' Tansy wailed and
Martin shrugged and responded.

'Save it for a more suitable occasion, you'll only spoil
un riding over to Vitifer.'

Reluctantly she gave in, merely adding a striped
ribbon of blue and green to her bodice and a matching
one to her hair. The Mine Captain, Henry Wilson, and
his wife Jane were outside to greet them, inviting them
to share in the supper of ham and beef joints, salads
and pickles spread out on a long table. The gooseberry
pies Tansy had been told of by Gertrude Warne took

pride of place down the centre of the table and she had herself brought a large dish of clotted cream, thick and crusted, to accompany them. After everyone had ate their fill the table was cleared; benches placed along the sides of the room and Billy Somers took up his accordion and began to play. After 'Tavistock Goosey Fair', 'Down in the fields where the buttercups all grow' and 'O'Kanes March' Captain Wilson spoke up.

'We have a well known Step Dancer among us. 'Twould give us all much pleasure if'n he would favour us with a dance.' He looked across to where Martin sat and Billy Somers played the first few bars of a hornpipe. Martin looked surprised.

'Why tis Uncle George's Hornpipe'.

He made no move to respond to Henry Wilson's invitation so Tansy rose and crossed the room to take a large dinner plate from the table, clean off the remains of food, rub it with her shawl and place it on the floor in front of the accordionist.

'There's plate all ready for ee Webber.' Henry Wilson smiled at him but still Martin hesitated.

'Haven't danced for so long, Captain . . .' Tansy whispered her encouragement.

'Just one dance would do, Martin. Everyone's waiting.' Reluctantly he rose, placed his feet on the plate and signalled Billy Somers to begin. With the flash and whirl of Martin's feet, Tansy was taken back to the Green at Lustleigh, realised with a shock how thin he had become. Now his then sturdy frame resembled that of Evan Williams, the Welsh miner who had beaten him to win the side of beef then collapsed and been taken back to Newton by Martin in his family's pony and trap. As the miners and their wives clapped with the stepping of Martin's feet she thought of that time only two years ago at the May Fair; remembered how disappointed she and Rosemary had been at missing the dancing when they had accepted a ride home to Newton with Martin instead. Tansy missed her friend – promised herself that she would write when she had time. Martin was breathing hard, his fact scarlet with the effort of dancing on a china plate instead of his mahogany board. As soon as the music stopped so did he.

'Well done, Webber.' The Captain spoke for all who again clapped and cheered and demanded more. Martin shook his head and, sensing his exhaustion, Henry Wilson suggested anyone to have a turn until, without the lightness of foot demonstrated by Martin, the plate cracked and shattered into pieces bringing an end to the fun. Now long sets were made for 'Strip the Willow' and 'The Dashing White Sergeant' which gave a chance for the women and girls to join in while the lads ran outside to play their own games and the little ones ran between the legs of the dancers until all were too tired and sought the benches and the refreshment which now appeared on the table. To bring proceedings to a close Henry Wilson introduced Jake Endacott known as a singer in the locality.

'What be going to sing for us Jake?' he demanded and Jake replied that he would give them three songs from the West. 'Come my Lads', 'Green Broom' and 'The Cuckoo' which proved very popular and, after much clapping from his audience, cries for an encore went up. Requests were made for many popular songs but Jack elected to sing that most in demand.

STRAWBERRY FAIR

As I was going to Strawberry Fair
Righto righto riddle tol de lido
I met a fair maid go selling her ware
Tol de dee
I met a fair maid go selling her ware
As she went on to Strawberry Fair
Righto righto tol de riddle lido
Righto righto tol de riddle dee

Here there came mutterings of 'tis my favourite' from the women.

> My pretty fair maid pray thee tell
> Righto righto riddle tol de lido
> My pretty fair maid what do you sell?
> Tol de dee
> Come tell me truly sweet damsel
> As you go on to Strawberry Fair
> Righto righto riddle tol de lido
> Righto righto tol de riddle dee

Nods of approval greeted this verse.

> Oh I have a lock that doth lack a key
> Righto righto riddle tol de lido
> I have a lock, Sir, she did say
> Tol de dee
> If you have a key then come this way
> As we go on to Strawberry Fair
> Righto righto riddle tol de lido
> Righto righto tol de riddle dee

Foot tapping now stopped and eyebrows were raised.

> Now between us I reckon that when we met
> Righto righto riddle tol de lido
> The key to the lock it was well set
> Tol de dee
> The key to the lock it well did fit
> As we went on to Strawberry Fair
> Righto righto riddle tol de lido
> Righto righto tol de riddle dee

Some of the women in the audience gathered up their bags and children and prepared to depart.

> Oh would that my lock had been a gun
> Righto righto riddle tol de lido

I'd shoot the blacksmith for I'm undone
Tol de dee
And wares to carry I now have none
That I should go to Strawberry Fair
Righto righto riddle tol de lido
Righto righto tol de riddle dee.

'Not suitable afore the children'.

'Best kept for the public house or the men's room at the Conservative Club in town.'

Martin too looked angry and drew Tansy out through the door to join the Osborne family and make their way home. Wilmot and Tansy found plenty to talk about as they crossed White Hill passed through the two stone circles that were Grey Wethers; where the children wanted to get down from Lucifer's back and play. The two couples parted at the track between the two farms with many expressions of enjoyment and promises to meet again very soon. Tansy commented on the version of 'Strawberry Fair' sung by Jake Endacott – a version she had never heard before and Martin laughed.

'Perhaps you should ask your friend, Sabine Baring Gould – tis he as is collecting up the songs they do say. Us've seen him at Warren House Inn night times taking down words from an old stone breaker working on the roads. Going to put em all in a book seemingly.'

Tansy looked shocked that a man of the cloth should collect up songs the words of which were so rude. Would she dare ask him about this next time he called? She thought not. This reminded her that he and his friend Robert Burnard had applied for permission to excavate the bronze age village at 'Grimspound' and she commented on this to Martin.

'I wonder if the History Men have started their digging at 'Grimspound' yet? T'would be good to go and see.' At the wistful note in her voice Martin decided to take her there the very next day. Packing bread, cheese and cider they saddled Lucifer and set off but, to Tansy's surprise, instead of taking the track from Bennett's Cross then descending steeply through the mine workings to Vitifer, Martin guided Lucifer along the Moreton Road, turning off across Shapley common to Hookney Tor where they dismounted and began the struggle to the top. When Tansy questioned his choice of route he exclaimed.

'Had enough of that Mine track. Soon be done with it now. Burrowing underground like a badger; tis no life for me, needs to be up auver, out on the Moor where a man can breathe.' At this speech, long for Martin, usually a man of few words, he began to cough, the dry racking cough that had been keeping both of them awake during the last few week ends. Only now did she realise the price Martin was paying to keep their heads above water; the price of the spring blizzard which had cost them the beginnings of a flock of sheep. He had lost weight, his face gaunt and thin, clothes hanging on his normally sturdy frame and Tansy vowed to herself that she would do her best to feed him up and restore his erstwhile good temper before the autumn arrived. She must visit Sarah Webber, see if she had a remedy for the harsh cough. Reaching the top at last Tansy gasped at the view of rounded hills set back in folds beyond each other so clear that Martin pointed out Yes Tor.

'Tis the highest Tor of all. Close to Okehampton. That's where there's a very large market. Where Lucifer came from.'

The sun moved across the landscape, lighting up newtake and copse then moving on to illuminate a stone farmhouse and buildings.

'Look there's Headland Warren down there, Warren House Inn, Bellever, White Horse, Cut Hill and if you look hard you'll see leats cut by tinners to collect hillside drainage.' He pointed immediately below them. 'Look that's Grimspound.' Tansy looked at a huge rough rock edged circle with a stream of water flowing through it.

'Let's get down there and have a closer look'. Too steep to ride the rough hewn tor they scrambled down where Martin let Lucifer crop the sweet grass while he sat on a rock and smoked a cigarette, watching a pair of buzzards circling ahead. Tansy was excited at the sight of the pound Sabine Baring Gould and Robert Burnard were planning to excavate.

'Tis more sheltered here than tis at Teignhead.' she exclaimed and Martin nodded in agreement.

'Good shelter from both Tors. The far one is Hameldown. See the water course flowing through the pound; that's the GrimsLake so they'd have had water to drink. But where they'd sleep and cook we'll have to wait till History Men dig it out afore us knows!'

'Why would anyone want to live here anyways?' Tansy wanted to know.

'Perhaps valleys were full of wild animals and bog land. They say in country was covered in forest years and years ago and wolves and deer roamed free over the land.' Martin threw away his cigarette and clicked his fingers for Lucifer to come.

'Let's climb Hameldown and have our vittles up there.'

It took half an hour of struggle through the tough sinewy heather, ferns and rock outcrops before they reached the cairn. Tired and hungry now they settled down to eat and drink and, lulled by the hot sun, dozed for a while until a group of horses and riders passed them and disappeared along the track.

'Where does that track go, Martin?'

'Can get to Widecombe if ee goes to the end and down through Kingshead Farm and so into the village where ee can get a good pint of beer at the 'Rugglestone Inn' or, if tis Christmas Day a glass of mulled ale at the 'Olde Inne' and truth to tell which ale house is the older I doesn't know!' At the account of these delights Tansy was all for making the journey to Widecombe-in-the-Moor but Martin persuaded her that it was too far to go that day; that there was

Hortense to be milked and the hens shut up for the night.

'It'll have to keep for another day' Martin promised and Tansy had to be content with that. She sighed and tossed her head.

'Always 'another day' she grumbled then, feeling ungrateful thanked him for bringing her to Grimspound and showing her all there was to see from both Tors.

'There be Nattadon and Meldon which hills are just above Chagford and if you look in the opposite direction at that long ridge far away, that's Great Haldon, which is beyond Newton but this side of Exeter.'

Tansy was mightily impressed thinking how small they were compared to these hills and tors in their serried ranks. As they descended to make their way home she saw yet another track and questioned Martin who would use this and why. He sighed and explained briefly, anxious now to get back to Teignhead his thoughts already on the day ahead when he must set off once more for his week's labour at Vitifer Mine.

'Tis a path used by Tinners, Miners and Moormen's ponies, worn over the years.' At last she was content.

'Has been a fine day; at least I now know what Sabine Baring Gould was speaking of when he promised to let me know when they do start on their digging here.'

Martin merely smiled at her and was rewarded with a hug and kiss while her eyes held the promise of a reward in the hours to come and, for the first night since coming to live at Teignhead, Tansy didn't think of Geoffrey Llewellyn when finally she closed her eyes in sleep.

13

JACOB BLACKSTONE'S REVENGE

Tansy had seen uniformed figures crossing the valley before, usually the khaki of the Reserves from their camp at Okehampton carrying out manoeuvres. However these uniformed figures wore the dark blue of the constabulary. Curiosity sent her out through the courtyard to see where they were headed, and, to her surprise, found them crossing the clapper and climbing up the stroll, where, on arrival, they greeted her.

'Mrs Webber? Mrs Tansy Webber?'

'Yes, I'm Tansy Webber. What can I do for you sirs?' The older of the two constables stepped forward, a piece of paper in his hand, and read from it in measured tones.

'I have a warrant for your arrest on the grounds that, on Wednesday, 15th March, you did take from Mr Jacob Blackstone a gold watch as pledge and have not returned this to him.' Tansy felt alarm fill her soul knowing she had neither returned the watch nor, in fact, thought about it since the day Jacob Blackstone, had brought her back to the Farm. She gave a nervous laugh.

'Tis a mistake because I have the watch here in the Dairy; tis quite safe, I'll get it for you. Only sorry that you have had such a false journey.' The men exchanged glances then the elder spoke up.

'So you admit you have Jacob Blackstone's watch here on the premises?' When Tansy nodded he continued.

'Then can you show us where tis?'

Tansy led the way through the Farm kitchen and into the Dairy where she climbed steps to fetch down the watch, still concealed behind cans on the upper shelf. She climbed down and offered it to the Sergeant who turned it over in his hands, before showing it to his subordinate.

'Here, Jones, look at it – fine, isn't it? Tis no wonder Blackstone wants it back. Surprised he didn't come and fetch it hisself!'

Tansy stood looking puzzled then blushed as she remembered how he had come to the farm after the day she had cleaned the shop floor, after the altercation here at the farm. Remembered how she had hidden inside and pretended to be away from home.

'Well, he did come to the farm but no mention was made of the watch, if he'd asked for it then I'd have given it him and saved the Law a deal of trouble.' She led the way back into the kitchen. 'Can I get ee some cider?'

When Jones would have accepted Sergeant Mortimore restrained him.

'If he came out to the farm? You say he didn't come for his watch?' Tansy nodded. 'Then what did he come for?' She felt embarrassed; how to explain that Jacob Blackstone only wanted one thing, not easy to explain the out come of her transactions with the blackguard! She shook her head.

'I can't say. Tis best you go back, give him his watch and ask him about his second visit here for I'll not say.'

'My orders are to place ee under arrest so you'd best come along of us.'

Tansy, not believing things had come to such a pass, stood her ground and refused to move. The men conferred for a moment or two then the Sergeant produced a pair of handcuffs and, before she could demur, fastened one . . . to her wrist. She gasped, surprised at the speed of the action, protested.

'You'm making a mistake Sergeant. I am no thief.

Jacob Blackstone gave me the watch as a pledge for services rendered in cancellation of a debt.'

Both men exchanged looks, a smirk growing on Jones' face. Tansy continued to protest.

'You can't take me away – there's animals to feed, the cow to milk and my man is working at Vitifer Mine.' Faced with this unexpected development the men hesitated not knowing what to do then the Sergeant began to drag her from the kitchen and out into the courtyard where Tansy continued to protest.

'How long will I be gone?'

'You'm going to Chagford Lock-up then brought afore the Magistrate in the morning.'

The bobby was all for waiting for Tansy to perform her duties visualising a mug of cider at the end of it but Sergeant Mortimore thought of the Magistrate who had given him the summons to execute; thought of the fiver Jacob Blackstone had promised if the watch was recovered and the woman confined to the Lock-up at Chagford before night fall. He did not intend to lose this prapper prize and again began to pull her across the courtyard.

'Then let me call at Fernworthy Farm and tell Mrs Osborne what's happening so she can come up and feed the animals and milk the cow?'

'I agree to stop at Fernworthy but us must be quick.

There's duties to peform in Chagford afore us goes off duty.'

'Then will you send word to my husband at Vitifer telling him where I am?'

The Sergeant nodded in agreement and as soon as Tansy had locked the door of the farm house the trio set off down the stroll, across the clapper, and over the moor to Fernworthy where Wilmot emerged to gasp in astonishment at sight of Tansy handcuffed to the Bobby and in custody. Tansy handed the key to Wilmot asking her to look after things at the farm, assuring her.

'I'll not be long – tis all a mistake!' Wilmot shook her head at the men.

'That it is! Why there's no-one more honest than Mrs Tansy Webber! You'll live to regret your actions this day' she said addressing the men. 'Is word to be sent to Martin?' Both men looked shamefaced; the Sergeant nodded and hurried Tansy off across the bridge and up the road towards town. People stopped to stare as Tansy was hustled through the main street where she insisted they stop outside Jacob Blackstone's Emporium where she refused to move however hard the Sergeant and Constable tried to drag her. At her shouts Thomas came out.

'I told un not to do it Mrs Webber!' he said looking embarrassed.

'Fetch him Thomas! I'll not go till he comes and faces me!'

Thomas went back inside the shop and a moment or two later his master came to the door, a sneer on his face.

'Thought ee could get away with it, didn't ee my beauty?' He said before Tansy could open her mouth. 'Have the law on my side now. See what Magistrate has to say!' Tansy, outraged at this speech, shouted at him.

'If anyone needs locking up tis you Jacob Blackstone – not I! Give him his watch Sergeant' she added but the Sergeant shook his head.

'My instructions are to secure property and thief at one and same time. Tis evidence of theft – the watch. Must be produced at Court. So ee must come along.'

Tansy, conscious now of a gathering crowd, realised that she must submit to the Law and allowed herself to be led to the Lock-up where she was confined to a small cell in which there was but a narrow bed, a bucket, just one blanket, a mug of water and nothing else. She felt cold and angry; how could Jacob Blackstone have done such a thing. She was hungry too, not having had a thing to eat since breakfast and, although it was still light, she felt suddenly tired, wrapped herself in the rough blanket which was none too clean and tried to sleep. Time passed; she dozed, awoke to the sound of voices and a key turning in the cell door. Sitting up to see the Constable followed by Martin who looked troubled and angry.

'What's up now Tansy? Brought from the Mine here – Sergeant Mortimore says you'm charged with stealing Jacob Blackstone's watch! I've told em there must be some mistake. What does it mean?'

Tansy looked embarrassed, not wanting to have to tell Martin the whole story of her transactions with the shop keeper. Not wanting the memories of their wedding day spoilt or her foolishness exposed.

'Exchanged his watch for some work I did one day just to settle some things I bought and for which, when it came to it, I didn't have the money.'

Tansy shrugged her shoulders and smiled at Martin, hoping he would accept her explanation but he was having none of it.

'Doesn't sound like a simple transaction to me. What work was it you carried out for Jacob Blackstone? And when?' As she hesitated he pressed her. 'I mean to know what's going on. Haven't come all the way from Vitifer to be swept aside with a half truth. So, come on Tansy, the full story if you please!' He turned to the Constable.

'I'm sure I shall get the truth if you will leave us.' The man nodded and left, locking the door behind him. Tansy realised there was nothing for it but to tell Martin the truth; watch his face turn to fury as she told him how she had scrubbed Blackstone's floor and how he had tried to abuse her while he Martin was staying overnight at the Mine. He paced the floor of the cell and Tansy was thankful that he didn't ask what it was she had bought which had provoked the issuing of the summons.

'Us'll soon sort the varmint out – just let us get at him. Tis him as should be locked up, not ee my maid! Us'll soon get ee out of here don't fret!'

Martin began to rattle the bars of the cell door and call for the Constable while Tansy dreaded lest Martin himself got into trouble. She tried to restrain him until the door was unbolted and he was let out, still shouting his indignation.

'Tis Jacob Blackstone should be in here Constable not my girl. There's no call to lock her up when ee hears what that varmint have been up to.'

The Constable refused to release Tansy until she had appeared before the Magistrate but did agree to let Martin fetch some vittles from The Three Crowns. With this concession both had to be content and Tansy resigned herself to spending the night in the Lock-up. Try as she might she couldn't persuade Martin to go back to Vitifer; instead he swore to spend the night at Teignhead and return to Chagford to attend the Court House in time for the Magistrates' Hearing in the morning.

Tansy woke as soon as it grew light, asked the Constable to bring her a bowl of water so she could wash her face and hands. Taking pity on her he also produced a comb and mirror, a mug of tea and some bread. Tansy felt all the better for this and Martin's support encouraged her in the belief that Jacob Blackstone wouldn't get away with his charge of theft so; when the cell door was unlocked she emerged with chin held high, prepared for whatever was to come. The Court House was but a short distance from the Lock-up and she was taken round the back of the building into a small room. From here she could hear the sound of people climbing the Court House steps to the public gallery and her thought went back to her visit to London where Norah had taken her from Goldsmith's college to hear the lecture on the Boer War; remembered how she had risen to protest against the treatment of horses in the heat of South Africa, remembered how she had caused a near riot and been hauled off to jail to be brought before the Magistrates next day. She smiled remembering the outcome – a caution. Then too it had been Martin who supported her. Why he had even come up from Devon to bring her home. She remembered too the wrongful accusation by Fanny Luscombe's sister, Janet, that she Tansy had stolen Miss Emma's birthday watch. Tansy shivered at the recollection of how she almost lost her good name. That time it was Geoffrey Llewellyn who had uncovered the real culprit, Janet Luscombe. What if word of that episode had already reached this Court? Two charges of watch theft would surely go against her even if neither were true. Through the door she could hear the proceedings begin with the treading of feet, banging of a gavel and she asked the Sergeant to tell her what was happening.

'Court has begun, three magistrates are sitting – Captain Christopher Smith Haig of the Devon Yeomanry, Lady Annabel Watson Hope of Gidleigh Park and Henry Westaway, a Mine Owner. You've a Solicitor to defend ee Mrs Webber and your case is third on the list.'

Before Tansy could absorb this information the door opened to admit a young man wearing a dark suit, white collar with a tab front which lit his saturnine features. He held out his hand and smiled at her.

'My name is Nathaniel Hext and I'm your Defence Lawyer. How do you wish to plead Mrs Webber? Guilty or not guilty?'

'How can I say until I know what the charge is?'

'The Sergeant should have told you these details when they came to arrest you.' He sighed and shuffled through his papers. 'It says here that on Wednesday, March 15th, 1901 you did take charge of Mr Jacob Blackstone's watch as pledge and have not returned it to him although he himself has fulfilled his own part of the bargain.' He looked at Tansy with raised eyebrows. 'Is this true?'

Tansy knew that this was, in fact, the state of things and, if Jacob Blackstone hadn't assaulted her at the farm but had exchanged the receipted bill for his watch then that would have been the end of it. How could she tell the underlying story in front of the Court. How to tell that the Store Keeper had come out to Teignhead a second time when she could have given back his watch? A second chance but one she had been too frightened to risk with Martin away and no-one within ear shot? She stuttered.

'Put like that Mr Hext, on the surface that is the truth of it but there are good reasons why I didn't give Jacob Blackstone his watch on each of these two occasions.' The young lawyer raised his eyebrows and asked.

'So are you going to tell me what these reasons were?' Now Tansy worried that they wouldn't have finished the story before the door opened and she would be ushered into the Court Room.

'How much time have we before tis my turn?' Nathaniel Hext encouraged her.

'There's time enough. Two cases are to be heard before your own' and when Tansy looked enquiringly 'one for poaching salmon from his Lordship's stretch of the Teign and the case of Osborne v. Roberts.'

At the sound of her friends' name Tansy looked startled.

'Is that the Osbornes of Fernworthy by any chance?' The young man nodded adding.

'Tis a dispute between two farmers about livestock. But' he added 'this must not be discussed outside the Court Room. Are they friends of yours?'

'Very good friends; looking after the Farm while I'm here. The best friends in the world!'

'Can we get on Mrs Webber? You must give a good reason to the Magistrates for keeping the gold watch or you will be found guilty of theft and sentenced to jail for a minimum of six months. So please'.

Half an hour later the door opened to admit Tansy to the Court Room where Martin was already seated in the public gallery next to Tom Osborne. Both smiled encouragingly at her. She looked at the figures on the Bench at once recognising the Vallances' friend and mine owner, Henry Westaway who immediately at sight

139

of her moved his seat back from the Bench indicating that he would take no part in the case as was the rule should someone appear who was known to them. Tansy noted that the public gallery was full, recognized Mary Hannaford who bought eggs and cream from her at the Dairy; the Minister from the Chapel in town also the farmer's wife from Thornworthy for whom she had bought lamp wicks on her first visit to Chagford when she came to Teignhead. The Clerk of the Court rose and read from his notes.

'The next case, your worship, is that of Tansy Webber. Number 3 on your list. Mrs Webber appears for trial today on the charge of stealing a gold watch to the value of £150 from Mr Jacob Blackstone owner of Blackstone's Emporium, Chagford. Mrs Webber has pleaded not guilty to the charge.'

Tansy studied the third member of the Bench; an elegant figure dressed in riding habit of grey with top hat perched over a sharp featured face which bore a look of concentration yet at the same time a look of kindness. Tansy felt she would get a fair hearing from this woman who was no longer young. Tansy realised the Clerk was addressing her.

CLERK: (Motions to defendant) 'Please stand. You are Tansy Webber?'

TANSY: 'Yes.'

CLERK: 'Your date of birth is the 4th April, 1872?'

TANSY: 'Yes.'

CLERK: 'You are here to answer one charge?' (Looks across to Defence Solicitor).

DEFENCE: (Nathaniel Hext) (Stands). 'Good morning your Worship. I represent Mrs Tansy Webber.'

CROWN PROSECUTION SOLICITOR (CPS): 'This is a relatively simple case Your Worship. The Defendant, Mrs Tansy Webber, was given a gold watch as pledge by Mr Jacob Blackstone at his premises on Wednesday, 15th March, 1901 in exchange for a receipt for work done on that day and, although Mr Blackstone fulfilled his part of the bargain by handing over the receipt Mrs Webber failed to fulfill her part of the bargain and the watch remained in her hands some three months since.'

CPS:(continues) 'I would like to call my Witness Mr Jacob Blackstone.'

CHAIRMAN OF THE BENCH:(Capt. Christopher Smith-Haig.) 'Yes please proceed.'

CLERK: 'Call Jacob Blackstone to Court Number 1.'

(Jacob Blackstone appears from the back of the Court and is conducted to the witness box. The Usher hands him a book and a card).

USHER: 'Please take the book in your right hand and read the words on the card.'

BLACKSTONE: (Holds the book and reads from the card).

'I swear that the evidence I shall give shall be the truth and nothing but the truth.'

CPS: 'Tell the Court the circumstances of the exchange of a receipted Bill for a gold watch as pledge which took place on Wednesday, 15th March, 1901?'

BLACKSTONE: 'On that day Tansy Webber came into the Shop and again could not pay for goods she had had on credit, some since the beginning of September last year.'

CPS: 'What happened when she couldn't pay?'

BLACKSTONE: 'She offered of her own free will to clean the shop floor.'

CPS: 'What was your reaction?'

BLACKSTONE 'I accepted her offer and said I would cancel the debt if she completed this.'

CPS: 'Did she agree to this?'

BLACKSTONE: 'Yes'.

CPS: 'Did she clean the floor and what happened after this?'

BLACKSTONE: 'It was late when she finished and I offered to take her home as twas getting dark and I didn't like the thought of her crossing the Moor alone.'

CPS: 'Did this offer cause you any inconvenience?'

BLACKSTONE: 'Yes, it meant I had to close the shop

earlier than usual but this I was willing to do to keep Tansy Webber safe!'

CPS: 'What happened next?'

BLACKSTONE: 'She insisted I give her my watch as pledge to be exchanged for the receipted bill at Teignhead Farm'.

CPS: 'Did you agree to this?'

BLACKSTONE: 'Yes'.

CPS: 'What happened when you arrived at Teignhead Farm?'

BLACKSTONE: 'She refused to give me the watch even though I had handed over the receipted bill.'

CPS: 'Thank you Mr Blackstone. Stay there please.'

DEFENCE:(rises) 'Earlier in your dealings with Mrs Webber did you ask her to have dinner with you at The Three Crowns Hotel? Remember you are on oath.'

BLACKSTONE: (looks toward CPS who nods. He mutters his reply). 'Yes, but she refused my invitation which was merely to seal a business arrangement.'

DEFENCE: 'Did you offer to cancel a bill for material for a wedding dress if she would have dinner with you?'

BLACKSTONE: (Getting red in the face, stutters): 'Yes'.

DEFENCE: 'Following her refusal on a second occasion when you tried to bribe her with dinner at The Three Crowns Hotel, did you threaten to tell her husband now working at Vitifer Mine of her debt?'

BLACKSTONE: (Now purple in the face) 'Yes'.

DEFENCE: 'Did you offer to take Mrs Webber home after she had cleaned the floor of your Emporium because she inadvertently let slip the fact that her husband was now spending his nights at the Mine?'

BLACKSTONE: (Struggling like a fish on a hook didn't answer).

CHAIRMAN: 'You must answer, Blackstone.'

BLACKSTONE: 'No, I did not'.

DEFENCE: 'Did you enter Teignhead Farm against the wishes of Mrs Webber and attempt to abuse her and in which act you were thwarted by Martin Webber's sheep dog?'

BLACKSTONE: 'No, I did not!'

DEFENCE: 'Did you subsequently visit Teignhead Farm at a time you knew Martin Webber, Mrs Webber's husband, to be away from home and what was the purpose of this visit?'

BLACKSTONE: 'I went to the Farm to collect my watch, a watch I use every day and have done since my Father left it me twenty years since. I was unaware of her husband's absence from home and, although I knew her to be at home, she didn't answer my knocks or answer the door. This is the reason we are here today so's I can regain my property.' (Here he looks round the Court with a self righteous air).

DEFENCE: 'That is all. (Turns). Have the Bench any questions for my client?'

TANSY: (Comes forward and is sworn in).

CHAIRMAN: 'Why did you insist on holding Mr Blackstone's watch until you got home to Teignhead Farm?'

TANSY: 'Because I was afraid of him; a fear upheld by his behavior when we got there.'

CHAIRMAN: 'Why was the watch still in your possession some months after he gave it you even though he had fulfilled his part of the bargain by handing over the receipted bill?'

TANSY: 'I was still afraid of him which is the reason I didn't open the door the second time he came.'

CHAIRMAN: 'Why did you not return the watch to Mr Blackstone at his premises in Chagford?'

TANSY: 'Although I come into town every Wednesday to sell eggs and cream I found it too painful to contemplate visiting Blackstone's shop ever again. I banished this unpleasant episode from my mind.'

CHAIRMAN: 'What happened when the Police officers called at Teignhead Farm yesterday?'

TANSY: 'I was amazed that they had come for the watch which I then remembered was still high up on

143

the shelf in the Dairy. I fetched it immediately and offered it to them but they were unable to accept it and told me I was to be charged with theft!'

CHAIRMAN: 'Thank you. That is all. You may step down.'

Tansy turned to go back down the steps to the back room but not before she noticed Lady Anne questioning the Chairman who held up his hand.

CHAIRMAN: 'Just one moment Mrs Webber. Lady Anne wishes you to tell us the nature of the abuse you say took place at Teignhead Farm the night Jacob Blackstone took you to Teignhead Farm in his trap?'

DEFENCE: 'If my client is willing to go over this unpleasant experience in Court then I have no objection.'

TANSY: 'When we reached the clapper Blackstone unhitched his pony and dragged both the pony and I up the stroll where he tied the pony to the ring and waited for me to open the farmhouse door. I then protested that it wasn't necessary for him to come inside. I waited a while but realising that he wasn't moving tried to get in and close the door. Martin's dog Moss came out barking at this intruder which had the effect of catching me between dog and man. Blackstone kicked Moss so savagely that he whimpered and ran to me for comfort. Afraid of what Blackstone would do next I hid his watch behind the peat blocks. I then asked him 'Tis time to exchange tokens then you'd best be on your way before tis too dark to see bog close to track.' However he made no move to exchange tokens but said 'He didn't scare easy, added that as my man was from home I'd be all on my lonesome and twould be best if he stayed and kept me safe.'

Now there was a murmur throughout the Court; Martin leapt to his feet and clenched his fists. Tansy, pale and perspiring at her ordeal felt faint and asked for water.

LADY ANNABEL: 'I suggest a chair be brought for the Defendant.' A chair was brought by the Usher. 'Now take your time Mrs Webber and tell us what happened next.'

TANSY: (Sipped water and wiped her forehead with her hanky). 'Again I said twas time to exchange bill for watch, told him to be off or I would report him to the Constable at Chagford.'

LADY ANNABEL: 'Go on, tell us what happened then.'

TANSY: I had drawn a mug of cider in an effort to calm the situation; now he swallowed it down, rose from the bench and came toward me. Moss growled and began to crawl across the floor toward him. Blackstone seized a spade from a pile of tools in the corner of the room and faced Moss who began to circle him, baring his teeth.'

LADY ANNABEL: 'Yes, yes, what happened then?'

TANSY: 'I was afraid he might kill Moss so when I saw Martin's gun behind the door I seized it and aimed it at Blackstone telling him it was loaded even though it wasn't. Told him I would shoot even though I can't and at last he gave in. He left, leaving the receipt on the table and it was only later that I realized I hadn't given him the watch.'

LADY ANNABEL: 'Thank you Mrs Webber for giving us such a full account of what happened.'

A hum of conversation rose from the public benches and the Usher called for silence as the Magistrates prepared to leave.

CLERK: 'The Court will convene in three weeks time, after they have conferred on this case. The prisoner will be allowed bail.' USHER: 'All rise'.

The three members of the Bench left the Court and Tansy was taken below where Nathaniel Hext asked if she knew anyone who would stand bail for her in the sum of £25. While Tansy sat and thought of all the people she knew who might gamble money on her not running away before the Court sat again, and could not think of a single person with that sort of money, the Sergeant came in.

'You are free to go Mrs Webber. Bail has been given.' Tansy, amazed that release should come so quickly, asked who had put up the money. At which Sergeant Mortimore smiled and reported that Mary Hannaford had taken up a collection outside the Court so it was she she had to thank. Nathaniel Hext shook Tansy by the hand and reminded her she must attend the Court in three weeks time or bail would be forfeit but that a notice reminding her would be sent.

'If you have Lady Annabel on your side then I think you have little to fear. It's a case of who the magistrates believe – you or Blackstone. Could do with another witness to clinch matters.' Hext added.

'If only dogs could talk' Tansy laughed then added 'Only person who was present at the shop during all the transactions with Jacob Blackstone was his assistant, Thomas Smith, but I wouldn't want him to risk losing his job on my account.' Tansy found Martin waiting for her, a broad smile on his face.

'Everyone was on your side Tansy. There's other women have been assaulted by that varmint.'

He hugged her to him but she pulled away declaring.

'I must just go and thank Mary Hannaford for standing bail then I wants to know all about the Osborne's case and this time I want no excuses.' Mary Hannaford smiled a welcome when Tansy entered the Dairy.

'I know what ee've come to say but there's no call for thanks. You'm not the only woman as has suffered Jacob Blackstone's tricks so it was easy to collect the £25 bail money, knowing of course that you won't let us down and will come back to Court to hear they Magistrates clear your name.' Tansy brushed a tear from her cheek at the thought of women who could barely afford to feed themselves and their families giving money to support her, she tried to speak her thanks but was prevented by the lump in her throat. Mary smiled at her and said.

'You know the old saying 'Do zummat, do good if ee can, but do zummat!'

Martin came into the Dairy to see what was taking so long, took Tansy home where she had a good cry on his shoulder before setting about milking Hortense and rescuing half set cream.

'Feel's I've been away years' she said and it was only after Martin had left for the mine next day that she remembered that the mystery of the Osborne's case still remained just that.

Three weeks to the day saw Tansy attending the Magistrates' Court at Chagford, waiting below the Court Room anxious to hear the result of their deliberations. Martin had taken the day off promising to report back to the mine workers' wives, Tansy's Father, Edward Drewe sat next Martin's Father, Amos Webber and the Osbornes and Mary Hannaford were in the public gallery awaiting events. Nathaniel Hext arrived and greeted Tansy warmly followed almost immediately by the assistant from Blackstone's Emporium, Thomas Smith. At once the Sergeant came and took him off to another room but not before he exchanged smiles with Tansy who raised enquiring eyebrows at Nathaniel.

'Our witness agreed at once to give evidence on your behalf. Seems he is not enamoured of Blackstone either.' He smiled and left Tansy alone to await her call to appear before the magistrates of whom just two were present. Capt. Smith Haig again took the chair and Lady Annabel Watson Hope, again dressed in grey riding habit with veil covering her face took a seat beside him. The third member of the Bench, Henry Westaway, sat in the public gallery evidence that he took no part in the proceedings but still anxious to witness the outcome.

USHER: 'All rise'.

CLERK: 'The first case on the list today is No. 1 – Jacob Blackstone versus Tansy Webber who has been accused of theft by the foregoing. Since first heard a witness has come forward to give evidence. Is it your

Worship's desire that this witness, Thomas Smith, be called?'

CHAIRMAN: 'It is'.

USHER: 'Call Thomas Smith.'

(The ritual of swearing in takes place and Thomas Smith stands in the witness box looking nervously about him.)

DEFENCE: 'Thomas Smith, were you employed by Jacob Blackstone in his shop at Chagford during the months when Mrs Tansy Webber purchased certain goods there?'

THOMAS SMITH: 'I was'.

DEFENCE: 'What happened on her first visit in September of last year'.

THOMAS SMITH: 'Mrs Webber (Tansy Drewe as she was then) came into the shop to buy some lamp wicks and saw some material she thought would make up into a wedding dress.'

CHAIRMAN: 'Yes, yes. Go on.'

THOMAS SMITH: 'He, Jacob Blackstone, offered the material to Mrs Webber on payment of a pound down, saying he would let her pay off the balance of £4 monthly. It was only after the Blizzard when Mrs Webber couldn't get in to pay the instalments owing that he, Blackstone, added interest. Also he sent me out to Teignhead Farm before the wedding with boots and gloves which she, Mrs Webber, hadn't asked for. He told me not to return with them. That if I did that would mean the loss of my job.'

CHAIRMAN: 'And was the cost of these items added to her account?'

THOMAS SMITH: 'Yes sir. This brought the debt up to £8.'

CHAIRMAN: 'Were you present when your employer invited Mrs Webber to 'The Three Crowns'?'

THOMAS SMITH: 'Yes, sir. She refused both times he asked her.'

CHAIRMAN: 'Were you in the shop on the occasion when Mrs Webber cleaned the floor?'

THOMAS SMITH: 'Yes, sir, I was'.

CHAIRMAN: 'What do you recall of that visit?'

THOMAS SMITH: 'She came in to buy a new skillet which my employer found for her and wrapped but, although she had paid for it there and then he wouldn't give it her reminding her she still owed him money. He then offered to take her home and when she refused he grew very angry. It was then she offered to clean the floor and he said 'that would settle the debt' but then tried to trick her by offering only a shillin an hour in payment.'

CHAIRMAN: 'What happened following this disagreement.'

THOMAS SMITH: 'He locked the shop door and she finished washing the shop floor on the understanding the debt was cancelled. At 6 o'clock he sent me away, this was an hour earlier than I normally finishes. That's all I saw.'

CHAIRMAN: 'I need to confer with my fellow magistrate.'

Lady Annabel and Captain Smith Haig rose and left the Court. The public gallery was now abuzz with comment and indignation while minutes passed and Edward Drewe and Amos Webber grew impatient to hear the verdict and Martin's anger rose to boiling point, this being the first time he had heard the full details of Tansy's transactions with Jacob Blackstone. Shortly the magistrates returned instructing the Usher to call Mrs Webber and Jacob Blackstone to come before them. Each sat beside their legal representative.

CHAIRMAN: 'Three weeks ago we heard the case of Blackstone versus Webber in which the former accused the latter of the theft of a watch. Since then a witness to the transactions which led to the loss of the watch has come forward. His evidence convinces the members of the Bench that the loss of this watch was brought about by his own behaviour. From their very first encounter it seems Mr Blackstone has molested Mrs

Webber until she became terrified by his presence. Call Mr Blackstone to the stand.'

USHER: 'Call Jacob Blackstone'.

He mounts the stand his face red and angry.

CHAIRMAN: 'Jacob Blackstone you are lucky not to be facing a charge of attempted assault. Your charge against Mrs Webber is dismissed but you will have to pay the expenses of this Court of which the Clerk will notify you. Do not come before this Court again. You may step down.'

LADY ANNE: 'Mrs Webber, please come forward.'

USHER: 'Call Mrs Tansy Webber to the stand'.

She climbs the stand, smiling broadly.

LADY ANNE: 'Mrs Webber the Bench sympathises with you over the protracted reign of terror exerted by Mr Blackstone. Although you should have found a way to return the Accuser's watch the Bench understands why this was not done. You are free to go without a stain on your character.'

USHER: 'All rise'.

The Magistrates leave the Court Room, Amos Webber and Edward Drewe embrace, Martin and Tom Osborne shake hands and Henry Westaway congratulates Tansy on the result. Mary Hannaford wipes her eyes but Jacob Blackstone slinks from the Court and within a few days a 'For Sale' notice appears on the door of Blackstone's Emporium! Martin looks at Tansy with new eyes, shocked by all she has gone through and as soon as the chores are done and both are sat by the fire drinking tea before retiring for the night, he speaks up.

'Promise me never to get involved with such vermin again, Tansy. If ee needs anything come to me. Never a lender nor a borrower be, tis what Feyther always says. I did love you in that blue dress on our wedding day Tansy, but, if I'd a know'd all you were going through to pay for it – why I'd a been happier to see you in the one you wore to the Ram Roast at Kingsteignton!'

Now Tansy laughed, thinking of the crumpled mess of muslin lying inside her box and, to tease him, she ran to the box and drew it out. Ripping off her plain work dress in a fit of celebration she put on the figured muslin and danced round the kitchen, the lamp light showing off her figure through the thin material till Martin's heart beat fast and when she came near he caught her in his arms to cover her face with kisses.

'One thing's for sure – I must teach ee how to shoot that gun but perhaps twas as well ee didn't try or Blackstone might be dead and ee afore the Magistrates on a murder charge.' Tansy laughed and remembered the figures on the Bench.

'That Lady Anne she was on my side when that Captain would a let things go.'

'I remembers her when as just a little tacker I rode my pony with the Mid Devon Hunt. She rode to hounds in a long black habit, side saddle too but galloped full tilt across Moor after Mr Reynard.'

Now Tansy's mood changed and she told Martin off for hunting down God's creatures even though she now knew this same fox could kill her chickens for the mere fun of it. Despite her change of mood Tansy made no protest when Martin pulled her on to the chuckle bed and began gently to remove the ruined muslin dress.

14

THOMASIN

Tansy loved the walk into Chagford, how the Moor gave way to lanes deep in blossom; primroses, celandines and violets in spring, bluebells then parsley, ragged robin, valerian and in June the overwhelming smell of meadowsweet. Wilmot regaled her with all the local sayings. Unlucky to take May blossom into the house, lilies only for funerals! Roses bloomed in the hedges intertwined with honeysuckle and the steady hum of bees. Happy to return from this lush valley, cross the bridge at Fernworthy Farm to tread the moor track to the clapper and experience a sense of peace and satisfaction as she climbed the stroll and entered the courtyard where chickens ran to meet her and Moss barked a welcome. Now, however, an event was to occur which would change her life dramatically. It happened one hot day in late August when she and Wilmot met at the clapper and climbed up Sittaford, the children nowhere to be seen and Tansy, used to their constant presence, asked where they were.

'Writing a story'.

'A story – did you tell them what twas to be about?' Wilmot laughed.

'Market day at Chagford! Tis to be finished by dinner time so we have an hour!'

On the way they sought out colours to share; the mauve of lousewort, blue autumn squill, red and blue berried whortle berries, white puffs of bog cotton among bright green moss, ferns uncurling beneath newtake walls where pennywort filled gaps between stones and the pink stars of saxifrage clinging to granite rocks.

'Tis one huge bouquet of flowers' Tansy exclaimed. She looked up at the mewing sound of a pair of buzzards circling overhead. 'Martin have told me they'm buzzards. What are they hunting for?'

'Young rabbits, worms and perhaps small snakes.' Wilmot told her.

'Snakes! Are there snakes up here?' Tansy shivered.

'Adders love the sun, lie out on paths in summer. Can't mistake them Tansy – black zig zag pattern down their backs. Quite shy they be and only bite if they'm disturbed. Usually slither away into the bracken when anyone approaches.' She looked at Tansy. 'You have a lot to learn my lover!' Together they reached Sittaford and sat on the rocks enjoying each other's company and the warmth of the day.

'Do you miss Tom during the week when he's at Vitifer?' Tansy asked and Wilmot nodded and sighed.

'We all misses him – tis two years now since the animals were took!' She stopped and when Tansy pressed her to go on shut her mouth and shook her head.

'What happened Wilmot? What happened to the farm – Martin once hinted at it having something to do with Thornworthy but he says he's sworn to secrecy.' Now Wilmot's gray eyes looked troubled.

'Weighs heavy on us all – I do long to tell some-one . . .'

Still she hesitated 'But Tom says tis best forgotten.'

Before Tansy could persuade Wilmot to unburden herself both saw a tall figure walking the track from Postbridge toward them. For a moment Tansy held her breath, the figure was too tall for Martin.

Her heart began a slow hammering as the women hurried down the hill to meet the man who appeared to be carrying a bundle on his shoulders. As he drew closer disappointment filled Tansy's heart as she identified his clothes with that of a working man, not the black of her priest. It was only when the tall figure reached the gap in the Newtake Wall that Tansy recognized the familiar frame of Tom Moore; on his shoulders a small child.

'Why Tom Moore what a sight for sore eyes!' Tansy exclaimed 'whatever are you doing up here?' He smiled and touched his cap to both women.

'Come to see you Tansy.' He looked pointedly at Wilmot who immediately took her leave when Tom Moore and Tansy made their way along the path and over the clapper to climb the stroll to Teignhead. It was only when Tansy had stirred up the fire, filled a pot and set it on the trivet that her guess at the reason for Tom Moore's visit was confirmed.

'How is everyone?' she enquired of Tom who had set down the child on his lap. He smiled and nodded.

'Very well, boys growing taller by the day.'

Tansy looked at the rosy cheeked child, now regarding her with blue eyes beneath a mop of curly brown hair. Tansy took a deep breath. 'So this must be Avril's baby?' Tom nodded.

'Yes, this be Thomasin'.

'The girl Avril always wanted? And Avril?' Tansy asked the question knowing full well what the answer was going to be. Tom's expression changed from joy to sadness.

'Yes, always wanted a girl and after losing Eleanor . . . couldn't seem to settle till us tried again . . .' Tansy hesitated

'And Avril?'

Tom shook his head, hugged the child to him and his voice became thick with emotion.

'Never fully recovered from the birth, Tansy. Lingered on through the winter then' (here his voice broke) 'then was gone.' He struggled to recover himself.

'Mother and Father been looking out for her till now

. . . managed till she began to run about . . . now, with Father gone, boys at school all day . . . well, Mother, she can't manage.' Tansy poured hot water on to tea, went into the Dairy for milk, poured a cup for the child giving herself time to collect her thoughts, prepare herself for the question she knew was coming. Tom looked at her beseechingly. Tansy enquired.

'You'm not at Vitifer any more then?' When Tom shook his head she hurried on 'Of course Martin would have told me if you'd still worked there.'

'No, moved on to Golden Dagger for a while but am working at Brick Works in Newton. Sorry to hear Martin lost the sheep . . . Mr Drewe, he told us what happened . . .'

Still the question hung between them and at last Tansy could bear the tension no longer.

'Brought Avril's baby for me to look after then, Tom?' Tom, relieved that he had not had to ask for the commitment he had sought, smiled broadly and lifting the little child from his lap, stood to cross the room, hold out the little girl to Tansy, who wiped her hands on her apron, opened her arms and her heart and accepted Thomasin into her life.

Tom Moore had stayed a while, settled Thomasin with Tansy promising to return with clothes and cot for her at the weekend, left with many smiles and waves. The little girl cried as her Father's figure grew smaller and smaller as he walked away down the stroll where he turned to give a final wave to her. To distract her from her grief Tansy showed Thomasin the lamb rescued during the blizzard and now grown big but still tame enough to be petted. Moss was used to Storm but at first flattened his ears at the little girl, sensing an intruder into his small close world but, when Tansy made a fuss of him, he eventually wagged his tail till Tansy felt it safe to set her down in the kitchen and begin on preparations for her stay. Thomasin was steady on her feet and Tansy showed her the hens shutting them up for the night, then began on the milking when the child ran as far away as her tiny legs would carry her, not liking the large animal. Hortense swished her tail and mooed till Tansy soothed both cow and child with her favourite lullaby.

> May God bless you goodnight,
> little cloud soft and white
> and roses of red
> shall make you your bed.
>
> In the dawn if God wills,
> you will wake sleepy head,
> In the dawn if God wills,
> you will wake sleepy head.'

After a little bread and jam, Tansy showed her pictures from 'Little Women' then settled her in the largest basket and covered her with her shawl, watched over her until she herself tired after all the day's excitement, succumbed to the night stealing over both woman and child.

When Martin came home the following Saturday Thomasin hid behind Tansy's skirts and refused to come out. Used to there being just the two of them she waited for this stranger to go away.

'Who might this be?' Martin enquired after hugging and kissing Tansy then drinking the cider she had drawn for him. 'Too small for one of Wilmot's girls I think.' He turned an enquiring gaze on her. Tansy hugged the little girl close and nodded.

'Tis Thomasin – Avril Moore's last baby.' She went on with a rush. 'Tom Moore came last Monday – mid-day twas – tells me he has finished at the mine – still you would know that. Working at Hammond's Brickworks over to Newton now so he can keep an eye on his boys before and after work.' Martin sat down and waited.

'Seems Dr. Owen's warning wasn't in vain. Told her he doubted she would survive another birth. Avril lingered on through the winter but was gone by spring. Now Tom's Father has died his Mother can't manage such a small child on her own . . .'

Tansy paused waiting for Martin's reaction.

'Does that mean what I think it do?' he demanded. Tansy's face took on a pleading look.

'Last time I saw Avril she made me promise to look after the child she was expecting if anything should happen to her. So this is she.' Again she put protective arms around Thomasin.

'So we have another mouth to feed?' Martin sounded serious but, even so, he smiled at the little girl who stared at him from Tansy's arms.

'Couldn't refuse, Martin, could I? She was a good friend to me when I needed one.'

'How long is she going to stay?' He asked then, as Tansy hesitated 'You mean to say you haven't set a time?'

'Didn't think of anything but making Thomasin here happy; finding her a bed for the night and stopping her tears when Tom left and she watched him walk away from her down the stroll and across the Moor back to Newton.'

'Tis just like you . . . I suppose I would have done the same . . . strange that the first little un be someone else's and not one of our own, still tis company for ee I guess when I'm away at Mine.'

'Tom's going to bring her bed and clothes at the weekend so all us has to provide will be vittles.'

Tansy was relieved that Martin had accepted Thomasin so easily without real complaint and, when he tucked her into the basket the following night and was rewarded with a smile from the rosy face, Tansy exclaimed.

'You'm a good man Martin Webber!'

She took his hand as together they went out to shut up the fowls, to check the animals and look across the valley as had become their habit each night that Martin was at home.

'At least you will be practised at looking after little uns when our own bairns come along 'though I never thought our Adam would be a father before I!'

Now he caught Tansy about the waist as she closed the henhouse door and swung her round to face him. Suddenly serious he spoke in a soft coaxing tone.

'Perhaps we should think about it – could be tonight we'll start our own family?'

Tansy alarmed at the prospect of having a bairn thought of the practical problems that Thomasin posed. How was she to get to Chagford and back each Wednesday. As if he had read her thoughts Martin asked.

'How are you going to manage the walk to Chagford, my maid?'

'She can ride on my shoulders or' (when he looked doubtful) perhaps I can leave her with Wilmot or take the sled.'

At this Martin's face looked full of alarm.

'No, no sled's too heavy for ee to drag so far.'

The unspoken question lay between them. Lucifer could pull the sled with both of them on it or she could settle Thomasin on the sled with the eggs and cream and ride Lucifer herself. She remembered how Martin and Adam had fixed the sled to the cob's harness for peat cutting but kept quiet now just in case Martin forbad it.

'This Thomasin will cost us, Tansy. Needs a pony and trap but us cannot afford either yet. That and the oven must wait till sheep shearing.'

Deep in thought they parted to finish their chores but later that night, as if babies were on both their minds, they made love – such sweet and gentle love prolonged until both fell into soft slumber which outlasted cock crow and the 5 o'clock chime of the wedding clock.

'At least' thought Tansy as she washed Thomasin's soft face 'Martin didn't say Thomasin must be sent back to Newton.'

*   *   *

Geoffrey Llewellyn came into Tansy's mind with the arrival of a large brown paper parcel; a parcel wrapped twice, tied with string, knots sealed with red wax. On opening this to find it contained not one but three books her delight was overwhelming. Who could be sending her such pleasure? The parcel contained nothing to tell her the name of the donor. She remembered her excitement at receiving 'Pride and Prejudice' Geoffrey's gift that Christmas they had shared at 'The Manse'. How she had read Jane Austen's masterpiece over and over till she knew it almost word for word! Now, with her days so full of activity there was no time for books during the day and she was too exhausted to read at night. Martin exhorted her to make the most of the long days, adding, time for reading when winter comes. Tansy turned the books over in her hands admiring the illustrations in Wilkie Collins' 'The Moonstone', became excited at the thought of reading Dickens' 'Great Expectations' whilst she knew a little of 'The Water Babies'. Her Mother quoted Charles Kingsley to her and Norah when they were young exhorting them to 'Do as you would be done by'! She smiled remembering the other book Geoffrey had given her that precious Christmas when she had invited him to make love to her. She went over to the shelf and took down 'A Child's Garden of Verses' which must await the arrival of her own children: but now here was Avril's child Thomasin to be the first to enjoy it. Tansy replaced it on the shelf but the new parcel she hid in her box with the emerald wedding dress; the box which had once conveyed her belongings to 'Courtenay House' when she was in service and now sat in the corner of the large kitchen where they ate, washed and slept. A secret to be kept from Martin, something to look forward to when days grew short, the Moor changed colour from gold and mauve to brown and white, animals were kept in at night, sheep herded into the sheepfold where walls were high enough to keep ewes from jumping out.

Yes, she thought, she could see herself sitting by the fire reading by oil lamp while Martin worked on accounts and planned the year ahead. He had bought her a spinning wheel at a farm sale hoping she would spin their own sheep's wool to knit into garments for them to wear, but Tansy wasn't sure she had enough patience for this. Sarah Webber seemed to enjoy the process and sat by the fire of an evening while Amos ended the day at the Half Moon at Manaton where talk was of beef prices and men arranged to travel round with the threshing machine from farm to farm. Sarah came to visit once a month and was pleased with the way Tansy had settled to such a different life from the one she had been used to, but Amos still stayed away bemoaning the absence of Martin's strong presence to help with the harvest. Now Martin's work at the mine was producing good money and when Sarah learnt this she suggested Martin join in the harvesting to bridge the gap between finishing at the mine and buying in new stock.

Tansy asked after Fanny and was told that she and Adam had moved into the other large bedroom at Staddens. Sarah had brought out the cradle which all her children had slept in and Fanny was at last sewing baby clothes and a cover for the cradle. Adam had taken to riding up to the Warren House Inn to meet Martin on a Friday night and this Tansy was not pleased about.

'You could get Adam to help bring bricks for an oven – twould only take a day surely?' she insisted but now Martin exploded with anger.

'Working hard enough all week – have earnt my beer – tis only one night after all – all the miners are there!!' Tansy missed her family who had come to visit at Easter and Whitsun but not since. Now she determined to take Thomasin to Newton Abbot where she could leave the child while she went to the monthly dance at 'The

Globe' hotel. Excited at her decision her spirits fell when she realised it would have to be when Martin was home unless she could get Wilmot to see to the animals. For the first time since she had married Martin she felt trapped.

15

AN UNEXPECTED VISITOR

Tansy was pegging out washing in the courtyard; it was a blustery day with a strong wind blowing from the west and clouds racing across a grey sky. Martin had finished working at Vitifer Mine, bought a dozen Scotch sheep reputedly hardier than the Dartmoor Longwalls lost in the blizzard. He'd also invested in six heifers all in calf, a pig which, when fattened up was to provide bacon and ham for winter. Tansy made good money from her hens' eggs, cream making and had learnt to turn any surplus milk into butter for their own use. More money had been added to the jar on the dairy shelf after Wilmot, Tansy and the children had walked to Vitifer to pick whortleberries. All had enjoyed the day, returning home with purple mouths and fingers although the children found the berries somewhat sour and when Wilmot sold them in the Dairy at Chagford she brought home boilings to make up for this disappointment and earnt three pennies a pint for the berries. Tansy dreamt of having enough money to furnish the Farmhouse properly and be able to bake in her own oven still lacking.

Now September and Thomasin had settled well to life at the Farm, was growing into a sturdy little girl who loved to ride on Lucifer, run in and out stables and shippen, unafraid of the animals.

Pegging out the last of Thomasin's white smocks to

dry Tansy straightened her back and saw a tall figure crossing the Moor from Fernworthy.

This figure wore dark clothes, not the brown of a moorman and, as Tansy paused to wonder who it might be, clouds split to let through a shaft of sun. A shaft of sun which lit the approaching figure and made Tansy catch her breath. Red hair-the figure had red hair!! It couldn't be anyone else but Geoffrey Llewellyn. Now approaching the clapper the figure came on, swiftly and steadily and Tansy held herself back from the desire rising through her to run down the stroll and throw herself into his arms. She managed to control her instincts, gathered up basket and pegs, called to Thomasin, ran into the house and shut the door. Inside she fetched a comb and, using a small mirror on the mantel shelf, tidied her hair while Thomasin regarded her with interest.

'Man come' she said 'not Dada. Not Martin.' Tansy nodded trying to still the racing of her heart as heat rose to her cheeks. She replaced the comb with hands that shook and waited for Geoffrey to climb the stroll and reach the door. Every second stretched into an age so that his knock, when it came, made her start. Swallowing down her excitement, she took Thomasin by the hand, crossed the room and opened the door.

'Geoffrey! Why what a surprise!' she affected ignorance of his approach. There he stood tall, black suited, giving her his familiar look, one that said he wasn't fooled by this show of ignorance of his arrival. Tansy felt foolish, perhaps he had seen her in the garden. He held out both hands and smiled, his smile lighting the green eyes. Immediately she took his hands in hers, noted how he had again grown a beard, looked like the Geoffrey she had worked with at the Manse. Was it barely two years ago? His gaze shifted to the child and surprise crossed his face and he dropped her hands.

Tansy determined not to satisfy his curiosity moved back from the door.

'Come you in. Norah not with you then?' she added. He stood his ground.

'No, she is teaching at Torquay.'

'Would ee like a drink of cider?' Tansy asked not trusting her hands to cope with the ritual of tea making.

'That would be good.'

She drew the golden liquid from the barrel in the corner and placed the jar on the table. Geoffrey sat, drank quickly but didn't take his eyes from hers. She felt her face flushing again and turned away, picking up the egg basket thinking that activity would ease the tension building between them.

'Going to collect eggs – do you want to come?'

He looked at her for a long moment then rose and crossing the room opened the door to let her through. Thomasin followed Tansy and the three crossed the courtyard as Martin rode in on Lucifer. Seeing Geoffrey he checked the horse and slid from his back.

'Why tis the preacher – what be doin out here?' Martin wanted to know holding out his hand in welcome.

'Norah has sent me to see that all is well as Tansy seems to have forgotten how to write a letter!'

For the first time since her wedding day Tansy felt pity for Norah who had written several times. Tansy felt ashamed of the unanswered letters which lay in the drawer of the kitchen table.

'And you – thought you were finished at Newton?' Martin asked.

'On the circuit in Wales:gone back to Merthyr if you must know,' came the reply.

Tansy remembered her first walk with Geoffrey when he was new to the Parish and how he had hinted at an unfinished romance at Merthyr. She felt cross with him – cross on Norah's behalf. Wondered if her sister knew about this old romance.

'Why Merthyr' she demanded 'I'd have thought there would have been a place on the Devon circuit for you!' Geoffrey frowned, ignored her question and instead turned to Martin.

164

'Tom Moore tells me you've been working at Vitifer these last few months?'

'Yes, that's all behind us now – lost first flock of sheep in Blizzard but now we'm doing really well. Do you want to see the animals?'

Geoffrey nodded and went with Martin leaving woman and child behind. Lucifer had taken himself into the stable and there Martin began his tour by feeding the cob and Tansy returned to begin on the evening meal but a feeling of fury had taken hold of her. How dare he turn up without warning. How dare he talk so openly of Merthyr. What was he doing there? No doubt he had forgotten what he had told Tansy about the affair he had had with the married woman.

She felt she had a right to know what Geoffrey was doing there and why he was sending books to his wife's sister!! So angry was she that she didn't notice Thomasin slipping through the half closed door and out into the farm. It was only when, half an hour later and she started to lay the table for supper that she noticed Thomasin's absence. Swiftly she went out to call the little girl, usually playing by the pond or digging in her own little patch in the garden.

'Thomasin! Thomasin!' She called but there was no response.

Now the men came back as she continued calling and searching the buildings between house and newtake. How could she have let the child wander off? She had let the closeness of Geoffrey banish the little girl from her mind? Thomasin had never left the surrounds of the farm and buildings before – always within sight or sound – fear began to grow in Tansy – could she have gone down the stroll to the clapper and fallen in the river deep now from recent storms? She began to run shouting back to the men.

'Thomasin's missing – I'm going to the clapper.' At once Martin followed her and moments later Geoffrey – his long strides taking him along the river bank toward Sittaford while Martin took the opposite direction towards the Great Mire leaving Tansy to search the valley.

Could she have toddled off along the now familiar path to Wilmot's house where she was used to stopping on the way to and from Chagford? Tansy called from time to time, waiting for the men to come back. The sultry weather had brought bees to visit the last of the summer's heather and damsel flies glinted blue above the river. The humming of the bees caused another fear to plant itself in Tansy's mind – what if Thomasin had been stung? She knew a bee sting could be dangerous. Or worse still the sting of an adder – the snakes basked on the sandy path across the valley. What if the child had been stung, had fallen among the heather? She started up the path towards Fernworthy Farm, looking back from time to time to see if either of the men had found Thomasin but each was still moving on his own; had left the river bank and was searching newtake walls. She hurried on only to be met by Wilmot who had seen her coming.

She could tell by the anxious expression on Tansy's face that all was not well.

'Tis Thomasin – she's missing. Martin and Geoffrey are searching the fields around the farm, they've already looked in the river. She's not come here?' Wilmot shook her head.

'That would be a long way for a little 'un to come on her own' She paused thinking of her own children, of the times she had suffered similar scares and always found them near to home.

'Are you sure she's not somewhere close home?'

Tansy disappointed not to have found her but relieved that the child hadn't wandered this far from home decided to go back to the farm and look again. She thanked Wilmot who offered to come with her . . . she called her children and together they retraced Tansy's footsteps across the valley and up the stroll. There they spread out and began to search each building. Tansy was just about to leave the barn when she noticed a slight movement in a pile of straw against the end wall. Parting the straw she found Thomasin fast asleep her arms clutching Moss who opened one eye and looked at Tansy. Sheer relief erupted in a storm of anger.

'You bad dog! You bad girl!'

She seized a stick and began to beat the dog who cowered away whining and barking. This in turn woke Thomasin who got up and placed herself between Tansy and Moss.

'Don't! Don't!' she cried trying to catch Tansy's hand. 'How dare you hide away from me!' Tansy now lifted the stick which fell across Thomasin's face and she began to sob. This pandemonium brought Wilmot, her children, Martin and Geoffrey into the barn. Martin at once seized the stick from Tansy demanding.

'Whatever do ee think ee's doing?'

Tansy, anger spent, relieved at the safe recovery of Thomasin now flung her arms around the little girl who began to cry. Tansy hugged her saying over and over.

'Forgive me. Forgive me. You'm safe – tis all that matters.' So saying she picked up the child and carried her out of the barn and into the house. Martin thanked Wilmot for her help and offered refreshment.

'No, no, Martin. We'd best be on our way.'

She laid a hand on his arm. 'Don't be too hard on Tansy. She was terrified at what might have happened – worry makes women behave in unusual ways.'

She gathered up her children and was gone. Geoffrey and Martin exchanged looks – perhaps remembering times when they had been the victims of Tansy's wrath. Geoffrey attempted to sooth Martins own anger at the reaction shown by Tansy towards the child.

'Worried out of her mind no doubt!' Martin straightened up from stroking Moss's head, his mouth tight.

'We were all worried Preacher but there was no call to hit both dog and child for falling asleep in a barn.'

'Didn't know as you had already had a child'.

Geoffrey added and was surprised when Martin burst out laughing.

'Tidn't our child Preacher!' Then Geoffrey lifted his eyebrows in query.

'Tis Tom Moore's – maybe you've not heard Avril died some months after Thomasin's birth – Tom's Mother and Father looked after her till George Moore died and Alice found she couldn't cope with a growing bairn . . . Well, Tansy had promised Avril she ud look after her girl (and Avril was sure she was having a girl) if anything went wrong . . .'

Geoffrey smiled and nodded

'Of course if anyone would keep a promise it would be Tansy.' Suddenly feelings of relief flooded his body, relief that Thomasin wasn't Tansy and Martin's child. This strange thought was followed by a longing to hold Tansy, to comfort her as she had comforted him on the dreadful night of the flood when he had found Avril Moore's baby drowned in the Courts at Newton. He hung back until Martin went off to milk Hortense then walked slowly to the house, letting himself in in time to see Tansy washing Thomasin's face with such gentleness that he stopped reluctant to intrude. Now Tansy washed the tears from the little girl's face and put butter on the bruised cheek. Next she rocked her to and fro until all was settled between them and Thomasin kissed her surrogate mother on the lips, slid from her lap to fetch a book and settle by the fire to turn the pages. Now Geoffrey was at a loss as to how to behave – tried to ignore the feelings of desire still uppermost in his being, tried to fight back his need to hold Tansy and as she rose to her feet with the bowl of water and saw him standing there, a desire matching his grew until all that stood between them was the bowl of water and the knowledge that each belonged to another. She turned to the sink and in the moment when the water flowed out of the bowl into the stone sink Geoffrey crossed the room and enclosed Tansy with his arms – she dropped the bowl with a clatter and turning met his lips with her own. A kiss which lasted but a moment until both heard Martin's step outside the kitchen and drew apart hot faced and breathing hard. Martin's attention was all for Thomasin who turned to him.

'Look Martin – tis little girls like me' and he sat down beside the child and shared the book while Tansy and Geoffrey moved guiltily apart.

'Tis time I was going.' Geoffrey announced and, although Martin pressed him to stay and eat with them, he demurred.

'Thank you, but I must get the train from Moreton.'

'Come again, Preacher. Bring Norah with you next time'. Martin added but Geoffrey was gone, leaving Tansy to recover from his visit, his kiss and the trauma of losing Thomasin. Martin watched as she served food, noted her flushed face, that she hardly touched the meal and, when she thought he wasn't looking, tipped it back into the pan.

'Surprised to see the Preacher. What did he want?' Martin, ever direct, wanted to know. Tansy shrugged.

'Came because Norah sent him. Tis true I haven't answered her letters.'

Neither she nor Martin really believed this the real reason for his visit and he called up Moss and was gone far longer than he normally took to check the animals. Meanwhile, Tansy remembered the parcel of books lying in her box; had forgotten all about them, hadn't asked Geoffrey if it was he who had sent them. When Martin came back and found Thomasin tucked up in her cot fast asleep, he moved toward Tansy who sat mending by the hearth. He took smock and needle from her hands, drew her toward him, looked into her eyes which would not meet his. knew that Tansy had still not got over Geoffrey Llewellyn. Bitterly he knew that he was still second best, hadn't won Tansy's heart. Wondered how long it would be, if ever, before she grew to love him without reservation, no longer thought of Geoffrey even while she lay in his Martin's arms?

169

'Preacher mentioned letters? Don't you think you'd best reply to them?' Martin asked next day, Tansy had brought out the envelopes and they lay on the table waiting for Tansy to deal with. 'Save them both a trip?' Martin's voice was sarcastic and Tansy flushed as she responded with feeling.

'P'raps you'd like to sit down and write all that's happened since we married and came to live here!!!'

He shrugged and said 'You've more time than I for such work!' but when he'd gone from the room the desire to write to Norah left Tansy and, again, she thrust the bundle of letters back in the drawer to await a calmer state of mind. Guilty feelings surfaced as Tansy knew she was glad she had not written to Norah – she would not have received Geoffrey's visit nor Geoffrey's kiss and knew in her innermost soul that if withholding letters meant another visit from him then that's what she would do!

16

WHORTLEBERRYING AT
DUNNABRIDGE

Encouraged by the success of their berry picking at
Vitifer Mine earlier Wilmot suggested an outing to
Dunnabridge Farm where her cousin Bertha lived with
her brood of children.

'Tis a lovely valley close by, the slopes of Bellever
Tor are always covered with wurts every summer and
beyond is the river, just right for a picnic. Us could hire
a wagon from Chagford and take any woman as wants
to go!'

'T'would be a good finish to the Summer.' Tansy
agreed, a day was settled on and a notice affixed to the
Post Office door. A small charge would be made to
pay for the wagon and when Wilmot, Tansy and the
children arrived at Chagford Square there were
enough excited families to fill the wagon and pay for
the journey there and back. Bert Arscott had decorated
the head brasses of the pair of horses with red ribbons;
a boy held the lead animal by the harness, children ran
about shouting with excitement until Wilmot, as leader
of the expedition greeted Harry Arscott who assisted
the women and children on to the waggon by means of
a short ladder. Bert, atop the wagon placed them in
rows, starting at the back. Sternly he forbad the taking
of the first two rows; the first where he would sit to
drive with Harry beside him, behind in the second row

he reserved for Wilmot, Tansy, Rebecca, Anne and Judd who sat bursting with glee at being right at the front. Tansy sat Thomasin on her lap where the little girl clutched her surrogate mother tightly, her eyes huge with excitement. Now the boy stood away from Bosun the lead horse, Bert Arscott reached forward with a thin whip to tickle Bosun lightly on the back and with a grinding of wheels, a struggling of hooves and a cheering from the boys of the party, the wagon moved off down the street. As hotels and guest houses were passed some of the women told of giving milk or cider to walkers and visitors to the Moor; even spoke of using best parlours to entertain the growing number of people staying in Chagford. Tansy thought with regret at the still empty tallet up the stairs at Teignhead, the absence of a proper bed and settle to screen the fire from draughts, of the absence of an oven to bake bread which would prevent her from taking advantage of this opportunity of earning money to add to their income.

When the narrow lanes had been negotiated, the smoothness of the Postbridge road eased the way, landmarks were pointed out including the plots of land shaped like playing cards above Vitifer Mine. They passed the Warren House Inn to descend Merripit Hill into Postbridge. At Two Bridges they crossed the turnpike bridge over the West Dart; some of the women complained that they had passed a signpost back along saying 'Bellever' and Wilmot, to calm them, rose in her seat to explain that they were expected at Dunnabridge Farm where refreshments awaited; this seemed to satisfy the women whose muttering ceased and when, on arrival at Dunnabridge, Wilmot's cousin Bertha came out to greet them, they immediately looked for the promised refreshments. On a long bench in the courtyard sat lemonade for the children, tea for the women, gingerbread and Tetti cakes for all and cider for the men. The horses were unhitched from the wagon, led to drink at the trough in the courtyard then freed to graze in the newtake. The day which had dawned cool was now hot with a September sun beating down; coats and hats were discarded and placed inside the sheep pound under the watchful eye of Bertha's best sheep dog, Jack.

Armed with pint pots and buckets a crowd of some twenty five women and children set off across the Moor; the boys in their corduroy knickerbockers, flannel shirts, worsted stockings and black boots, braces of red making splashes of colour; the girls in striped cotton dresses covered in white pinafores which, by the end of the day, would be splashed with berry juice, had hair tied back with yellow and blue ribbons, legs covered in thick stockings and boots. The boys made straight for the top of Bellever Tor; the girls, more biddable, began on the serious work of the day. Tansy herself was anxious to climb the Tor from where, according to Martin, she would get a fine view of Sittaford and know how far from home she was. So she worked fast and, only when she had filled her bucket which took a couple of hours, felt free to climb the Tor, leaving Thomasin with Wilmot and the girls. At the top she found the sun had brought a mauve haze to the far hills Kes Tor stood out proud above the valleys but which hill was Sittaford remained a mystery and after enjoying the freedom of the moment she called the boys to come down from the rocks where they fought each other in mock battles.

'Tis time to go to the river for our picnic' she invited and the thought of vittles soon saw the party settled by the bridge at Bellever. Now the girls joined in the play, abandoning boots and stockings to splash and paddle in the river. The boys tried to catch sticklebacks but the coldness of the river sent them back to the bank where Bert and Harry Arscott had set down the baskets of food they had brought from Chagford. Pasties and pies were washed down by lemonade for the children and cider for the women and men. After they had finished the children returned to playing in the river and the women, some of whom were miners' wives, talked of the

173

April Party at Vitifer, expressed surprise at the bawdy nature of Jake Endacott's singing of 'Strawberry Fair'. One mentioned the Reverend Sabine Baring Gould who was known to be collecting tunes and words of these old songs from workers across the County.

'Surprised if'n he collected that version of 'Strawberry Fair' she added 'him being a parson and all'. Now another came forward with her story.

'Sally Satterley, over to Jolly Lane Cot at Hexworthy, she do know lots of they songs; taught her by her Granny so they say. The Reverend have been to visit but, as she can only sing while she'm about her work; he has to trot after her with a notebook and pencil.'

Everyone laughed as they imagined this picture but Tansy felt she must support her hero.

'The Reverend, why, he's a real gentleman. Called in to bring a photograph of our farm, taken by his friend Robert Burnard. Ever so polite they were.' On a flash of inspiration she added. 'Got 15 children I believe.' This statement impressed the women as no-one among them could top this achievement; and perhaps it was the thought of the hard labour involved in the having and raising of such a large family together with the strength of Bertha's cider that had something to do with the fact that many fell asleep. These events may have been responsible for the fact that when they awoke the time they had arranged for their departure from Dunnabridge had long since passed; Bert and Harry had already gone back to harness the horses for the return journey, carrying the empty food baskets with them.

'Us could go home past 'Snaily House' someone suggested.' This gave rise to the telling of the story of the two sisters who lived at 'White's Slade' but, when they became too old to cross the Moor for food, lived on snails alone until they died and were found among thousands of empty shells. That's why they changed the name to 'Snaily House'. Wilmot now brought an end to this further delay by urging the party to hurry but now little legs were tired; what with the early walk to Chagford some from outlying farms and cottages together with all the running about and the smallest of the children had to be carried by the biggest of the boys. The harvest of berries was split between the women but now the walk seemed twice as far and to encourage flagging spirits the women began to sing.

'I'll sing you one-o
Green grow the rushes-o
What is your one-o?

One is one and all alone
And ever more shall be so.

'I'll sing you two-o
Green grow the rushes-o
What is your two-o?
Two is two and . . .

Wilmot's Judd was the first to hear the drumming sound. Tansy held up her hand in a call for silence as the ground began to vibrate under their feet. Wilmot said.

'Tis hooves – horses, I reckon.'

Nearer and nearer the drumming came; looking behind they saw them – the horses – galloping toward them in a long line which stretched across the width of the valley. Women gathered up little ones and made for the sides of the valley.

Most made it but there were still children in the middle and as the horses drew closer Tansy took action; calling them to come to a cluster of rocks.

'Come quick – come here to me. Run!!' She made them crouch down among the stones and held her breath as the galloping came nearer and nearer. Would they stop before they reached the rocks; she raised her head, saw them coming straight for them. Horses of brown, grey, black and piebald blurred now with nostrils flaring, tails streaming behind, manes flying then, at the last moment, the line split into two, passing each side of their refuge. So close Tansy felt the heat of their galloping bodies, the sound of their pounding hooves, saw the saliva from mouths hit the rocks. She rose in time to see the two stallions who were driving the mares and then they were gone. Only when the sound of hooves had died away completely did the children rise and ask.

'They won't be coming back will they, Tansy?' She said. 'No, they won't be coming back.' not knowing if this was true, suddenly longing for Martin who would now be explaining what they had witnessed, what it had meant. She wanted to be home. Wanted to tell him about this adventure. Shakily the party re-grouped and as quickly as they could, made their way back to Dunnabridge, where mothers fetched coats to wrap children against the cooling evening.

Bert and Harry Arscott were waiting, horses harnessed, anxious to get back to Chagford where Tansy was delighted to see Martin waiting for them with Lucifer chained to the sled. The whortleberries were to be deposited at the Dairy for sale next day Wilmot's children and Thomasin rode the sled while the adults walked and talked over the events of the day. At Fernworthy Tansy took her place on the sled with Thomasin while Martin pointed out the North Star, the evening star. As he led Lucifer across the clapper he looked back and smiled to see both had fallen fast asleep.

17

FAMILY MATTERS

Geoffrey Llewellyn's visit had thoroughly unsettled Tansy – days after and still she couldn't concentrate on anything, couldn't read to Thomasin without drifting off. Ruined a pan of cream and broke eggs, sought Wilmot's company but fell silent and distracted until her friend demanded to know.

'What's wrong Tansy? You hardly seem yourself at all? Seems there's something as has upset you these last few weeks? Has it to do with the red headed man?'

So astute, thought Tansy, Wilmot had touched at once on the subject that was worrying Tansy; the reason why she couldn't sleep, spoke sharply to Thomasin when there was no need, was avoiding making love with Martin on the pretext of a bad head and, when that excuse began to wear thin, complained of toothache until Martin lost patience with her and told her to see the Doctor the very next week when she took eggs to Chagford.

'Can't afford the five shillings!' she retorted, took a spade and began to break up used ground ready to plant onions in the garden. What to tell Wilmot she did not know. What reason could she give for the ache that had arrived in her heart the day Geoffrey visited Teignhead. She settled for a half truth.

'The red haired man just reminded me of my life back at Newton.' Then she burst out. 'Tis unsettled me

Wilmot that's all. Used to work together in the Parish, twas a life full of interest and excitement!' Adding 'Married to my sister Norah now. She went to College, I went into Service. Supposed to be a teacher; now she's a Minister's wife. Twas my wages helped send her to Goldsmith's.'

'Well, that was a great thing to do for your sister, Tansy. Your family must be very proud of you.' Tansy felt ashamed of her outburst. After all she could have had her own turn at training for something worthwhile; it was her own fault that she had run away and married Martin instead. She swallowed hard and tried a smile which slipped and slid away; she rose hurriedly and left for home.

Her mood changed when next day she received a postcard from her Mother showing a snow covered Courtenay Park and in the background the Station at Newton Abbot.

'Coming out Wednesday next on morning Post Van. Will walk from Fernworthy Farm. Love Mother.' Tansy was filled with alarm; for her Mother to leave Newton on a Market Day was unheard of. Market Day regarded as sacrosanct was only to be missed in time of death or illness. While Tansy was delighted to learn of her Mother's visit she spent all the time, between receiving the card and meeting her Mother at Fernworthy, worrying over the cause. Was someone ill? Her Father perhaps or the twins? She discounted these suppositions knowing nothing would remove Eva from their side should either one of them need her. It was with great trepidation therefore that she set off next day, which was in fact Wednesday, to meet the Post Office van at Fernworthy which was as far as it could get and beyond which the track became stony, narrow and certainly not suitable for motor vehicles.

Tansy's spirits soared at sight of her Mother dressed in her smart chapel suit, a large basket in her hands. Tansy took this from her hands and gave her Mother a hug.

'Tis so good to see you Mother. Is all well at home?'
Eva smiled and nodded looking down at Thomasin.
News of the little girl had travelled fast and Eva was
eager to see her whilst Tansy, in her turn, was anxious
to know the real reason for her Mother's visit. Both
women took one of the little girl's hands and walked
across the Moor, swinging her up between them until
she crowed with delight.

'So this is Avril's girl?' Tansy nodded.

'Looks like the boys don't she? How long has she
been here and how long is she staying?'

They began on a long exchange of news from
Newton, Tom Moore's change of work from mine to
brickworks; how Rosemary Brimmacombe was faring at
college in London, how Johnnie was apprenticed to the
Carpenter, William Avery, and now making coffins as
well as furniture.

'Perhaps he'll make us that Settle soon?' laughed
Tansy. At the Farm all was admired and praised and it
was not till they had eaten the fairy cakes and pasties
that the reason for Eva's visit became apparent.

'Tis lovely to have you here Mother, but is there
anything wrong at home?' Her Mother gave her a sharp
look before answering.

'If you'd taken the trouble to answer Norah's
many letters you would know what has been happening
to her since she left College. As you didn't deign to
reply I understand she has stopped writing. Why was
that?'

Tansy flushed with guilt, conscious that, even after
Geoffrey's visit, she still hadn't been able to bring
herself to answer the pile of letters still lying in the table
drawer.

'Just been so busy what with the animals, the walks to
Chagford and now Thomasin. Never seem to get time
to sit down and write . . .'

Her voice tailed off and she sat winding her hands in
her lap. Eva drew in her breath, a look of disapproval
crossing her face. She hadn't mentioned Geoffrey's visit

179

once and Tansy began to wonder if her Mother was in fact aware it had taken place.

'Norah passed her finals with honours in June, she and Geoffrey have rented a small house in Torquay where she has a position at a private school in the Warberries. She seems to be quite happy there.'

'Why has Geoffrey gone away then?' Tansy asked 'Couldn't he get a Parish near Norah's school in Torquay?' Eva looked startled.

'How do you know he has gone away?' Tansy stuttered.

'He told us when he came here – just a week or two ago -didn't you know?' She added hastily in response to the shocked expression on her Mother's face. 'He said Norah sent him to make sure that we were alright!'

Eva Drewe's eyebrows rose, her mouth set in a thin line.

'No, I didn't know Geoffrey had been out here and I wonder if Norah does either. No, there's quite a lot your Father and I don't know about him seemingly. So I suppose you know that he has gone back to Merthyr and is Minister at a chapel there?' Tansy nodded but said no more wondering why loyalty to Geoffrey now assumed first importance in her mind.

'Whatever's wrong between them then?'

'Norah's not happy that he's gone back to Wales – says he's trying to find a good place so they can move and settle there. Norah thought he would move round the Devon circuit so that she could move with him and teach in Church or Board Schools wherever he's spending each two years. He comes home but of course it has to be during the week when she's teaching.' Eva paused looking at Tansy. 'When you worked with Geoffrey did he ever tell you why he left there?'

Tansy was shocked. Why shouldn't she tell her Mother what she knew. At least pass on what he had told her when first he asked her to show him round the Parish? Surely he should have told Norah – dear trusting Norah – before they were married that there had been someone before her. She made up her mind to tell her Mother what she knew.

'When I first met him he did hint at an affair with a married woman – the wife of an industrialist I believe but' now she rushed on 'he said it was all over before he came to Newton.'

'I trust he was telling the truth because Norah is very upset – feels he has deserted her and at a time when she needs him most. Now it was Tansy's turn to look surprised.

'Didn't tell you Norah's in the family way then?' At this news a flood of jealousy filled Tansy's body – jealousy at the thought of Geoffrey and Norah making such love that made a child.

'How will Norah be able to teach when she has a child to look after?' Tansy burst out. At last her Mother did look pleased.

'She will come home to have the bairn and afterwards there's to be a place for her at Bell's School while Geoffrey's still looking for a place in Wales.'

Tansy felt doubly angry – angry that Geoffrey hadn't told her this news when he came to visit the Farm and angry that things had been arranged so that life would go on for Norah even in his absence and without his support.

'Then you are going to look after Norah's child?' She paused and sighed. 'Just like I'm looking after Avril's'. Sensing her distress Eva rose and put her arms around Tansy.

'At one time I thought it was to be you and Geoffrey who would be sweethearts?' and Tansy lowered her face quickly but not before Eva had recognized the admission in Tansy's eyes. 'Life doesn't always happen the way we would like it to.' Eva rose and began to collect up her basket and jacket. She added 'You'm happy enough now with Martin aren't ee my girl?'

All Tansy could do was nod and try to hide the feelings of hurt and anger which had taken possession of her. They talked of matters at Newton and Chagford and Tansy saw her Mother off from Fernworthy with many messages of love and affection for her Father, Robert and James and for Norah, adding a late apology at not having answered letters; promising to write soon and last of all sending an invitation that Norah and Geoffrey should visit Teignhead Farm together.

When she settled Thomasin to bed – a cot now – Thomasin was surprised by tears which dropped from Tansy's face as she bent over her.

18

CHRISTMAS AT TEIGNHEAD

A Christmas card from Sabine Baring Gould heralded the Festival and asked 'I trust the books pleased?' which solved the mystery of the parcel but disappointed Tansy whose belief that the books had been from Geoffrey Llewellyn had perhaps kept the flame of passion more alive than it would had she known the donor's true identity. She sighed and propped the card, an engraved and hand coloured account of Bob Cratchet's family Christmas, on the mantel. It wished the recipient 'A Merry Christmas and a Happy New Year' and was addressed to 'Mr & Mrs Tansy Webber' which amused Tansy but caused Martin to grunt and pronounce.

'Now there's more animals to see to us should stay here at Teignhead this year.' She protested.

'Not go home! Not see Father, Mother or the twins! Then there's Thomasin here. She should see her Dada and her brothers, shouldn't she?' At this the little girl looked up from her play.

'Dada? See Dada?' Martin was cross.

'Trust you to upset the apple cart Tansy. Twas you said 'Home is now at Teignhead' I do recall?' and, when she nodded, he added 'Then this shall be our first Christmas at home and I'm sure Thomasin will be happy to be here with us and Meg.'

Both adults looked down at the child playing happily with the fat puppy born to the Osbornes' collie bitch and chosen with care by Tansy. Moss joined them by the hearth raising his head to listen to sudden storms which sang through the stand of trees sheltering the Farmhouse and, while the ashes had shed their leaves, hawthorn and rowan been stripped of berries by birds, bronze leaves clung tenaciously to beech and only the firs remained green.

At Martin's pronouncement that they must spend Christmas at Teignhead, Tansy set about making the festival as pleasant as she knew how. Leaving Thomasin with Wilmot she made a special trip into Chagford where shops were bright with festive fruits and meat. Geese, partridge and hams hung in butchers' shops and Tansy used some cream money to buy a ham, 3 oranges, some dried raisins and figs, a new pocket knife for Martin and 4 sugar mice, one each for Thomasin, Rebecca, Anne and Judd. Leaving those for Wilmot's children with her friend she took Thomasin home and hid her treasure in the dairy. Meanwhile Martin had hung swags of holly and ivy from the ceiling beams and on Christmas Eve he brought home a plump rabbit, still warm, for Tansy to skin and prepare for stewing with onions, carrots and herbs from the garden. When all was tender she set the pan aside ready to heat up on Christmas Day on their return from Church. This they did and found it delicious followed by a plum pudding sent out by Eva Drewe and, after this repast, pots were removed from the hearth and Martin placed an ashen faggot above the fire. This he had made from one of the ash trees, five feet in length and two feet deep and tied around with withy bonds. This he placed on the hearth where it crackled and snapped into a roaring blaze which filled the wide chimney with bright flames.

'Now' announced Martin 'each time a withy bond snaps we shall drink a toast to the coming year; draw a jug of cider Tansy, if you please.'

Just as Tansy was feeling the absence of family and friends on this special day, there came the sound of feet and voices outside followed by a rapping at the door and Tansy ran to open it to Tom and Wilmot Osborne, Rebecca, Anne and Judd whom she greeted with much hugging.

'Just in time' Martin said and Tansy realised it was he who had invited their neighbours to join them. Her heart swelled in gratitude as she filled mugs with cider and Wilmot produced a basket of yeast cakes which she encouraged them all to dunk into the cider before toasting the coming year. Each time a withy bond snapped the company cheered and when they were finished they played 'Blind Man's Buff' and 'Spinning the Plate' until the childrens' heads were beginning to nod and it was time to wrap adults and children in warm coats for the walk back across the moor to Fernworthy. Tansy and Martin watched the lantern light as it moved to and fro with the progress of the walkers who sang as they went.

> 'In the bleak mid-winter
> Frosty wind made moan,
> Earth stood hard as iron,
> Water like a stone:
> Snow had fallen, snow on snow,
> Snow on snow.
> In the bleak mid-winter, long ago.'

Sad that the company was gone Thomasin asked for a story and Tansy remembered a poem her Father had taught her years ago. Martin knocked the remains of faggots together, added peat till it caught, they drew close and Tansy began to recite.

> Magic of night
> A world grown still,
> Restless shepherds
> Upon a hill.

> 'A tremor of wind
> The fields among,

Suddensome light,
Celestial song.

Savants three
Who had journeyed far
To fathom the portent
Of a star.

A babe asleep
with haloed head
Pillowed on hay
In a manger.

Soft eyed kine
Disturbed and a-stare
At the wonder astir
'Neath a lanthorn there.'

Thomasin clapped her hands before Tansy wrapped her warmly and laid her in her cot, watched by Martin who said.

'Not such a bad Christmas day then was it?'

Next day Martin was up early to harness Lucifer and set off to join the Mid-Devons while Tansy fed cattle, sheep and chickens and, after milking Hortense, walked Thomasin across to Sittaford hoping for a sight of the red coated riders and hear the sound of the horn telling that hounds had found; although in her heart of hearts Tansy prayed that the fox would escape back to its earth.

Christmas Day had brought Postee with an invitation to 'Staddens' for Twelfth Night's Wassailing and it was a clear cold night with a full moon which lit tracks and walls and the orchard where Amos, Sarah, Adam, Fanny and the baby, which, sucked at Fanny's breast and was a wonder to Thomasin, Tansy and neighbours alike, awaking sudden feelings of such tenderness in her heart that for the first time Tansy looked at Martin with longing that he would soon give her a baby. The gathering was now joined by labourers from the village bearing shot guns.

'Ho, Martin us can begin now you'm here.'

Amos declared and all circled the first apple tree, a Tom Putt, while Martin sang

> 'Let every man take off his hat
> And shout out to th'old apple tree
> 'Old apple tree we wassail thee
> And hoping thou will bear'

and all joined in

> 'Hats full, caps full, three bushel bags full!'
> Hip, hip, hip, hurrah!'

At each 'hurrah' a man fired his gun into the air. Then all moved on to the next tree 'Slap me girdle' and the ceremony was repeated. Unseen by Tansy Amos and Adam had gone back to the house and now brought out and set down a bucket of hot cider with toast floating on top.

'Hang up the toast our Adam' Amos invited 'Robins'll eat it and keep away worms'.

After the cider had all been drunk the men left for the next Orchard and the Webber family went inside to eat a cold supper but, as Martin and Tansy left, Amos grasped Martin by the hand and declared.

'Never thought to have to hire in labour to my own farm when I have two healthy sons to work it! May this year see you return and abandon this sheep nonsense!' Whereupon Martin broke free from his Father, bade his Mother and Brother farewell, and, setting his lips defiantly, answered 'Ee'll wait forever for that Feyther!' Then gathered up Tansy, Thomasin and was gone to ride happily across the Moor singing the chorus as they went till on arrival at Teignhead, Tansy wanted to know what 'wassail' meant.

'Health be to you' that's what means, but can't say

more,' and Tansy promised herself she would ask Sabine Gould if he could tell her when the custom began. She longed to see the tall figures of the History Men crossing the clapper especially now she had been to the site of the Bronze Age village at Grimspound; anxious to know if the digging was soon to begin.

19

RETRIBUTION

Early in the New Year Tom Osborne announced his intention of leaving the Mine at Vitifer to start up a herd of Red Devons. This he did one Sunday when Wilmot invited Tansy, Martin and Thomasin to supper ushering them into the Parlour for the first time. Tansy gasped at sight of the long polished oak table set about with blue and white china, sparkling silver, pewter tankards for the men and tea cups for the women. Anne and Judd stood behind chairs until the Webbers were seated then took their places at the end of the table. All were wearing new clothes and there was an air of barely concealed excitement about the room. A rose coloured glass lamp lit the table sending shadows about the walls of the low ceilinged room. Family portraits hung from the picture rail and paintings of violets and roses in gold plaster frames were interspersed with swags of dried flowers. Tansy enjoyed the sheer luxury of the surroundings after the daily bareness of walls at Teign-head. She noticed a harmonium in the corner of the room and looked forward to hearing it played by and by. Cider was passed round in a big stone jug and tea for the women accompanied carved ham, a whole cheese and pickled onions. Home made bread sat on a wooden platter with a dish of butter by the side. The last item was an Apple Cake, its top covered with sugar and baked brown in the oven. They ate till they couldn't eat another crumb when Tom rapped the table with his knife for silence.

'Welcome to you, our best of neighbours. Tis a joy to have'ee living close by and tis to share our good fortune we've asked 'ee to supper tonight. Idn't that so, Wilmot?'

Wilmot smiled and nodded, beaming round the table at them all.

'Tis, indeed, a treat to have 'ee here but now Tom has something to say.' She smiled at Tom encouragingly and sat back.

'Encouraged by our Mine Captain, Henry Wilson, Wilmot and me, well we talked to the lawyers and took our neighbours at Thornworthy to Court over the killing of the herd two year ago.' Tansy was startled at this statement and looked at Martin who smiled and nodded as if he knew what Tom was talking about.

'Us've just been informed that our case has been won in County Court and we'm to receive compensation to the tune of £500 with costs.'

Here Martin cheered and applauded while Tansy sat puzzling over what this was all about.

'Enough to clear our debts. Re-stock the farm once more and, best of news for me, never to have to go underground ever again.'

Again Martin cheered and banged his fist on the table, drummed his feet on the floor.

'I'm pleased that you'm pleased' said Tansy 'but can someone here tell me why you had to go to Court and who is paying you £500?'

Tom sat down, passed pipe and tobacco jar to Martin and, after filling his pipe and lighting it, began.

'For the sake of Tansy and the children tis only fair to tell what happened from beginning so you will all understand.' Here Wilmot brought in fresh tea, refilled Tansy's cup and her own.

'Our other neighbour, Andrew Roberts, came to Thornworthy to take over farm from his Uncle, Josiah. Josiah had no children of his own. That were about four year back. No sooner had he arrived than he declared it his intention to grow corn; refused to listen when us told un he was wasting time and money by trying. Us all told him arable was only possible in the Teign Valley with it's shelter and warmth – not on upper slopes above Chagford. "Stick to sheep and cows" us told un but he took no notice.'

Martin nodded and sucked at his pipe.

'There was no stopping him and, after begging advice from the Teign Valley farmers he carried out tillage. First off he cut a wide but shallow furrow with a single broad plough share which turned turf but didn't cut it free. This turf was allowed to lie and wither before being harrowed; broke it up into soil particles and a mixture of dead grass and root fibre known as "beat".'

Again Martin nodded, puffing smoke rings to amuse the children who had begun to fidget at the length of the story.

'This was raked up and burnt to produce an ash which, mixed with dung, compost, soil from the hedges and roadways as run-off, hedgerow mosses and moulds, and later slaked lime was ploughed in using a deeper plough share to produce a tilth.' Tansy who was listening to this account of preparing ground with great interest, now wondered if she and Martin could grow corn.

'Go on, Tom.' she pressed him and Martin reading her mind interrupted.

'Don't get carried away with the idea Tansy – just you wait for rest of story before ee starts making plans!' How well he knew her.

'Well, when he'd prepared ground he cast seed corn onto ridges, then harrowed and finally turned it by hand. His first crop, oats, was good if sparse; next year he planted barley which he fed to his animals and the third year he planted wheat. All summer he weeded growing corn.' Martin explained to Tansy.

'Real back breaking work that be.'

'Well' went on Tom 'Andrew Roberts' corn did grow;

good weather helped, an early warm spring led to a hot summer with regular night rain and by August his field was looking good, full of golden stands waiting to be cut and stacked to await threshing.' Now Tom seemed unable to continue so Wilmot took up the story.

'Then it was our cattle strayed across the South Teign where they was in habit of drinking mid-day: avore turning back up auver to be milked later in the day. This day the leader, Strawberry, spied a gap in newtake wall, saw the ripe corn, broke through into the field and began to eat.' Tansy was horrified, even with her slight knowledge of farming she knew this was a disaster. She demanded.

'That's terrible – whatever happened next?'

'Strawberry being the leader, all other cows followed and began to eat corn, their bodies swelling up with the unused feed. Then Andrew Roberts came on the scene carrying a gun as does all farmers.'

'First he fired into the air and it was the sound of shots that drew Tom to the river. By the time he got there Roberts had begun to shoot the cows, first he shot in legs but when this didn't deter the rest of the herd he shot to kill.'

'Surely he could've driven them back through the gap in the wall?' Tansy asked.

Wilmot shook her head, Tom's bent under the anguish of retelling the moment when he saw his herd destroyed. She went on.

'No he wouldn't wait for help; in such a mood of anger at the destruction of his corn he just shot and shot till every last one of Tom's herd lay groaning among the trampled corn. Star, Primrose, Heather and Snow lay their legs twisted beneath them and Tom had to finish them off. Some were bellowing, some in calf, some only injured and still alive.' She fell silent and Tansy stunned by the story still couldn't understand why it had happened.

'Couldn't have got them through the gap once their bellies swelled up; corn builds up steam in their insides and unless us could have slit their bellies they would have been sick to death.'

Silence fell over the remains of the party meal. Tom seemed to recover now the telling was over, reached for the Cider jug only to find it empty. He rose to fetch more while Wilmot finished the story.

'Lost more than our herd, Tansy. Couldn't pay the seed merchant or farrier, lost our good name which, in a small community like this takes a deal of getting back.'

'That's terrible' agitated, Tansy rose to pace about the room. Now she understood why Martin hadn't told her the story before; he knew how angry she would have been on the Osbornes' behalf. Tansy bit her lip knowing her own response to Andrew Roberts' actions would have been to send her to Thornworthy to berate Roberts himself. Now all had become clear. Tom returning with fresh cider seemed now to have recovered his normal good temper.

'Case of pride coming before a fall, I do reckon.' he said 'Hasn't grown corn since!'

At last Tansy understood why such bitter feelings existed between Fernworthy and Thornworthy; understood why Martin had refused to discuss the matter, why he had forbidden her to call at the Roberts' Farm again, why that farm prospered and the Osbornes' didn't.

Wilmot rose from the table to clear empty plates and dishes, Tansy joined her and together they carried them through to the kitchen to wash and stack. They had almost finished when a sweet sound reached them from the parlour; Tansy ran back to see Rebecca sitting at the organ while Anne stood to turn the pages of her music. The notes of one of her favourite songs filled the air; 'Home Sweet Home' a song that Norah had often played at the Drewe home behind the Post Office. A song which brought so many memories of her family, of her friend Rosemary Brimmacombe and a lump rose in Tansy's throat. She realised how much she missed her friend; missed the precious times when both had sat on one of the 148 steps between Southernhay and Courtenay Road, times when secrets were shared in the knowledge that the contents would be safe from the outside world. Tansy decided to write that very night; and arriving at the farm she scrabbled through the kitchen drawer among Norah's letters (still unanswered) for her friend's address. Promises to write had been exchanged but not kept as each girl embarked on a new life, Tansy here on the Moor, Rosemary in London. All her longing to see her friend poured out as she pleaded with Rosemary that she come as soon as ever possible. Come and stay for as long as possible; surely they had holidays from College and Tansy waited and waited for a letter but, when it did come, it was to promise a visit in June when College finished for the summer. Tansy had to be content with that.

20

CRANMERE POOL

Tansy learnt the calendar of a year when snow fell
fitfully on sheep in lamb but confined to enclosures,
heifers in calf were fed in the shippen and the pig
grew fat in a stone pen. February saw Martin joining
moormen to swale bracken covered hills, the burning
producing ash to fertilise pasture. March brought warm
winds from the South West and early lambs, fieldfare
flying in large flocks and Martin out shooting crows for
fear they would peck out his sheeps' eyes. The bodies
he hung on gates as a warning to other crows in spite of
Tansy's protests. A warm April saw green breaking on
sycamore, rowan, willow and beech although the last
year's beech leaves clung leechlike to branches. Early
summer brought new calves, delighting Tansy and
Thomasin when they sucked their figures with rough
tongues, christening them with names like Dinah,
Cherry, Bindy, Nancy and Strawberry. The bull calves
would be taken to market in six months with the
exception of Billy who, Martin declared, would, when
mature enough, run with the cows and save paying to
see a bull thus providing a new season's crop of calves.
Now the sheep shearing had been good and produced
enough money to employ Johnnie Brimmacombe to
stay a week, build a bed in the tallet for Tansy and
Martin, a larger cot for Thomasin behind a division
which made a small second bedroom. As prophesied the

oak in St Paul's Road had indeed fallen, Johnnie had obtained enough wood to make a settle to stand between the farmhouse door and the fire. He also made shelves to fit the large shell cupboard on the right hand side of the fireplace. All this proved of great delight to Tansy who was able to display her treasures and books beneath the round stone decorated curve and rewarded the young man, not only with the Five pounds promised but also with hugs and kisses. Adam came for a day or two to help Martin build an oven in the alcove to the left of the hearth bringing with him Fanny and the baby Mary who gurgled and laughed when Thomasin tickled her cheeks and pushed her about the courtyard in her own doll's pram. Fanny expecting another child already was feeling sick and pleased to sit by the fire while Tansy waited on her, becoming moody and silent when Fanny taxed her with her lack of fertility herself wondering why she was not having a child after over two years of marriage? She thought also of her sister whose first child would come soon, fathered by Geoffrey Llewellyn. Was it her fault? Was it Martin's? If she'd been married to Geoffrey would she now be pregnant? Was the difference the love aspect? She was fond of Martin and their love making was good so why hadn't it produced a child?

Still, she thought, it was pleasant to have Fanny's company and together they made the first bread in the new oven, visited Chagford on market day to sell Tansy's cream, eggs and now butter, calling in on Wilmot on the way home. The Osbornes' farm was now alive with the new herd of Red Devons, pigs, chickens and men worked to patch the leaking roof and re-glaze the broken windows. Wilmot was tending to beehives in the small orchard beyond the house and the children, now equipped with new boots, had begun to attend school in Chagford every day. It seemed to Tansy that Wilmot had put on weight, her cheeks glowed with good health and when they sat together in the kitchen

196

she broke the news that she was expecting a fourth child; she blushed and smiled with pleasure.

'Us've all got children coming now except Tansy here.' Fanny thoughtlessly declared making Tansy feel even worse and she rose at once saying they should get home as the men would be wanting their vittles. Wilmot came quickly across the room and put her arms around Tansy repeating the words of Eva Drewe.

'Children doesn't allus come when us wants them, Tansy. Be patient and you'll get your heart's desire.' They left to cross the moor, Tansy carrying Mary on her back and Fanny holding Thomasin's hand. Tansy was silent over supper and surprised Martin by making love to him fiercely into the night, both of them enjoying the luxury of their first full sized bed.

Martin and Adam worked hard to widen the stroll as far as the clapper bridge to make it possible to drive a pony and trap right up to the courtyard. This proposal took Tansy's mind off her childless condition for a while and she made many plans to drive far and wide until Martin pointed out that ponies couldn't cover such long distances in a day as horses could. At that she contented herself with plans to drive with Thomasin to 'Staddens' to visit Martin's mother and ask her advice on keeping bees and getting babies.

Martin, sensing her unhappiness, took her to Tavistock to buy a pony. Much discussion had taken place between Martin and Adam who declared a Dartmoor would be the best, good tempered, tough, tireless, suitable for Tansy to drive in the trap or indeed to ride across the open moor and both agreed a bay or chestnut would not need so much grooming as lighter colours. However, the first pony Tansy saw that took her fancy was white with grey markings and, try as they might to dissuade her, this was the one she insisted was the one she wanted.

'I like the look of it' she declared 'I like it's coat' and try as they might neither brother could change her mind and, when several farmers were interested in it, she became even more determined to gain possession of it. After heated bargaining the price reached eight pounds Martin said they could bid no more and Tansy held her breath. The Auctioneer shouted the price once, twice and at three times the gavell fell and the pony was hers.

'Tis a Piebald, Tansy' Adam said 'That be a cross between a Shetland and a Dartmoor but' he added as Martin fetched the creature from the ring 'tis a handsome creature for all that and just the right size for ee my maid!'

Tansy got to know the pony while Adam and Martin moved on to the agricultural sale, returning with a quite smart trap which was painted with oak leaves and red and gold curlicues. The brothers had brought tackle with them and when all was attended to Adam offered to drive all home but Tansy would have none of it.

'If I'm to drive to Chagford the sooner I learn how the better. If I could drive Tom home from Newton to 'Staddens'

I'm sure I can drive' here she paused considering for a moment 'then I'm sure I can drive Robin soon as think of it'.

She lifted her chin and seized the reins from Adam and Martin recognizing the familiar sight of Tansy facing a challenge, winked at Adam, encouraged her.

'We're sure you can do it, Tansy, but at least let me lead the way I'll keep Lucifer to a trot and Adam will ride with you then if' here he paused 'Robin is any trouble plenty of help be handy.'

All went well and as they crossed the moor from Fernworthy two figures emerged from the stroll; these proved to be Sabine Baring Gould and Robert Burnard bearing news that they had at last received permission to begin excavating the Pound at Grimspound and inviting Tansy to go at any time when a team of students from Cambridge would be joining them shortly. They would need accommodating nearby, some were to stay at Manaton, some in Chagford. Tansy at once offered to take someone in until Martin pointed out that the Farm had limited space and beds whereupon she sulked all night until he reminded her next day that with the pony she could go to Grimspound whenever she liked adding.

'As long as vittles be on table and animals fed and cows milked.' Whereupon Tansy flung herself upon him with hugs and kisses.

'You'm an angel, Martin Webber, really you are. How many husbands would give their wives such freedom!' While Martin smiled ruefully, coming at last to the conclusion that, without this giving of freedom, perhaps he wouldn't keep her. In his thoughts he matched hers, thinking surely it was time she swelled up under that white starched pinnafore. A child would bind her to him, prevent her escaping, as surely she would if they didn't produce a child soon. Both loved Thomasin, now coming up to three years old, but she was not their child and would he supposed return one day to her family at Newton. He sighed and took the dapple grey pony from his harness and led him to the stables for his first feed of hay.

Late May saw two sets of visitors at Teignhead; Norah and Geoffrey with their baby boy, Bryn, come to say 'goodbye' as they now had a parish near Merthyr and a house to go with it. After a moment's awkwardness, blood ties between the sisters broke through their recent estrangement and the sisters fell into one another's arms; spoke at the same time in an effort to bridge the gap which had opened up when Geoffrey had chosen Norah instead of Tansy. Tansy hugged the child now grown fat and aware, hugged the little boy with red hair, blue eyes regarding Tansy with a serious expression; her heart skipping a beat as she observed his likeness to Geoffrey. Martin was from home but returned in time to share supper with his sister and brother-in-law, relief flooding his veins when he learnt of their imminent departure for Merthyr. They left exchanging many invitations for Tansy and Martin to come to Wales and these were acknowledged and reciprocated but all four of them knew this was most unlikely. The animals to be tended, the journey involved set against parish work and teaching would keep them tied to the lives they had chosen and Tansy shared Martin's unspoken feelings of relief that this would be so. Memories of times shared with Geoffrey came back to haunt Tansy in the days to come and in spite of the joy of riding Robin nothing could stop the mood of depression falling once more as she waited for signs of a child only to be disappointed.

No amount of cheering by Martin and Wilmot could lift her mood which affected everyone who came Tansy's way. This blackest of mood finally lifted when Nathaniel Hext, her Defence lawyer at Jacob Blackstone's prosecution, arrived with an invitation for her to visit Grimspound now that excavating had begun.

'What are you doing out here?' Tansy had asked and the young man had got down from his pony to explain.

'I've been at Shovel Down with Baring Gould and Robert Burnard. It's not so far from here; they believe it was a military position. Think it cut off access from the Northern part of Dartmoor to the upper part of the Teign valley. There was a hut village at Teigncombe.'

'Where are you from?' Tansy wanted to know.

'Exeter is my home but I'm staying at 'The Bullers' Arms' for the time being. I'm taking a holiday while the Court is in recess. Chagford is a jolly place to stay and near enough to ride out each day.' He looked at Tansy with a penetrating gaze.

'What is an intelligent young woman like you doing living out here in the wilds?'

This remark caused Tansy to bridle. How dared he question her presence at Teignhead. She felt the colour rise in her cheeks and responded with fire.

'Tis a good life up auver away from the confines of town. Out here I can breathe free. Whenever the mood strikes I can ride across the Moor in whichever direction I please. Then there's the birds and animals for company. Tis a busy life with cream, butter and bread to make. Eggs to collect and all of what I make I sell in Chagford. Then there's herbs and vegetables to see to in the garden.' As she paused for breath Nathaniel Hext held up his hands.

'Whoa, whoa! I can tell that you are busy but . . .' here he looked unconvinced. 'Is it not a lonely life?'

At this Tansy tossed her head and retorted.

'Not many a day passes without a caller and' she added 'I've very good neighbours at Fernworthy!'

The young man smiled at her spirited defence of her life and she noticed for the first time that he too had the high cheekbones and long lashed eyes that had attracted her to Geoffrey. Nathaniel was smaller of stature and with blonde, not red, hair falling to his shoulders. He had removed his soft felt hat to speak to her and, in his corduroy trousers and tweed jacket looked so very different from the sombre clothes he had worn in Court. Then she hadn't noticed that his eyes were a mix of green and grey, that his smile was a slightly lopsided affair and it was this feature that caused her heart to jump.

'What do you do for entertainment then?' he asked as he prepared to mount his grey pony. Tansy felt it to be no business of this inquisitive young man but again pride drove her to defend her choice to live on the Moor.

'There's allus something happening. Dancing at Vitifer Mine, Fairs at Chagford and Tavistock. Then there's wassailing in the New Year, races at Huccaby and the Hunt.' Now Nathaniel Hext placed his foot in the stirrup and swung up on to the pony. He raised his eyebrows.

'Not seen you at the Hunt! Not seen you at the County Ball either?' Here he pulled on the reins and the grey turned full circle in the courtyard. He smiled at her, a teasing expression in his eyes. 'Like dancing?'

Tansy, beguiled by this slim young man, would only

nod her head. 'Then we must arrange a dance at Chagford during the Dig. Students are coming from Cambridge I believe.'

'Yes, Sabine Baring Gould called and told me they'm staying in some of the farms.'

The note of regret that she was taking no part in this was apparent in her voice.

'Aren't you taking any?' He looked beyond her to the house. 'Couldn't you have some here?' Tansy shook her head.

'Not enough room just now . . . but' she added 'I have plans!'

The grey began to pull at the bit, Nathaniel steadied the creature, raised his hat to Tansy with 'See you at Grimspound soon then?' was gone leaving her with a feeling of deprivation at the lack of dancing and company. The time spent building the herd, the flock, learning the ways of a moorman's wife and looking after Thomasin had absorbed her utterly until now. Why then did she want to follow this man to Chagford, dress in her wedding dress which lay still unused in the chest upstairs, dance and dance until she dropped with exhaustion. Hear again the music of 'The Lancers', be whirled off her feet, dance a stately waltz and let rip in a polka? She and Martin had never danced, she didn't even know if he could waltz or polka as well as step dance? Suddenly, nothing felt good and seizing Thomasin by the hand she ran from the house to dance the little girl round and round the courtyard. Thoroughly unsettled she must do something, go somewhere. Thought of Cranmere Pool. Martin always promising to take her there but never fulfilling his promise. Well, she would go and find it for herself.

How many times had Martin shown her the gate in the farthest, largest enclosure.

'Whitehorse Hill that be' he had pointed 'over there is where Varracombe rises.'

Tansy pressed him to tell her how much further it

was to Cranmere Pool and showing signs of impatience he had added.

'Over to the right is Moute's Inn which is a turf cutter's hut . . . but ee don't want to concern isself with that. I'll take 'ee in the summer when the ground be dry.'

But he hadn't yet taken her after two summers and she had pressed for further directions which Martin gave with reluctance.

'You'm going close the East Dart in about half an hour, tis often wet and boggy there. The Pool be another half hour's ride straight ahead.'

Gritting her teeth Tansy settled Thomasin on the pony in front of her and set off. As the heifers, calves and sheep were grazing beyond the newtake she left each gate open pending their return. Why, she thought, it would only take an hour to get there and the same coming back. They would be back before Martin who was away buying feed and selling fleeces from the newly shorn sheep. Thomasin caught her excitement and laughed and giggled as they rode up through the newtakes and out on to the open moor. They reached Moute's Inn easily where they paused to look for the East Dart and when Tansy saw the silver splash of the river head she made towards it. Skirting the ground surrounding it she kept slightly to the right and rode on. There was nothing now to guide her to the Pool and slowly she climbed a ridge ahead from where she could see a high Tor in the far distance. At a loss as to which way to go Tansy dismounted and lifted Thomasin down from Robin. A movement to her right attracted Tansy's attention to the pair of riders coming toward them. She waited hoping they would be able to direct her to the Pool. This proved the case when they reached her and to her surprise and delight proved to be Lady Annabel Watson and a gentleman dressed in riding clothes.

'Why tis Tansy Webber I do believe! Whatever are you doing so far from home?' Lady Annabel reigned in her mount and her companion did the same.

'Now I have a pony I can ride about the Moor. Thomasin and I wanted to go to Cranmere Pool – tidn't too far from Teignhead but . . .' here she paused looking embarrassed 'I'm not sure which way to go from here . . .'

Lady Annabel laughed and introduced the man riding a handsome chestnut stallion.

'Lord Brookesborough is staying at Gidleigh Park and, like you, wished to visit Cranmere Pool so if you care to join us we can go on together.'

Waiting for Tansy to remount they set off at a slow pace in order that she could keep up and after ten minutes saw the Pool shining silver ahead of them. Their luck held as the ground surrounding it bore tufts of reed and cotton grass but was dry enough to cross. At the large pool all dismounted and Lady Annabel who had been before told them.

'There's a glass jar somewhere about' and, after searching the banks it was Thomasin's bright eyes that spied it and Tansy who lifted the jar free from the bank. Lord Brookesborough unscrewed the lid, too tight for Tansy's strong fingers. Lady Annabel it was removed half a dozen calling cards and looked through them.

'Nobody I know – all from away – as far afield as Bath and Bristol. People are starting to come and walk Dartmoor. It's becoming easy to travel about now roads and railways are linking up.' She turned to the man at her side. 'Shall we add our cards to the jar?' Both produced calling cards, gold edged and important looking but before replacing the lid Lady Annabel turned to Tansy and asked.

'Is there something you would like to place in the jar my dear before we go.' She added 'I must say you've done extremely well to come here on your own.'

She smiled encouragingly at Tansy before both riders mounted their horses and waited for Tansy to make her contribution. Now she was at a loss, having nothing in her pocket but a hanky and, unusually, no ribbon in her hair. On an impulse she pulled the gold band from her wedding finger and placed it inside the jar. Tansy heard the sharp intake of breath from Lady Annabel who asked.

'Are you sure about this? It's of no importance to leave something. Just a game really.' Tansy's answer came at once.

'Yes, my lady, I am sure. Why, tisn't far from home and, now I know the way, I can come and fetch it with Martin . . .' she paused then added for Lord Brookesborough's benefit 'my husband. Always promising to bring me here so it will make a good reason for both of us to come together.'

No more was said as the three riders retraced their tracks until at Whitehorse Hill they parted; Lady Annabel and her companion to set off across Gidleigh Common to the Park, Tansy and Thomasin to descend to Teignhead Farm covering the last-part of the journey at a very brisk pace, so brisk that by the time they entered the courtyard Robin was in quite a lather, foam coming from his mouth. Martin waited for them, his face dark with fury.

'So you'm back, having left open all the gates as well as the top gate leading out on the Moor. Where have you been? No, don't tell me! There's cows wants milking, animals to be fed and sheep and calves brought back from outside newtake walls.' So saying he left in the direction of the far field. Tansy slid from Robin's back, rubbed him down and gave him a rack of hay. After milking she began to peel potatoes noticing the band of white skin on the third finger of her left hand. A band of white which stood out against the brown sunburnt fingers and she wondered if she would live to regret her sudden decision to go to Cranmere Pool and, even more, her sudden impulse to leave her ring behind. Whatever had possessed her. She knew Martin had bought the ring when first he had fallen in love with her and kept it for two years until, at last, she had agreed to become his wife. she rubbed dirt from the potatoes onto the white band, swallowing anxiety as she heard his footsteps on the stone slab of the porch as he returned.

Silence grew between them as they ate supper broken only by Tansy who asked.

'Are all the animals safe?'

Martin's response merely.

'No thanks to you.'

Nothing more was said, no caresses exchanged and Tansy's escapade didn't seem such fun after all as she wondered what Martin would say when he discovered the ring was missing.

Next day Martin still refused to ask where Tansy had been merely commenting that she had a lot to learn if she was indeed to succeed as a farmer's wife; that ponies shouldn't be ridden to the point of the distress suffered by Robin on his return from her jaunt over the Moor. Tansy, now brought to stubbornness herself became determined not to tell Martin where she had been and waited, not with trepidation but something akin to glee, for the moment he would at last notice the ring missing from her left hand.

Days passed with a lasting coolness between them and it was Martin's Mother who noticed the missing wedding ring and drew it to Tansy's attention on her monthly visit to Teignhead.

'Lost your ring Tansy?' Sarah Webber asked as she and Tansy picked herbs in the garden. In the middle of telling her how Marigolds, Comfrey, Elder and Self Heal could be chopped fine and enclosed in lard used to rub into bruises and cuts she noticed the absence of the ring even though the white band had now turned brown in the sun. The girl at once hid her hand behind her back; not wanting to tell Martin's mother where the ring was, she prevaricated.

'No, tis not lost. Doesn't want to lose it as my fingers seem to be thinner now. Tis safe!' Sarah Webber had to be content with that but added.

'What does Martin think to that then, maid?'

Tansy blushed and admitted that he hadn't noticed she wasn't wearing it and had forgotten to tell him. Sarah broke the uneasy silence by remarking that the garden was so sheltered it would be a good place to keep bees, and Tansy, relieved to drop the subject of the missing ring asked.

'Where would I keep the hives?' She pointed to the garden, vegetables growing one side of the path, gooseberries and herbs the other.

'Hill farmsteads usually kept bees in skeps?'

'Adam said something about skeps when first I came to Teignhead. What are skeps Mother?'

'Usually straw skeps were kept in alcoves in the courtyard wall or even in the wall end of a building. Could be there is one such here if we look for it.'

Friends again, both were happy to search, pulling an old rose away from the wall until Tansy protested that Sarah would be scratched by the thick thorns and took over. Soon rewarded by the cleft in the wall behind.

'Tis big enough for several skeps' Sarah exclaimed. 'Heather honey is very good and if you had more than you could use would sell well.'

'What are skeps? Are they in place of beehives?'

'Yes, I've already said they're made of straw then placed in the wall with slides underneath and openings to allow the bees to fly in and out. Get Martin to cut down this old rose and get some skeps and slides – should do well here in such a sunny place. Must confess never kept skeps myself but twas the only way years ago afore hives were thought of. I'm sure you could get the straw baskets somewhere – p'raps Webber's might keep them and I'm sure Martin could make some slides for the bees to crawl in and out.'

'Where would we get the bees from, Mother?' Tansy asked.

'Tis said to be unlucky to actually buy bees. You could exchange them for cream, eggs and butter p'raps?'

'In terms of money what would a swarm cost?'

'Swarm could be worth ten shillin, skeps say two,

then you would need a reed covering – should allow altogether fifteen shillin for the first swarm.'

Excited at a new venture Sarah and Tansy restored Martin's good humour by involving him in their plans but when Sarah learnt that Martin had given Tansy permission to visit Grimspound she pursed her lips and shook her head, firmly believing a woman's place to be at home tending the dairy and keeping man and children clothed and fed. This she communicated to Martin when he saw her off from the clapper, adding that what Tansy needed was a bairn to keep her contented and at home. At this Martin shook his head and assured his Mother that both he and Tansy wanted children, that he was sure it was only a matter of time before he filled Tansy's belly and that the best way to hold her was to give her a free hand.

'Leave the stable door open and the horse won't bolt!' he added, smiling at his mother, who looked sceptical adding.

'No good will come of this Grimspound business, Martin, you mark my words!'

21

GRIMSPOUND

On Tansy's first visit to Grimspound there wasn't much to see, just labourers attacking overgrown turf walls with pickaxes; hard work but welcome at a time when jobs were scarce with men returning from the Boer War finding previous jobs filled by outsiders or young men grown to maturity.

In answer to her enquiries as to why anyone in their right mind would want to live in such a place, Sabine Baring Gould amused her as he regaled her with early beliefs that; it was a secure defensive site against bears, wolves, warlike tribes or perhaps Roman invaders. Another theory that it was the fortification of a permanent settlement, a temple to the Sun, a safe storage place for tin built by Norsemen. The wall of the Pound was already proving hollow and the students debated its use; a secret passage for concealment from an invading enemy or, lastly perhaps protection for cattle against bands of robbers. As always Tansy went straight to the heart of the matter.

'So your excavation is going to find out what, in fact, this Pound is really for, who lived here and how long ago it was built?'

The great man, still wearing his clerical garb of black frock coat and trousers smiled down at her while Robert Burnard replaced a slide to take Tansy's photograph.

'That, young woman, is it in a nutshell. Come back in a couple of weeks and there will be more to see.'

'Tis larger than any other Pound we've seen' said Robert Burnard 'of course there was plenty of loose stone all around; they only had to drag it down from Hookney or Hameldon Tors'.

'T'would have been very hard work though surely?' Tansy wanted to know. At this moment Nathaniel Hext arrived and was deputed by Baring Gould to show Tansy around the site. This he undertook with alacrity.

'Easiest way to explain the position is to climb Hookney Tor; from there we shall have a good view of their water supply and we can relate it to the paths that cross the site. These paths have, of course, been worn away over the centuries.' He held out a hand to help Tansy climb the rugged track but this gesture was ignored.

'I've been here with Martin' she exclaimed setting herself to climb the opposite Tor from Hameldown where she had brought a picnic with Martin who had pointed out the landmarks. Now she was about to discover what lay under the surface. Her worn boots slipped from time to time and she would have fallen had not Nathaniel Hext steadied her.

'We're on the Miners' Path to Headland Warren' he commented Tansy nodded.

'That's near Vitifer Mine where Martin worked after the Great Blizzard killed our sheep.'

She pointed to the valley bottom. 'That road wasn't always there was it?'

'Cut in 1874 apparently to act as a pass between Princetown and Widecombe.'

'However did they survive those early settlers? Where did they get water? Ours' comes from a leat to a potwell just outside the farmhouse door!'

Tansy was now thoroughly involved with the life of the inhabitant of Grimspound.'

Nathaniel pointed.

'We've crossed the Grim's Lake ford on our way up –

this would have supplied their water, look you can see the line of it. we could follow it downstream to the road. Would you like to go down to the road bridge?'

Again, he offered Tansy his hand and this time she took it and together they leapt the little falls and pools which descended the short distance to the bridge while he passed on all he had learnt from the History Men.

'This is called Firth Bridge and was built by a man called Frederick Firth who was lord of the manor of Blackaton when the new road was built.

'See the Grims Lake disappears between those new-take walls to join that leat and then joins the river Webburn at its marshy beginning.'

Tansy, cheeks glowing, felt alive and interested in all that Nathaniel told and showed her. After a pause to look around them they began the slow climb back to Grimspound, skirting Hookney Tor this time to share in the vittles provided by the students' landladies. Tansy, conscious of the stir she was causing as the only woman at the site and remembering that Wilmot was looking after Thomasin, merely drank a small amount of beer before saddling Robin and leaving for Teign-head. Martin was in the yard when she rode in through the opening; he noticed at once how much better she looked, banished the black mood of the past weeks, eyes alive, face glowing and said.

'If visiting men digging up the earth like badgers gives ee so much pleasure then, why, p'raps ee should go there every week!'

'What have they discovered so far then?'

Tansy shook her head, feeling as if she had been on a long journey instead of merely a few miles and a few hours.

'Nothing to speak of. Labourers are still moving turf from stones so it will be a while yet before they break into the secrets of what lays under ground!'

'Then what took ee so long my maid? Been gone hours our Tansy?' Guileless as ever Tansy explained.

'Sabine Baring Gould was there, also Robert Burnard

211

with his camera set up on a tripod to take photographs. No, it was Nathaniel Hext, you know the Defence Lawyer who defended me at Chagford who showed me the water supply, the miners' track leading down to Headland Warren and the valley road across Firth Bridge. Very interesting it was!' She smiled at Martin winningly. 'Can I really go there again next week? By then they may have discovered how the settlers lived?'

Martin, regretting his sudden earlier suggestion that she should visit each week, didn't want to back off, so merely nodded and went back to feeding Lucifer and Robin while Tansy set Thomasin down and went inside to begin on preparing supper.

On Tansy's second visit some weeks later an enclosure wall nine feet deep and in places five feet high had been cleared but the most impressive sight of all was the entrance to the pound. This had been cleared of fallen stones giving an entry of seven feet wide, each side lined with huge slabs almost nine feet high. The floor of the entrance way was paved.

'However did they manage to build such an imposing entrance?' Tansy wanted to know. Nathaniel Hext appeared as if by magic to greet her and assume his earlier role of guide.

'Two or three men with levers and trigging stones could raise a ten foot slab into a vertical position and, by tilting it at an angle and levering each end alternately, move it over short distances.'

'They must have been very strong.' She admired the paved floor of the entrance. 'Where does it lead?'

'Faces South east up that hill and Sabine thinks cattle were probably confined within the Pound and driven out through this entrance to reach pastureland uphill, then driven back at night to stock pens over there.'

Nathaniel pointed in the opposite direction. Tansy was impressed by the amount of clearing that had taken place since her first visit. She admired the exposed walls and noted the large stones set on edge, some laid in

212

courses, in order that she could tell Martin that these wall builders worked in a similar way to he and his generation. Fallen stones were being gathered together into piles by the students, a lively group of young men dressed in corduroy trousers and flannel shirts, sleeves rolled up over muscled arms, faces reddened by sun and wind they worked under the supervision of Robert Burnard and Sabine Baring Gould, the former stopping to move and set up his camera to record progress. Both men were excited commenting that this their first attempt at excavating an ancient site was proving rewarding although no pottery had yet been found. They now dismissed the possibility that the pound had been built for military purposes sited as it was beneath overlooking tors which would, of course, have made it indefensible. A theory of a pastoral community was beginning to emerge.

'It's thought this Hut was a cattle stall – perhaps with a straw roof for protection.' Tansy showed her disappointment.

'What about the farmers? Where did they live? There must have been someone to drive the cattle out each day and tend them?' She felt there wasn't much to show for four weeks of work and, when her offers of assistance were once again rejected, she rode home. However, she couldn't keep away and on her third visit entrances had been exposed to several houses, two pairs of houses joined, some entrances screened by shelter walls and all facing south west the prevailing weather direction. Fallen stones were thought to be lintels from doorways. Platforms appeared at the side of some huts. Tansy shared the excitement of the students who gathered round.

'Could these platforms have been beds?' she asked. All attention now moved to a small newly cleared building. A layer of charcoal was being cleared and a paved floor appeared.

'There's no hearth but the charcoal proves fire was made.' Theories and opinions came thick and fast.

'Perhaps a communal kitchen?' proved the most popular solution.

'However would they cook without a roof?' Ever practical Tansy saw things from a woman's angle.

'Yes, there would have been roofs, probably made of reed or straw but so far we've not found post holes to support them.'

It was in the middle of the Grimspound Dig that Rosemary arrived at Moretonhampstead to be met by Tansy who suggested they make a detour to see what the History Men had found. Rosemary was at once interested as she, like Tansy, regarded Sabine Baring Gould with great awe, finding pieces of his music coming before her at College. The young women caused a sensation when they abandoned Robin and the trap at the foot of Grimslake to scramble uphill where they were greeted with much admiration by Nathaniel Hext and the students, especially when they discovered Rosemary had come from London. She merely laughed and remarked that Cambridge was in itself a very fine City and added that it was one of her ambitions to attend a service in King's College Chapel.

Tansy now defended her home town stating that Passmore Edwards had built a very fine public library in Newton Abbot which included a technical college and art school.

'Now there's talk of covering the Lemon and Town Mill!' she claimed whereupon Rosemary looked dismayed.

'Well' Tansy continued 'perhaps now the Library is opposite and so large more people will visit, more horses and now motor vans – perhaps there's need for a road through to Wolborough Street?'

Rosemary, however, was more interested in all that was going on here at Grimspound; the twelve huts in which it was believed men had lived. Entrances to these were paved, with door jambs up to three feet high, all entrances faced south west, two pairs semi-detached, several screened by shelter walls. Hearths were usually central or opposite the entrance. Some huts were partly paved. The only finds were charcoal, proving cooking had taken place, a broken flint knife, a flint scraper and a polishing stone. All were disappointed that there had been no finds of pottery.

'There's not much more we can do now. Some of us are taking the summer vacation to travel abroad. Some as far as Egypt.' Now Tansy gasped in envy.

'Do you mean to the tombs of the Pharoahs?' Nathaniel nodded.

'I may join them if I can get permission from my Chambers. Why, Tansy, would you like to come too?' She nodded, eyes alight with envy.

'If only I could!' She realised Rosemary was looking at her with something that added up to reproach. She realised she was being selfish to neglect her friend at their first meeting.

'Rosemary has just arrived, her luggage lies in the trap at Firth Bridge so we must get her back to Teignhead.' With much waving and good wishes the women began their descent by the Grims Lake, taking more time to allow Rosemary to descend the rocky path with her damaged leg. Nathaniel Hext ran after them.

'Before we break up for the summer we are having a dance at 'The Three Crowns' next Friday. Why don't you both come?' When Rosemary would have shaken her head in dismissal Tansy thanked him for his invitation and promised to be there without fail.

Stopping to pick up Thomasin on the way home Wilmot offered Rosemary the use of the harmonium on hearing that she was an accomplished player. Meeting Thomasin for the first time Rosemary and the little girl took to one another and by the time they had covered the distance between Fernworthy and Teignhead a bond had been forged which stood both in good stead over the years to come.

Martin, too, was pleased to meet Rosemary again knowing how much she meant to Tansy who promptly showed her the pieces of furniture her brother, Johnny, had made for them. Tansy showed Rosemary up to the bigger of the two rooms but she protested that she was not going to deny the couple their bed. Instead she shared the smaller room with Thomasin and declared herself very happy with the arrangement. Descending to see the Dairy, the hens, the pig, stables where Lucifer looked at her with his golden eyes and neighed in greeting, Martin took on the tour of the newtake, the pounds, the sheep newly shorn and the heifers and their new born calves, while Tansy cooked supper and dreamt of pyramids and dancing in her wedding dress.

Rosemary's visit proved a happy one as they exchanged details of their new lives, sharing the chores then wandering about the moor or taking the trap and visiting Chagford and Bellever where Tansy regaled Rosemary with a description of the whortleberry picnic. In return Rosemary described the dark rooms of the College, the professor who demanded manuscripts be handed in every week but the joy of wandering about London, saving up for a boat ride down to Greenwich with new friends and how she longed to show it all to Tansy.

Tansy, meanwhile, spoke of the Friday night dance at Chagford, sensing an appropriate occasion to wear her turquoise dress.

'History Men are finishing at Grimspound, Martin.' She announced at the first opportunity. Martin merely raised an eyebrow and continued with his meal.

'Students going soon but avore that they'm having a party at 'Three Crowns' and have invited Rose and me to go.' This seemed to need some comment and Martin asked.

'Not husbands then?' Tansy blushed and shook her head.

'Well, they don't know you Martin but' (here she smiled winningly at him) 'I'm sure you'd be most welcome if'n you'd like to come.' Now she added 'Have to wear your best suit. If you'm coming?'

Martin raised his eyebrows.

'Does that mean what I think it do?' Again Tansy blushed then rushed on.

'Well, it seems a suitable time to wear my wedding dress. (She turned to Rosemary) 'Haven't worn it in the three years since.' Rosemary, sensing the challenge in Tansy's voice, rose to the occasion.

'What a shame Tansy. Where is it?'

Tansy rose from the kitchen table, abandoning meal and Martin, took her friend by the hand and led the way upstairs to where her box was stored. Shaking it out she held it against herself.

'Looks as good as ever.' Rosemary exclaimed. 'You should wear it to the Dance. Do you think Martin will come?' Tansy lifted her chin in a gesture Rosemary found familiar from childhood days.

'I don't care if he comes or not. I'm going and I do so want you to come with me!'

Rosemary laughed. 'I would love to but I won't match your elegance. However if you don't mind a companion dressed in a plain frock then that's settled.' Here she hesitated at the bedroom door. 'But I do think you should do your best to persuade Martin to come too. Would Wilmot have Thomasin for the evening? She seems such a good neighbour to you.' Tansy hadn't given a thought to Thomasin and, truth to tell, had enjoyed the admiration of the students at Grimspound. She had also taken a liking to Nathaniel Hext with his talk of Exeter and knew she would miss him when he left for Egypt. Was he serious when he had suggested she went with them? To see the Pyramids learnt of at School would be the experience of a lifetime! Was this the chance she was waiting for? There was nothing to stop her; no child to nurse. No child of her own. Something told her in a year's time it would be too late.

As the evening of the Dance drew near Tansy's excitement grew tangible. She hung her dress in the courtyard so that the creases would blow out in the wind and thought how much she and Rosemary had

217

enjoyed their time together; how the dance would see the end of the latter's visit. Rosemary had confided to her that she more than cared for one of the Tutors; blushed and stammered when Tansy pressed her for a description and a name. Tansy urged Martin to see to the animals earlier than usual, set out his chapel suit and a new shirt purchased from Chagford especially for the occasion. She helped Rosemary to get dressed and Rosemary helped Tansy into her turquoise wedding dress which to Tansy's relief still fitted. Both swept back hair from faces with Tansy binding her unruly curls with a broad taffeta ribbon; she combed Rosemary's into a neat pleat at the back but coaxed enough hair into a pretty fringe over her forehead.

Sarah Webber had given Tansy a pair of emerald drop ear-rings and lent her a necklace to match and Martin had surprised her by bringing her a scent bottle shaped like a camel containing sweet smelling perfume. Rosemary produced pearl ear-rings and necklace to match, a present on her twenty first birthday from her piano teacher at Newton to wish her luck at College.

Martin looked handsome as he brought the pony and trap to the door and helped the girls to climb up. His suggestion that shawls would be a good idea against the chill of the night was brushed aside by Tansy who was determined to arrive at The Three Crowns in style. He shrugged his shoulders and set off at a brisk pace in order to meet Adam whom he had asked to accompany them; Fanny sulked at 'Staddens' too advanced in pregnancy to join in the dancing. Adam remembered Rosemary from their visit to the Kingsteignton Ram Roast a couple of years before when their party had been drenched in a terrible thunderstorm and was looking forward to meeting her again. He also looked forward to a night free from Fanny's moans and, as they heard the sounds of music emanating from the Hotel, all four felt their spirits rise.

22

DECISIONS (2)

Nathaniel Hext acted as host at the Dance, welcoming all at the door.

'You must be Martin Webber, Tansy's husband?'

He extended a hand smiling warmly. 'I remember meeting you at the Court Room here at Chagford.'

Martin responded.

'You did well by Tansy but after all she was innocent of the crime! All credit to ee my friend for proving it!' Cordial relations established Martin whirled Tansy away in a waltz and she was surprised and pleased at how well he danced. He had to give way to a long line of students waiting their turn to dance with Tansy who struck such a stunning figure. She felt it would have been fitting for Martin to show a little jealousy but he had met a group of young moormen and was soon deep in conversation with them at the Bar. When supper was announced it was Nathaniel Hext who took her arm and found her a place at the long buffet. Hungry though she was Tansy took small helpings of the Pressed Beef, Tongue and Potato Salad returning late for a little Compote of Fruit and feeling she must keep a clear head drank only Aerated Water. Talk was of the Students' forthcoming trip to Egypt and Tansy learnt that they were to embark a merchantman at Plymouth for Alexandria from where they would take a felucca up the Nile to Gizeh.

'I've never been on a large boat!' Tansy exclaimed 'Will it be rough?' Whenever people spoke of boat crossings these seemed always to be rough and not to be undertaken lightly. Nathaniel tried to reassure her.

'Once clear of the Channel there's the Bay of Biscay which can be rough but all accounts I've heard have been of fine weather where one could sit out on the deck and watch for birds which always signify the approach of land. At the Straits of Gibraltar one leaves the Atlantic for the Mediterranean where the temperature rises and the sea more likely to stay calm.'

Tansy is filled with a longing to take this journey, to see one of the Seven Wonders of the World.

'How long will you be gone?' she asked and, after pondering a while and talking to the other students, he estimated three months from the middle of July. Three months would take up to the middle of October when preparations for the coming winter would be taking place. She sighed and Nathaniel noting the drop in her spirits immediately asked her to come and dance.

'I've asked the band to play a Schottische but they don't seem to have heard of it. So they've offered to play a Polka instead.'

The band struck up a lively tune and he and Tansy covered the room with great pace and energy and Martin watching from the bar was pleased to see her enjoying herself. Time passed swiftly for both of them and Martin had gained much good advice from the company so felt the evening well spent. He reclaimed Tansy for the last waltz and they made sweet love on their arrival at Teignhead. Rosemary had taken her case with her in order to go to 'Staddens' with Adam where she would stay the night and catch the train back to Newton from Lustleigh next day. During the next few days Tansy dwelt on the invitation repeated by Nathaniel to join the trip to the Pyramids thinking it would stay a dream until the coming week brought the removal of both barriers to her acceptance.

The first came in the form of a letter from Tom Moore; this announced plans for his wedding to a Chudleigh girl, Mary Hannaford, to which both Martin and Tansy were invited. It ended with a post script to the effect that he would be coming to collect Thomasin and her belongings the following Saturday so that she could meet her new Mother. Tansy ran to the barn to show Martin the letter.

'He can't do this!' she declared 'Why Thomasin's been with us nearly two years.'

'All the more reason she shall have as much time to get used to the idea of leaving us.'

'But only a week, Martin! How could he? A week's not enough time for me!'

Now Tansy burst into a storm of tears and Martin dropped his hay fork and held her close, realising how fond of Thomasin she had become. He held her in his arms until the flow of tears began to slow.

'Tis a shock to both of us my maid. Best to tell Thomasin at once. After all we knew t'would happen one day and, if she's to have a new mother to replace Avril and return to her brothers, we must do our best to prepare her for what's to come.' Tansy, recognizing the truth of Martin's words, dried her eyes and went to find Thomasin who was playing with Moss in the courtyard.

'Thomasin, come here there's a good girl. I've some-thing exciting to tell ee. Today Martin and me, we've had a letter – a letter from your Dada!' Now Thomasin looked up her attention arrested.

'Dada coming?' she asked.

'Yes, Dada coming Saturday. Coming to fetch you back home to Newton and the boys!' Thomasin looked puzzled.

'But I here . . .' she looked surprised.

'Dada has found a new mother for you!'

Now Thomasin began to look worried, a frown creasing her young face.

'You my mother, Tansy'. She looked positive and, as if to underline her declaration got up from Moss's side and ran to Tansy where she threw her arms round her laughing and smiling. Tansy realised this parting would be hard, harder than she had realised when Tom Moore's letter arrived. She cradled the soft body in her arms realising how much she would miss the child who had been such a comfort to her when Martin was away. Almost like her own child except for the fact she hadn't carried her for nine months or gone through the pain of childbirth with her. She put the little girl away from her and tried again to make the child accept the parting to come.

'I am not your mother, Thomasin. Avril was your real mother but she died and Tom, your father, brought you to me to look after. This I did promise your real mother I would do if anything happened to her.' Thomasin looked puzzled and Tansy realised this was too much for the child to understand – later perhaps when she was older. Tansy sighed and rose to her feet. 'We must pack up your clothes and books ready for when Dada comes on Saturday.'

But now Thomasin's face dissolved into a furious bout of crying, tears streaming down her face. She stamped her foot and screamed at Tansy.

'No, no. Not going with Dada. Staying here with you Tansy.'

Then she ran away out through the top gate with Moss at her heels and Tansy herself collapsed on the garden bench distraught. Saturday came bright and sunny and Tansy tried once more to pack Thomasin's things but, as fast as she placed them in the basket Tom had first brought them in, so the little girl took them out again. As the time drew near Tansy prepared a simple meal for Tom Moore, wondering whether he would bring his new wife with him. Hoping against hope that he would not; feeling that the parting would be even harder if Thomasin had to face a stranger. When Martin announced that he could see Tom coming Thomasin ran away and hid in the barn with Moss and refused to come and greet her Father.

Tansy was somewhat comforted when Tom told them the woman he was to wed came from country stock at Chudleigh and that the whole family were to move there and share a smallholding belonging to her mother and father. Tom would continue to work at the brickworks in Newton and the children would all attend school at Chudleigh. Tansy asked for a description of Mary Hannaford and Tom produced a photograph of a plump young woman with long dark hair and a warm smile and Tansy felt she would make a good mother. Thinking of the ready made family of five Tansy wondered how she would cope with any babies she and Tom might themselves produce in addition to the four boys and Thomasin. When Tansy found Thomasin she promised they would often see one another but, at the moment of parting, both woman and child dissolved in tears and it was Martin who handed the child up to Tom Moore as he prepared to leave in the trap.

'Bring her to see us Tom, won't you? Bring her soon!' Martin and Tansy waved until Tom and Thomasin disappeared from sight; immediately Tansy left the farm to climb Sittaford Tor where she gave way to her grief. When she awoke each morning she went into Thomasin's room, forgetting for the moment that the child had gone. This provoked fresh tears and Wilmot and Martin grew concerned at the effect of losing Thomasin was having upon Tansy. Wilmot spoke to Martin about Tansy going to Egypt evoking an angry response from Martin who demanded to know how he would manage without Tansy. Wilmot had been showing Rebecca now about to leave school, the arts of cooking and dairying and felt it would be good practice for Rebecca to stand in for Tansy but Martin wouldn't agree; afraid in his heart of hearts that if Tansy went away she would never come back.

When the following week Nathaniel Hext called with a leaving date and told Tansy that one of the students had diphtheria and had had to pull out she sensed an opportunity.

'Do you think I could go in his place?' she asked. Nathaniel considered.

'I don't see why not, the History Men both thought you as good as a man when you worked with us at Grimspound. Besides it wouldn't cost anything – the trip is paid for by the University.' Tansy pleaded with Martin.

'Please, please Martin, do let me go. Tis only for a short time!'

So Martin agreed and when Tansy met Lady Annabel in Chagford Tansy told her she was going to the middle east and asked if she herself had ever been. Lady Annabel nodded and commented.

'You are going at the hottest time of the year – what have you to wear?'

Tansy shook her head, her face clouding at the paucity of her wardrobe.

'Nothing specially for hot weather, just my skirts and blouses.'

'You will need a topi, that's a pith helmet, canvas shoes. Why not come up to Gidleigh Park and I'll look out some very thin cotton dresses for you. Perhaps I can find a bag to take them in!' She smiled at Tansy, a smile of approval. 'How is that young husband of yours going to manage without you? Or is he going too?'

This idea is completely new to Tansy who passes on the comment to Martin that evening. He looks at her for a long time then shakes his head.

'No, tis your trip. Tis you as wants to go, not me. All will be well here with Rebecca to do the milking and dairying and Adam coming up to cut peat us'll manage while you'm gone.' Suddenly, in an unusual gesture, he held out his hands to Tansy, closing them around hers and, for the first time, noticed that her wedding ring was missing. Surprise registered across his face and he looked down.

'No ring, Tansy?' She blushed but stayed silent.

224

'Lost it have ee?' She shook her head.

'Then why aren't you wearing it?' His face flushed with anger. Tansy recovered quickly.

'Tis safe. No need for you to fret!'

'Then tell me why you'm not wearing it and if you're going to wear it on this trip you'm intent on going on?' He let go her hands and waited for her explanation. Always a believer that the best method of defence is attack Tansy jutted out her chin and demanded.

'Will you still be here when I return?' Martin's face registered surprise at the question.

'Course I'll be here, planning to stay here for ever I be. Why do you ask?'

'Then you're the one who can find my ring!' Surprised Martin asked.

'If you say it's safe you must have hidden it? You haven't answered my question. Are you going to wear it to Egypt or not?' Now Tansy, tired of the argument, answered shortly.

'Can't wear it if tis hidden can I? I've placed it somewhere you keep promising to take me but never do. If you can find it by the time I come back I will stay with you until I die'. Martin, now alarmed at the seriousness of her words, pressed her

'And what if I can't find it? What then?'

'I will know you do not truly love me'.

'And . . .'

'I will leave you and Teignhead for good!'

When a few days later Nathaniel Hext came for Tansy, placing her box on the floor, he touched his hat to Martin and called out

'Don't worry, I'll look after her!'

Martin watched them disappear down the stroll to reappear and cross the Moor toward Fernworthy. Suddenly he laughed out loud thinking how typical of Tansy to leave him on tenterhooks. Leave him with a puzzle; at least she was coming back but did she mean what she said about the missing ring? Three months without her! At least life would be simple with just the animals to look to and neighbours for company. Again he thought of the missing ring; the ring he had bought when first they had met at Lustleigh May Fair, bought in the hope that one day Tansy would marry him. Drat the girl! He had better things to do than waste three months hunting for a ring! Sighing with resignation he turned in through the porch and poured himself a jug of cider.

Sarah Webber continued her monthly visits to Teignhead bringing home cooking and clean clothes to replace those taken away. She bit her lips and forbore mentioning Tansy's absence. Rebecca Osborne proved to have learnt her milking and dairying skills well and, in Sarah's opinion, would make an excellent farmer's wife if the time came.

Adam, like most people who came into close contact with Tansy, missed her and brought a swarm of wild bees to fill the skeps Martin had acquired from a farmer at Chagford. Adam, who had climbed a tree to collect the swarm, suffered several stings in the process but, when they were settled, told the bees.

'She be coming back. Has to don't she?'

It was close the end of three months, during which Martin had received post cards stamped 'Cairo' and signed 'With love from Tansy' that Martin remembered the lost ring. Wondered how seriously he should take her threat? Embarrassed he asked Adam

'Adam, have eee any idea where the mommet's put the dratted ring?'

'Don't ee remember where ee was supposed to take un and never did?' Martin shook his head, and Adam offered.

'Why not ask Wilmot Osborne. You know how women do love a secret!'

But Wilmot, privy to Tansy's secret, had promised her friend not to tell although, knowing all that rested on the finding of the missing ring, had half a mind to tell Martin. Torn by not wanting to lose a dear friend or

226

seeing her parted from a good husband, she settled on compromise by offering a hint.

'Told me she'd been there once with Thomasin' she paused 'just before the dig started at Grimspound.'

'Is that the best you can do to help me?' Martin asked and stood puzzling until the memory of Tansy leaving gates open, then returning with a hard ridden pony rose to tease him. He'd been angry at her reckless behaviour but hadn't asked where she'd taken Thomasin. It wouldn't hurt to ride out and check the cattle beyond the newtake and he saddled Lucifer, called Moss, walked the cob up through the enclosures to the top gate. There he paused, wondered which direction Tansy had taken, remembered the blizzard when Tansy had come with him to search for the missing sheep. He clicked his tongue, squeezed his knees into the cob's sides and walked on slowly until he reached Moute's Inn. Lucifer dropped his head and cropped the grass while Martin pondered the mystery.

Tightening the reins he walked on up White Hill from where he could see the head of the East Dart. Would Tansy have come this way; what was in front but Cranmere Pool. Surely, he thought, she wouldn't have found her way alone there. He rode Lucifer up the slope till Great Links Tor came into view and steered right across the bog and there was Cranmere Pool. Fortune had favoured him, the marsh was dry and he reined in Lucifer as memories flooded back of Tansy pleading for him to bring her here for a picnic and a swim. Now he remembered how he and Adam had laughed knowing the pool to be too shallow.

But the ring? Where could she possibly have hidden it here? Without confiding in Adam he had already searched the house and dairy remembering how she had hidden Jacob Blackstone's watch on the highest shelf of the dairy. Wilmot's words came back to him and he felt convinced he was on the right track. He knew of the existence of the jar; dismounting from Lucifer he strolled the edges of the pool while Moss stood, ears pricked, waiting to see what his master would do next. Martin had almost given up when a shaft of sunlight shone through the grey sky and began to move across the moor until it was directly overhead. The shaft reached the opposite bank lighting up the jar he was seeking; he covered the distance in three strides. The lid was stiff and beginning to rust from long immersion in water and peat but eventually it gave way under his strength and packed inside were calling cards from all over the South West. Fascinated Martin leafed through them until he happened on the gilt edged one from Lady Annabel Watson Hope of Gidleigh Park. Wasn't she the magistrate who had exposed Jacob Blackstone at Tansy's trial? He felt it must be an omen.

23

HOMECOMING

As the coast of Devon drew nearer and the air cooler Tansy went below to her cabin to change into the light but warm clothes she had worn on her departure three months before. The journey home had been rough in the onset of autumn gales and Tansy had shared the sickness some of the passengers had suffered. Now recovered she felt excited at the thought of seeing family and friends, and of course Martin, again. The train from Plymouth had brought her to Newton and, after stopping overnight with Eva and Edward Drewe and the twins, she had taken the branch line to Moreton next day gazing with delight at the gold and bronze leaves throughout the Wrey Valley. At Moreton she took the new motor bus to 'Staddens' where Sarah and Amos Webber were relieved to see her back. There she admired the new baby born in her absence and congratulated Adam and Fanny.

Martin was astonished to see a familiar pony and trap crossing the moor from Fernworthy; amazed when he recognized his Father holding the reins and Tansy waving at him. This arrival, so unexpected, had Martin standing rigid in the courtyard waiting for the conveyance and its passengers to alight. Not knowing who to greet first he held out his arms and it was Tansy who stepped into them; a Tansy looking tanned and plump. Moss barked and jumped around them both while

Martin couldn't take his eyes off Tansy realising just how much he had missed her. He set her down and turned to Amos now tying the pony's bridle to the hitching ring on the farmhouse wall.

'Well, my lover, us've brought ee's maid home though I thought I should a'come to fetch her away long avore this!' He proffered a hand and Martin took it in both of his, a lump rising in his throat at the unexpected arrival of his Father. He struggled to find words to express his joy at having Amos here at Teignhead at last while Tansy looked from father to son, then took the closest hands and placed them together.

'I'm sure you're pleased to see your Feyther, Martin.' She turned to Amos. 'He's longed and longed for ee to come. Aren't you going to welcome your Feyther to Teignhead, Martin? Show him how well ee's done? Show him stock and newtake? But first off I'll fetch ee a mug of cider!'

'Us'll have it after, maid' Amos declared gruffly turning to Martin who straight away left the courtyard to show his father the farm and Tansy made a fuss of Moss whose welcome continued. He pranced back and forth, round and round Tansy, making small whining sounds in his throat until she knelt on the ground and wrapped her arms around him.

'Tis so good to be home! There's only one person missing and that's Thomasin'.

Even this loss didn't quell her joy. Woman and dog entered house where Tansy threw her hat onto the table and whirled around. She removed her jacket and washed the dust and sweat of travel from her face then fetched water from the pot well and filled saucepan and placed it on the trivet. She looked at the mantel shelf, noticed the clock had stopped and all her treasures covered in dust. She laughed knowing she would be here tomorrow to set all to rights and went to greet Rebecca, milking Hortense and heifers that had calved in her absence. She asked after Wilmot who had had a baby boy, called Sylvester. Rebecca reported that all was well at Fernworthy and showed Tansy the money earnt from the sale of cream and eggs.

'I hasn't managed to make more butter than us have needed here but I'm learning'.

Rebecca removed her apron, hung it on a peg and prepared to go home to Fernworthy.

'Tell your Mother I'll be down tomorrow. There's so much to tell!'

She went inside, quickly taking down a ham from a hook in the ceiling, fetched three plates, carved ham to place on the plates, adding cheese from the dairy and bread from the crock. Now Martin and Amos returned deep in conversation and Tansy invited Amos to stay for supper and the old man, loathe to leave them, agreed. He sat but not before turning to Tansy with a question in his eyes which she answered with a shake of the head. Martin pressed his Father to take pickles from the jar and Tansy poured cider for them all. When the three of them had finished their vittles Martin asked.

'Did ee have a good trip then, my maid?'

'Marvellous it was, Martin. I do wish you could have seen the Pyramids; wonderful colours the bricks are – not just gold but green and blue as well. Tis awful hot though from the time you wakes in the morning till late at night when suddenly it turns dark and cold, cold as a Dartmoor blizzard!'

'What about Nathaniel Hext then and the students?'

'Gone back to Cambridge to begin the new term; one to write a paper on Grimspound for his degree, another to write on the Pyramids; he hopes to become an archaeologist and go back to work for Sir Flinders Petrie. The money to explore the pyramids comes from the Egyptian Exploration Fund which has only just been formed. Sabine Baring Gould and Robert Burnard – why, they would have found it truly enthralling – pity neither of them could go.'

'And Nathaniel?' Martin persisted.

'Gone home to Exeter to take up with his Court work.'

'After such excitement Tansy are you content now to settle down here with just me and the sheep?' Different emotions crossed Tansy's face as she struggled to express all she felt in a few words and failed. Amos broke the silence by rising from the table to make his farewells.

'Now you've at last come to Teignhead' Martin said shaking his Father's hand 'you'm to come again and often. I'll be glad of ee's advice from time to time even if our farming is different so don't ee forget!'

'Take care of one another' Amos kissed Tansy on the cheek turned to Martin saying 'Take care of this young 'oman. She's precious to us all.'

Then he's gone and the couple watch until he disappears from view then the couple turn back into the farmhouse, each suddenly shy of one another after being apart such a long time and for the very first time.

'Shall us have tea, Martin?' Tansy asks. Martin nods and sits at table while she fetches cups and saucers from the shell cupboard. Twice both begin to speak, then stop to smile shyly at one another. At last the tea is brewed and ready to pour. Tansy fetches the clock and gives it to Martin to set right and rewind. Then both sip their tea, Martin's large hands clumsy round the dainty handles of bone china, Tansy's small hands healed after being away from the rough work of farm and dairy for three whole months. Both stop the other from drinking the very last drops of tea.

'There's something at the bottom of the cup for you, Martin' Tansy proclaims smiling at him. He lifts a small object from the bottom of his cup and reciprocates with.

'There's something at the bottom of *your* cup too, Tansy' and she lifts a small object from the bottom of her cup.

'Whatever is it?' he wants to know 'Looks like a beetle!' Tansy laughs.

'That's exactly what tis. The Egyptians made it into a sacred beetle though of course tis really a dung beetle!' Martin laughs.

'Got plenty of dung beetles here haven't us though not one with emerald eyes!'

He strokes the smooth stone sculpture then rises to place it on the mantel shelf. Now it's Tansy's turn to admire the object Martin placed in her cup. When did you get the flower engraved inside – it wasn't there before.'

Martin takes the object from her hand and slides it onto the third finger of her left hand and, on an impulse raises her hand and kisses the ring.

'Tansy by name and Tansy by nature – always stay as wild.'

'Wouldn't ee have me otherwise?'

'Not for the world!'

'I knew you would find it!' Tansy says 'but where did you have the flower engraved inside?'

'There's a jeweller in Chagford and I only got it back yesterday!'

'There's something I've been longing to do since I got home' Tansy said 'and that's climb Sittaford Tor. Will you come with me?'

Together they climbed to her favourite place and there she turned to Martin to say.

'I have another secret to share with you' then taking his hand, placed it on her stomach. 'What is it we've longed for ever since you placed this ring on my finger?' Martin looks puzzled for a moment or two then his face clears.

'A child of our own, Tansy?' When she nods, he asks.

'When?'

'Next Spring – some time in March – before the lambs'. Martin's smile doesn't leave his face for several days and Tansy sings about her work. She had told her parents and Martin's on her way home and now the news travels to the Vallences and Cook at 'Courtenay House' and Wilmot and Tom Osborne find themselves already asked to stand as God parents.

'And the names, Tansy?' Wilmot asked.

'If tis a maid twill be 'Bryony' but if tis a buck then Martin shall decide.'

So it was left to nature and Tansy, her travels undertaken at last, settled to life on the moor declaring how much she had missed the changing colours, shifting shadows caused by the sun, the wind in the stand of trees close Teignhead Farm. How she had found the middle east quite barren, without a single tree, too hot and that she never wanted to leave the moor ever again.

'There's just one thing left to do then, Tansy' Martin declared 'and that's go tell it to the bees'.

BIBLIOGRAPHY

ERIC HEMERY, High Dartmoor, Robert Hale

TOM GREEVES, Tin Mines and Miners of Dartmoor, Devon Books

VIAN SMITH, Portrait of Dartmoor, Robert Hale

BRIAN LE MESSURIER, Crossing's Dartmoor Worker, Peninsula Press

STEPHEN H. WOODS, Dartmoor Stones, Devon Books

STEPHEN WOODS, Dartmoor Farm, Halsgrove

IAIN RICE, The Book of Chagford 'A Town Apart', Halsgrove

BICKFORD H.C. DICKINSON, Sabine Baring-Gould Squarson, writer, folklorist

MOLLY PERHAM, Devon Country Recipes, Ravett, London

QUEENIE NEWCOMBE, A West Country Kitchen, BBC

CHRIS SMITH, A West Country Christmas, Alan Sutton Ltd

WREN TRUST, Songs of the West for words of 'Strawberry Fair' 1 St James Street, Okehampton, Devon EX20 1DW

THE 20th CENTURY ENCYCLOPEDIA, Cresset Press

Dialect words used in this story

ee	you
Feyther	Father
potwell	small well commonly outside farmhouse doors
skillet	three legged pot for heating over open fires
tidd'n	it isn't
we'm	we are
vittles	victuals (general term for food)
maid	young girl or woman
buck	young boy or man
in country	valley farms
up auver	on the Moor
bain't	be not, am not
avorc	before
crib	food carried to work
prapper job	proper job (job well done)
set down	sit down
directly	unspecified time